SAVAGE HEART

By

M.G. Scott

Published by Digital Vine Media LLC
ISBN: 978-0-9896009-2-7

Dedicated to my family who form the inspiration for my storytelling

Chapter 1

Devastation.

Sabrina Katz thought it, felt it, lived it. Everyday. And as she ran along the foothills near Neskowin, Oregon, she knew today would be no exception.

The trail edged right. Sabrina stopped, her heart beating a runner's pace, and glanced at her watch. A weak smile worked its way onto her lips, temporarily easing the agony that was always with her. She started up again, the gravel underfoot crunching louder with every step.

Another look at her watch: Could it really be true?

It is, she thought. She was on pace for a nine-minute mile—a time unthinkable just a month ago.

With her heart beating more rapidly, she headed down toward the water. Glancing to her left, she caught a final glimpse of the foothills and smiled again, this time a little wider. The Pacific Northwest was more beautiful than she ever imagined it would be when she made the gut-wrenching decision to leave the only home she knew—New York City.

She veered right, following the trail as it led toward Neskowin's small downtown area, and felt the peace of the ocean as the waves crashed against the empty beach—a beach she figured in a few hours would be bustling with early June tourists.

As the trail neared sea level, Sabrina glanced casually at the wooden sign announcing the entrance to the Neskowin Beach State Wayside and momentarily cheered to herself. She was only a mile from her goal—the corner of Breakers Boulevard and Salem Avenue.

The path nudged her west, toward a statue of a boy that stood in the middle of the sand, no more than seventy-five feet from the water. As she half-wondered why it was there, her eyes caught something else in the sand. Normally, she would've glanced right over it, but something about how the shallow waves lapped around it made her pause.

Pondering whether the early morning run was making her delusional, she slowed to a walk and took a few steps off the trail toward the water.

Was it a washed up log from high tide? Or maybe a buoy came loose from the storm they had last night. She took a few more steps and suddenly the reality of what her eyes told her smacked her in the gut.

It wasn't any of those things. It was a body.

Chapter 2

Just for a second, Sabrina stared at the corpse. A damp shirt still covered the upper torso, but that was it—no shoes covered the gangly toes, no pants over the pasty yellow legs. It just lay there in a clump, wretched at an angle no living human would ever want to be in.

Sabrina fumbled for her cellphone—something she always carried with her since the attack on her sister—and punched in 9-1-1. Two seconds later, the dispatcher answered.

"This is the Oceanside 911 center. What is the emergency?" the calming female said.

"My name's Sabrina Katz," she hurriedly said. "I just found a body while running near the beach. I think it's male, but I'm not entirely sure."

"Okay. I'm verifying my Caller Location Information," the dispatcher replied. "I have you just west of Breakers Boulevard and Mount Angel Avenue in Neskowin. Is that correct?"

Sabrina turned toward the street and squinted at the sign. "I think that's right."

"I'm sending an officer and an EMT right away."

"Please hurry! I don't know who it is, but it doesn't look good. If there's anything you can do to save him…"

"Miss?"

"Yes?"

"We're going to get there as fast we can." And then the dispatcher said softly, "I'm going to stay on the line until the emergency personnel arrive. Is that okay?"

"Yes, yes. Of course."

"Good. Now do you know CPR?"

"I do, but it's been a few years."

"That's okay. I'll walk you through the steps," the dispatcher replied. "The first thing I need you to determine is a pulse. Can you put your index and middle fingers in the soft spot between the windpipe and the muscle?"

Sabrina walked the ten feet to the body and swallowed hard. "Yes," she replied meekly. She turned away. Seeing the still body from this angle didn't sit well. She took a deep breath and gathered herself. *Remove the emotion,* she thought. She turned back and made herself look at him again.

He had the outline of a beard that was at least a few days old. His face was pasty white, and his mouth was slightly open, as if capturing a thought frozen in time. Sabrina knelt on a knee and placed two fingers on the right side of the neck. The cold, heavy skin made her shudder, but she was determined to see this through. "I can't feel anything. His neck seems a bit clammy."

"Okay," the dispatcher responded dejectedly. "The emergency personnel should be there momentarily."

As if synchronized, Sabrina heard the sirens of multiple vehicles to the south, along Breakers Blvd. "They're coming."

"They'll take over from here. If you need anything else, call 911 again."

"Thank you. I will." Sabrina ended the call and stared at the lifeless face. *C'mon,* she thought, *show me you're alive.* But the whites of his eyes just stared aimlessly into the early morning sky, unable to soak in life.

Whoever he was, he was gone forever. She was sure of it.

"Whoa there, lady. What do you think you're doing?" a man in a white polo said as he grabbed her arm.

"Just trying to save him," she retorted, as she stared at the bulky hand wrapped around her wrist. Suddenly, swarms of medical workers and police started attending to the body. "I was out for a morning run before heading into the newspaper, and came across the body."

He let her go. "So you're the one who called it in?" He looked at his Blackberry. "Sabrina Katz?"

"I am," she replied curtly. "Any idea who it might be?"

Ignoring her question, he said, "You gotta move back. The area's being quarantined off."

She rubbed the sand off her hands and pushed herself up. She followed the officer back toward the running trail. "Can I get a moment of your time?"

He kept walking, toward another group of emergency workers.

"How rude!" she yelled after him.

That made him stop. He turned toward her, waiting a second while she caught up to him. "Listen lady. I don't know who the hell you are, but I've got a lot on my plate." He wiggled a finger in her face. "We don't get bodies washing ashore all that often."

On his shirt, she made out the emblem of the Lincoln City police department. "Look, I'm sorry. But I need your opinion."

"On what?"

She brushed an errant clump of hair away from her eyes. "Whether you think this will be written up as an accidental drowning or not."

"Why are you asking such—" He stopped and then said, "That's what you meant by heading into the newspaper. ... You're a reporter."

"I am," Sabrina confessed. "For the Neskowin Beacon." *And it's my first day.*

"Well, I don't have time for this bullshit. We'll let you know when we release the report." He turned and walked away.

"You're going to say it's an accident, aren't you?"

"That I haven't confirmed," he called over his shoulder.

"Yeah, well, it's not."

He stopped and turned. "How the hell do you know that?"

"I don't. All I can say is it's women's intuition."

A small chuckle. "Women's intuition? How the hell am I going to buy that?" He waved his hand at her. "Don't bother answering. I don't want to know." He studied her for a moment. "You're not from around here, are you?"

"Good catch. I'm a New Yorker. Well, ex-New Yorker."

"Well then ... the Pacific Northwest should be a shock to the system."

"That's what I'm looking for."

He stuck out a burly hand. "Sam Urbina. I'm a detective with the—"

"Lincoln City Police Department." She nodded toward his shirt. "I gathered that."

A smirk. "You certainly are a quick-witted one."

"It's called survival."

Another officer stepped up to the detective and handed him a paper form with markings and notes written on it.

The detective browsed the form, which Sabrina could only guess was an outline of the scene. "You'll have to excuse me," he mumbled.

Sabrina eyed the detective as he walked toward the body with the officer at his side. The officer knelt down, pulled back the white cloth covering the body, and pointed to his arms and legs.

A few minutes later, the detective returned. "Interesting what you can find when you do this long enough."

"Oh?" She was intrigued by what he knew. Besides, it kept her mind off far worse things. "And what's that?"

"We're not going there, Ms. Katz," he said sternly. "And especially when I haven't discussed it with the coroner."

"Isn't there something you can tell me?" She couldn't go back empty-handed. She had already blown off her first meeting with her boss, the newspaper's editor. But this had to be an easy excuse. Wouldn't a body lying on the shoreline be a definite newsmaker?

He shook his head. "I only just met you, but you're a damn bullhead, that's for sure."

She smiled. "That's not the first time I've heard that."

"And probably not the last, Ms. Katz."

"Just call me Sabrina."

He peered at her, as if trying to read her intent. "For some reason, I like you," he said after a moment. "So today's going to be your lucky day. How about a bit of an insider tip?"

Sabrina's eyes lit up. Anything to lessen the blow her new boss was going to throw at her. "And what's that?"

"That I think your women's intuition is right: It doesn't look accidental."

"So it's a homicide?"

"I'm not jumping to any future conclusions."

"Suicide?"

Urbina shrugged a shoulder. "We'll see. I haven't heard a thing from our friends up the coast regarding a missing person yet."

"That's all you're going to tell me? That it maybe wasn't an accident?"

Urbina smirked. "It's a body that washed ashore. It does happen on occasion along any coastline. And the cause can be anything: boating, storms, fishing, swimming, para-gliding, or just plain suicide. But my bet on this one is it's suicide. I've seen enough of them to know."

Sabrina shook her head. "Maybe I need to give up on my intuition." After all, his experience was nowhere near hers. "So how long will you keep the case open?"

"I'll give it forty-eight hours. We'll see what the coroner says. If nothing turns up, then we'll close it down. Let the family claim their loved one and move on."

"And what about an ID?"

"We'll start a scan in the next hour or so. Hopefully a missing persons report will produce a match. If not, then we'll post it ourselves and see what happens."

The group of officers huddling near the body disbanded. One of them came over and tapped the detective on the shoulder. "Sam, they're about ready to load the body."

Urbina nodded and then turned to Sabrina. "You'll have to excuse me."

"Good day, Detective," Sabrina replied, and then added, "I hope we meet again under different circumstances."

"I have no doubt," he replied over his shoulder. "I have no doubt."

Sabrina watched with interest as the coroner's team went to work. Much like a paramedic readying his patient for the trip to the hospital, the team loaded him onto a backboard for the trip to the coroner's office. As they worked the board's straps, a swift wind kicked in, momentarily lifting the sheet off the body.

Although it wasn't more than a few seconds, seeing the remnants of a once vibrant soul made her shudder—and stirred the tragic memory that was never far from her thoughts.

It was the reason she moved to the Pacific Northwest from New York. Now three thousand miles away from her closest friends, relocating was a small price to pay for starting a new life, a new beginning—one she desperately needed to escape the gut-wrenching emotions she felt shackled to.

A nudge by the crowd brought her back to reality. She stared at the corpse as they carried it toward the ambulance. However this man died, his family was about to experience the same fragility of life she endured two months ago.

If only she could've stopped her own sister's murder.

Chapter 3

Gina Hyde exited Highway 5 and then headed toward Charles Avenue—a well-kept street on San Diego's southeast side.

She stopped in front of her small bungalow and pushed herself out of the hybrid. Flashing her face toward the late afternoon sun, she wondered if a minute of tanning would do anything for her chapped skin. For early June, the weather in San Diego couldn't have been more perfect.

Her mind wandered to yesterday, the last day she hoped to ever see her boyfriend. After he stumbled in drunk for the umpteenth time at two in the morning, she had had enough. She just couldn't go on living like this.

I am not spending the rest of my life with this man, she thought.

But today was a new day. She was headed in a new direction. She wasn't exactly sure where, but that's what made it so exhilarating. And besides, she was days away from school getting out and the teaching headaches that went with it.

Gina turned toward the front door and strolled up to it, while at the same time hunting for the key in her purse. Finding it, she slipped the key into the deadbolt lock and turned. Nothing happened.

That's weird, she thought. She was sure she had locked the deadbolt.

Shrugging it off, she unlocked the lower lock and swung the door open. The familiar scent of her favorite vanilla candle floated toward her nose as she dropped her bag near the overly cheerful kitchen. She sighed. *Another exhausting day teaching the circus known as high school kids.* She pulled a glass from the pale yellow cabinets, poured the sun tea full to the rim, and slumped onto one of her two kitchen chairs.

Something wasn't right.

Maybe her senses were being overly cautious, but she sensed something. Her eyes searched the room and found the calendar dangling over the stove—a daily reminder of what she had to overcome. Everybody told her the second year was half as hard as the first. But to her, this year was worse.

And then she saw them.

Two diamond earrings, neatly pinned into a black velvet cloth, lay on her kitchen counter. She gasped at the site of them as they had to be nearly two karats each and sparkled like a prism of glass. For a moment, she forgot the reason for throwing him out yesterday, but then she saw the handwritten note lying against the cloth and it snapped her back to reality. She leaned toward the counter so she could make out the words: *Come back to me 'Gin. I can't think of spending the rest of my life without you. Love with all my heart, Gregory.*

In a fit of anger, she crumpled up the note and threw it in the garbage. How dare he try to win her back? She had given him more than enough chances to get his act together and every time he said he would. The problem was they were always empty words.

She was done with him. She had thrown him out yesterday after finally getting the courage to stop the abuse—both verbal and physical—that she received almost weekly from him. She felt her still swollen cheek. Gregory was a control freak—and a closet alcoholic. Besides, the mood swings drove her nuts. There was no telling what he would do when he had too much to drink.

Suddenly, her cellphone buzzed from inside her purse. She reached into the bag and grabbed the phone. She eyed the caller ID and cursed to herself. "What don't you get? I don't want to see you any more!" she yelled to the unanswered phone.

But after the fourth ring, she decided she needed to make it perfectly clear he wasn't wanted in her life anymore. She answered it with a deliberate press of her thumb. "What do you want?" she barked.

"Did you see the earrings I left for you?" Gregory said in a silky voice—a tone he used whenever he knew he was wrong.

"I did. And they went right into the trash." Gina bit her tongue as she hoped he didn't catch the lie. *What girl in their right mind would throw away diamonds?*

"C'mon 'Gin! I'm going through a tough time right now. Won't you at least let me explain?"

"Explain what? I've already given you enough chances, and I'm done."

"Please," he pleaded. "Something's bad happened. I just found out yesterday and I need to tell you."

She bit her lip. *Was he really serious or just being conniving like his typical self?* She had hoped her conversation with him yesterday would've been the last, but now he's dragging himself back into her life like a lost puppy. She was sick of it. Every time she tried to make a stand for herself, he would plead for sympathy and she would give in, and it always turned into a bigger mistake every time.

"Look Gregory, I'm moving on."

"But 'Gin. I love you. I need you … badly. I've told you that a hundred times."

"Yeah, and you've also been abusive a tenth of that."

"I'm going to counseling," he replied defensively. "You know that." Gina sensed the tension in his voice.

"Then what do you call your state of mind now? You sound like a wreck."

"Grief."

"I'd call it desperation."

"I've got to talk to you. I'm coming over right now. … And I don't plan on going anywhere."

"The hell you are. I'm done with you … and the alcohol. I'm moving on … to a life that doesn't include you." She spat the last few words for effect.

He breathed heavily into the phone. "You're right," he said more calmly. "I am a wreck. But it's because I don't know what to do."

Gina rolled her eyes. "I don't care what—"

"It's my sister.   She's just been diagnosed with cardiomyopathy."

She paused, trying to register if he was being truthful or just saying whatever would put her defenses down. She had become close to Blair over the past few years and almost thought of her as a sister. But somehow she had the feeling he was playing games with her. "You're full of shit."

"You don't believe me?" Anger was clearly in his voice. "Why the hell would I make up something like that on my sister?"

"I don't know. Nothing surprises me with you."

"Please! Let me come over."

"What don't you get? I don't want to see you again!" Gina threw the phone down and ran into her bedroom. Tears dribbled down her cheek as she sat on her bed. She swiped at her eyes, pushing away the tears and hopefully the last emotional outburst with Gregory. She looked around the room and her eyes settled on the photograph next to her bed. It was from Costa Rica. A getaway her fiancé had surprised her with. She had her arms wrapped around him as tight as love would allow.

What could've been better than spending the week with the man she loved? *Breaking up*, she answered to herself.

Enough was enough. His anger—while he always apologized for it later after sleeping off the alcohol—stirred a collage of emotion that made her physically and emotionally tired every time it happened. She just refused to deal with it anymore. She would take the earrings to a pawn shop and see what she could get for them, she decided, and she would do it tonight.

Gina pushed herself up. Suddenly, lightheadedness rushed through her. She started walking toward the end of the bed, but she clumsily stumbled along the way. Feeling as if she wasn't going to make it to the doorway, she reached out, hoping to grab the bedcover. When her hand finally found the fabric, she slumped back onto the soft queen-sized bed. She turned toward the bright window, hoping the incoming light would stimulate her eyes.

But it didn't do any good.

The helpless feeling that the world was collapsing in on her scared her. Thinking she didn't have but a few seconds before passing out, Gina leaned back on the pillow and closed her eyes.

"Why is this happening to me?" she whispered to herself.

Before she could answer her own question, darkness folded in on her.

Chapter 4

Sabrina sighed as she looked around the sparse newspaper office located in downtown Neskowin.

She was already in trouble.

Barely twenty-four hours into her new job she was already at odds with her editor and boss, James Blogg. He had been a little, okay a lot, irritated that she had showed up late her first day on the job. But what was she supposed to do? A body washed ashore. She wasn't just going to ignore it.

That face.

She just couldn't shake it from her memory. His eyes, frozen with the agony of his last moments, left a quirky impression on her. She didn't know a thing about him but would he really take his own life? It was probable of course, but there was something about him that suggested it wasn't an accident or a suicide ... but a homicide.

She was sure of it.

James Blogg surged through the door carrying a camera in one hand and a binder of papers in the other. Sweat was rolling off his broad chin onto his shirt and loosely wrapped tie. It was still jacket weather—a late spring chill had come in from the Pacific—but he obviously didn't need one. He glanced at Sabrina as he headed to his office and then stopped. He turned around and walked up to her makeshift desk.

"I like the copy you sent over," Blogg stated. "Nice start to the career."

Her piece focused on the statue sitting near the beachfront. After her run yesterday, she decided to revisit why the town had honored Little Johnny with a statue. What she found out from interviewing an old-timer townsperson as well as searching the newspaper archives made her glad she picked it as a first article. Little Johnny became a hero one night and paid the ultimate price for his bravery. Back in the 1930s, there was a nunnery that had started on fire, and Little Johnny, no more than twelve at the time, had run into the nunnery where fifty young women slept. Unfortunately, six died and he was one of them, but he had become a hero for how many he saved. No doubt there had been many stories written about the statue in the past, but her goal was to make it different by showing the human side of Johnny.

"Thank you," she replied. "I guess we'll learn soon enough whether the readers like it or not." Sabrina looked at his round face with black disheveled hair tossed every which way on his balding head. He wasn't for a moment attractive, but his reasonable tone almost made her forget the fight they had yesterday. "I didn't expect a compliment from you so soon after we spent the afternoon yelling at each other."

He hunched over her desk. "Let me tell you something Sabrina. One thing you'll soon learn about my style is I don't dwell on the past," Blogg said in one breath. "We've all got jobs to do. Making a small-town newspaper succeed is damn hard enough without us fighting about it."

Sabrina flashed a smile. "I'll take that as a suggestion to get to work on my next story."

Blogg tossed the camera he had been holding onto her lap. "Not so fast. You're not done yet. I said it was a nice start. But I need more."

She stared at the camera. "A picture? I thought it was ready to go."

"Nothing's ever ready in the newspaper business. And yeah, I need a picture of the statue you wrote about in the article … down by the water."

"I know where it is," she shot back. "I'm a reporter, not a staff photographer."

A laugh ruptured from his belly. "That's the funniest thing I've heard all day. If I had a staff photographer, I'd use 'em. You keep this up and you can be my staff comedian too."

"I'm serious."

He grimaced. "Sabrina, let me give you one piece of advice. We all have to roll up our sleeves and pitch in. It's the price we pay for making this small-town paper work."

She turned the camera over. "I don't know how to use—"

He cut her off. "I'm sure you'll figure it out." Blogg stood straight. "Now if you'll excuse me, I've got a paper to run." He headed toward his glass-framed office no more than twenty feet from her desk.

She refused to leave until she knew what happened yesterday. "Have you heard from the coroner yet on the body?"

Blogg stopped cold in his tracks and turned around. He flipped the binder he had been carrying onto an empty desk and pointed to it. "It's all right there. They ruled it an accident." He then walked into his office and closed the door.

She glanced at the bound report and wondered if he meant it was okay for her to read it. Thinking that's exactly what he meant, she leaped from her chair and collected the binder before sitting back down.

Final Report of Autopsy—Coroner Case Number 92-18048, Sabrina read on the cover. *This is it*, she thought. But why would Blogg have it? Then she realized he was probably researching the report for a follow up article in tomorrow's paper. She turned the page where the coroner had summarized the results. Sure enough, Blogg was right. The coroner had ruled the death an accident.

Sabrina continued reading. The body was a Caucasian male. He was about six feet two and a hundred eighty pounds. He had sandy-blond hair with one recognizable feature on his body: a missing toe on his left foot—the third Distal Phalange to be exact. The coroner wrote, based on how the foot healed, that it was a childhood accident, possibly from his teenage years. The coroner concluded he died twelve hours before washing ashore. That meant there was nothing she could've done to save him. She counted back with her fingers—that would put his death on Sunday evening. All the abrasions and markings on his body were due to the trip down the ocean shoreline and there were no signs of foul play anywhere on the body. Blood samples indicated the presence of alcohol only.

The last paragraph made her pause. While autopsying the heart, the coroner found ventricular fibrillation had occurred. The coroner ended the report by concluding the cause of death was sudden death caused by cardiac arrest.

So it definitely wasn't suicide as the detective ruled out. But it wasn't a homicide either. And somehow, he had ended up in the water after his heart stopped. *Seems odd*, she thought. She wondered if he often went down by the ocean's edge on a Sunday evening.

She shook her head. Why did this case bother her so much?

Whether it was suicide or an accident, it just didn't seem realistic to her. She obviously didn't know the man but why be standing near the ocean on a Sunday night? The problem was, she only knew one part of the truth—the hours after he died. And that urge to find his side of the story just wouldn't leave her.

Maybe it had something to do with her sister's death. She felt like a powerless bystander when her sister was tragically killed—and guilt that she could've done more to save her. Although her sister lived with her in their cozy two bedroom apartment along Manhattan's upper side, they were both busy with their lives—Sabrina as a fledging chef at the top of her class in culinary school and her sister a successful marketing executive. But somehow, on that devastating night, she had been so caught up in her own life that she walked right by the killer and didn't notice a thing. It made her sick with guilt that she dropped out of school and started drifting through life. She kept telling herself there was no way she could've known that man was the killer, but it didn't do any good.

To this day, the killer has never been found.

Sabrina grabbed the phone and dialed the Lincoln City Police Department. She needed to get the detective's take on the report and see if he believed what the coroner concluded.

"Lincoln City Police Department. How can I help you?" a woman's voice said.

"Yes. This is Sabrina Katz. I was the one who found the body on the beach yesterday and I'd like to speak with the detective on the case?" She kicked herself for not remembering his name.

"Oh? Yes, let me get him right away."

While Sabrina waited, she grabbed a pencil. After a ten second pause, the detective's voice could be heard. "Hello? This is Detective Sam Urbina. Who am I speaking with?"

"Detective Urbina, this is Sabrina Katz—the reporter you met yesterday morning up here in Neskowin."

"Yes, I remember. The New Yorker."

"I'm calling about the body—"

The detective cut her off. "Look, this is the third call I've received today on this. The coroner issued her report and as far as I'm concerned, the case is closed."

"Oh?" Sabrina responded, surprised. "So that's it? No more investigation?"

A pause. "Look, Ms. Katz. The coroner ruled it an accident so I washed my hands of it."

"I don't get the sense you believe that. Maybe it's my women's intuition."

A sigh. "We're not going to start that again. ... Are we?"

"Am I right? Does that mean you think it could be a homicide?"

Another pause. "It was his eyes. There was something about them that seemed to suggest he knew this was coming. The report said he had a heart attack and fell in the water. If that's what it's ruled, then we'll go with it. I've got five other investigations I'm doing and if I can get one off my plate, the others will be all the better for it."

She jotted down his comment. "So you think it could be foul play?"

"Don't go there, Ms. Katz. I don't want any quotes showing up in the newspaper based on speculation."

She smiled. At least he was warming to her thoughts. "Have you had any contact with next of kin?"

"Nothing."

"No missing persons report has cropped up?"

"We're still working that. Given it's been in the paper now, we expect somebody will come forward and ID the body." A pause. "Nice work on the article, by the way."

"I didn't write it," she replied flatly.

"Oh? Well, tell whoever did that it was a fine write-up."

"I'll see what I can do," she lied. "Thank you for your time, Detective."

"Any time."

She put the phone down and looked at the words she had written. The phrase "something in his eyes" seemed to draw her attention. She circled it and then wrote homicide next to it with a question mark. She didn't have any proof, and maybe she was going down a rat hole, but it just seemed plausible to her.

Her thoughts were interrupted by a heavily bearded man storming into the small office. He wore a flannel shirt and a pair of old jeans that were shredded along the cuff line. He took a peek at Sabrina's petite figure curled up on the chair, grunted, and slumped into the desk next to her.

Sabrina took a sip from her Diet Coke and followed his body language. "Having a bad day?"

He flipped on his laptop computer, ignoring Sabrina's question.

She pushed herself away from the desk and stuck her hand out. "I'm Sabrina Katz."

He didn't bother looking at her. "I remember Blogg mentioning we were going to have a new beat writer … doing puppy dog stories. I almost hung up the phone I was laughing so hard. 'In Neskowin?' I said. He said he knew what I was thinking but that's the way it was going to be. 'We did a survey and if that's what the readers want, that's what they'll get.' " His voice was gruff and raspy, as if he were a three-pack-a-day smoker.

What an ass. "I don't think I'm going anywhere. So you might want to extend a welcome."

He slowly turned his head. "Look lady, don't get sassy with me. The editor hired you, but that doesn't mean we have to accept it."

"What do you mean 'we'?"

"Us. The staff. You're going to be nothing but a nuisance."

That hurt. "I do have a name, you know. It's—"

He looked through her eyes, as if he could see everything she was thinking. "Listen lady, I don't give a damn." He slammed the lid down on his laptop and pushed away from his desk. "Now if you'll excuse me." He walked out of the office and disappeared into the sun-bleached afternoon.

Sabrina slumped back into her chair. Now she was getting it. She wasn't exactly being welcomed with open arms at the Beacon. And she didn't know why. Why were they so against her? Did they feel threatened by the only woman on the payroll?

The door squeaked open. It was the same Beacon employee returning with a cup of coffee. He stepped into the office and leaned against the milky-white framed window.

She glared at him, wanting to confront him with both fists flying.

"Why do you have to be such a jerk?" Sabrina blurted.

He shrugged. "Life is what it is."

"So I mean nothing to you?"

"Only if you stay out of my way."

She felt confused and angry at the same time. "Out of your way from what?"

"From us doing our jobs. We have hard news we need to track down and I don't want some gardening story getting in the way of the real stories."

She was livid. "I guess had you been doing your job then Blogg wouldn't have brought me in. But apparently that wasn't the case." She held up the coroner's report. "Had you been doing your job then why am I getting so many calls about the poor reporting you did on the body that was found yesterday." Sabrina knew it was a lie—even the detective said it was a good story—but she was intent on stoking the fire as much as possible.

He glared back at her. "What the hell are you talking about? The facts are all there for our readers."

She held up the coroner's report. "You wrote about the body and the circumstances. Big deal. I can read that from what the coroner said. What about a follow up?"

The reporter grunted. "Follow up? This isn't an exposé. It's an article based on the facts and the facts are what they are. It's one and done."

"Don't you think you should be investigating a bit further? Maybe where the victim came from? What his family and career were like?"

The reporter lurched forward, grabbing for the report. "Ever hear of minding your own business?" he hissed.

Sabrina pulled away. "Not so fast lumberjack."

Blogg's office door flew open. "What the hell is going on out here? I bet our neighbor three doors down can hear your damn voices."

"I told you we were going to have problems, Jim," the reporter replied. "You bring in a know-it-all reporter who thinks she knows how to write a hard story and this is what we end up with."

Blogg eyed the two of them. "If I wanted to babysit five-year-olds, I would've gotten a job as a kindergarten teacher. So the two of you better get your act together or you'll both be gone." He pulled the coroner's report from Sabrina's hands. "And you need to back down Sabrina. You're not an investigative reporter." He was clearly ticked.

"Don't the readers want a little more than just the facts about a body?" Sabrina shot back. She was not going to back down, especially when she didn't even start this fight.

Blogg banged his fist on a table. "Look, that's what I've got Getty for." He flipped a finger in Getty's direction. "That's why he's here, and he's not going anywhere."

"Hopefully you will," Getty snickered.

"That's enough Getty," Blogg barked at him.

Sabrina's anger stormed through her spine. "Have it your way," she sneered. She threw her empty soda can at Getty and stormed out of the office. She paused in the bright sun and realized she needed to let off some steam or she would regret her actions. She headed across the street toward the coffee shop.

"Sabrina!" Blogg yelled after her.

She ignored her name as she landed on the other side of the street but then thought better of it. She spun around and almost bumped into him. He was panting and looked uncomfortable at the same time, and it couldn't have been from the hard sun.

"What is it?" she replied sharply.

He paused, as if searching for words. "Look, we've got to keep our readers happy."

"What is that supposed to mean?"

"Do you honestly think we could support a staff of four when we only have thirty thousand readers?" He didn't wait for an answer. "No way."

"So what are you saying?"

He leaned up against the building. "Our largest donor is a widowed woman in her sixties who's tough as nails. Without her philanthropy, we're a dead man walking."

She cycled through what he was saying. "I would assume that's a good thing."

"Well, yes, if you don't piss her off with what you're writing."

"And are we?"

"Not right now. She wanted you and that's why you're here—to write features and entertain the town. Catch my drift? Your article on the Little Johnny statue is gonna tickle her to death."

She looked toward the coffee shop window. She was being told what to write because this woman was paying her check. "Why are you telling me this?"

"Because I want you to understand why Getty's ticked off."

"I see." It was becoming all too clear. He used to be the top dog at the paper and now the lady who calls the shots has a new favorite. "What if I sniffed around on my own time? Who would that hurt?"

He peered at her. "I see where you're going with this and that's not going to happen."

"Why not? The lumberjack doesn't have to know."

He laughed. "Lumberjack? The answer's a no. Like I said, our donations will go down the toilet if she knows you're working hard stuff."

I've already opened that door, she thought. "What if I disguised it as a feature?"

He shook his head. "You're a persistent one, aren't you?"

"I guess I was just born that way."

"The answer is still no. I don't want any of my employees going behind my back. If you want to get on my bad side, that's a damn good way to do it."

She was getting nowhere and all she had was a hunch that his death was no accident. There was also no way she could go to bed at night knowing a killer was possibly out there. How could she?

"If I investigate his death on my own time—"

He threw up his hands. "Just get the damn Johnny photo." He turned and walked back across the street and into the office.

In her mind, that might almost have been a yes.

Chapter 5

Gina looked around the waiting room and half-smiled at the various beiges covering the walls and chairs. Doctor's offices always seemed to be doing whatever they could to make their waiting rooms more enticing to the patients. The only thing they couldn't overcome was the fact that nobody every truly wanted to be there.

She looked at the bandage and cotton wrapped around the inside of her elbow. An hour earlier, her internist had requested a blood draw to get to the bottom of her symptoms—the nausea, fatigue, and lightheadedness she felt—and now she was waiting to see Dr. Engle for the second time today, which hopefully would put an end to the questions.

Gina thought back to the other day when she had passed out on her bed. She thought the anger and stress she felt about her ex caused her to faint but now she wasn't so sure—she had definitely gained weight over the past few months but she just thought it was all related.

"Ms. Hyde?" one of the doctor's assistants called.

Gina perked up and waved. "Yes." She hurried up to the assistant who led her down a hallway and into an examination room.

"Dr. Engle will be with you in a few minutes," the assistance said as she pointed to the examination table. She closed the door, leaving Gina to ponder what the doctor was going to say.

After a few minutes, there was a tap on the door and then it opened. A short, middle-aged woman stepped into the cramped room and sat down on a stool. She patted one of Gina's hands before saying, "How are you feeling now?"

"I feel pretty good. No nausea or lightheadedness, but I'm still a bit tired."

Dr. Engle smiled. "That's understandable." She cracked open the laptop sitting on the desk and started typing on the keyboard.

Gina wasn't quite sure what she meant by "that's understandable", but she figured she'd know in a few minutes regardless. "I do appreciate you seeing me again today. I'm sure you've got a hectic schedule."

"That's what I'm here for," Dr. Engle said as she continued typing, "to make you feel well."

Wondering if Dr. Engle might have a prognosis, Gina blurted out, "Did you find anything?"

"Mmm," she replied. She turned the laptop screen toward Gina and pointed at a graph. "This graph shows your hCG count. Do you know what that is?"

Gina nodded as a knot started to form in her stomach. "It's a hormone that women create when they're pregnant."

"That's right. It stands for human chorionic gonadotropin. And do you see how the line I've mapped against your count goes up…week after week … then tails off?"

A slow nod.

"Well, right now your hCG level is at a hundred and five thousand international units per liter. Based on the levels, I'm estimating you're at fourteen weeks."

Gina could feel her eyes bouncing from side to side. She was freaking out. Who was the father? How was she going to pay for it? How could she support herself, let alone a child?

"Do you remember missing your periods?"

Gina heard her say something, but her mind was racing with so many other thoughts.

"Gina?" Dr. Engle said. "Are you okay?"

"Yes. I mean, no." She buried her head into her hands. "I don't know what I am."

Dr. Engle caressed her back. "I know. If you weren't expecting it, it can be quite traumatic and maybe it feels like the whole world is on your shoulders. I do want you to know, though, there are options."

Options? There aren't any options. She didn't have money to take care of the baby, and she certainly didn't have money nor did she feel comfortable having an abortion. Gina picked her face up and stared at her doctor. "I don't know what I can do."

Dr. Engle reached in and wiped a tear from her face. "Well, I think you need some time to think about it. It may come as a shock today, but you may gain a different perspective tomorrow." She turned toward her desk and picked up a pen. "I tell you what. I'm going to write the name of a very reasonable clinic on the north side of the city. It's a private clinic affiliated with the BioHumanity corporation. If you feel like that's your best option, I've heard nothing but good things from other patients who have gone there."

Gina eyed the yellow note Dr. Engle gave her and read it aloud, "Humanity North Planned Parenting."

Dr. Engle nodded. "All I ask is you don't do anything on emotions alone. Think about it and make a rational decision. Can you promise me that?"

"Yes. Of course."

"Okay." A small smile worked across the doctor's lips. "In the meantime, I'd like to see you back here in a week for a checkup."

"Thank you, doctor." Gina left the examination room and headed back the way she came.   Near the office entrance was a small courtyard that led to the hospital. A strange curiosity crossed her mind: Was Gregory telling the truth about his sister Blair? Could she be here now if Gregory was telling the truth?

She didn't know, but investigating sure took her mind off the shock of being pregnant. She headed into the hospital. "Excuse me," Gina said to a broad, gray-haired lady sitting behind the welcoming desk.

"Yes, dear?" the woman replied in a perky voice and a smile to match.

"I was looking for Blair Archer's room. Do you by chance know which one it is?"

"Well, let me see here." The woman typed a few strokes into the computer and then put on a set of reading glasses. "Archer," she said softly. "Ah, here it is. She's in room 2950. That's the Heart Center located in the west wing on the second floor," she said as she pointed over her right shoulder.

"Thank you," Gina replied softly as she headed toward the elevator. So Gregory was telling the truth for once in his life. For a moment, she felt terrible at how she behaved. Then her stubbornness quickly returned. How was she supposed to know after all the lies he told over the years?

She reached the second floor and headed toward the Heart Hospital's main entrance. She wasn't quite sure what she was going to say to Blair but she made up her mind she had to see her.

Besides, Gregory had to be the father. It was the only possible explanation. That also meant Blair would be the baby's aunt and Gina would become a part of the Archer family.

That is, if she decided to keep the baby.

After announcing herself to the nurses, the hospital's wide doors opened and a nurse directed her to a room along the left wall. Gina peered into the open door, praying that Gregory wasn't there. He wasn't. Blair was resting alone, watching a small panel TV that hung from the ceiling.

"Hi. Blair?" Gina said softly.

The female voice startled Blair as she rolled over. "Gina. I'm so surprised to see you. I didn't even know you knew I was in the hospital."

"Of course, dear. Your brother told me on the phone yesterday."

"Oh."

An awkward pause followed as Gina sensed Blair knew they had split but didn't want to bring it up. Gina quickly changed the subject. "How are you feeling?"

The small smile quickly changed to a sullen sigh. "I'm okay, considering."

"When did you find out?"

"About a week ago I was having trouble breathing. I didn't think much of it—thought it was maybe my asthma returning. After the doctor ran a few tests, he came back with the news that I had cardiomyopathy. To top it off, it was the worst kind."

Gina moved to the bed. "What does that all mean?"

"Well, it means my heart is really, really weak. If I don't get a transplant soon, then I'll go into cardiac arrest with very little chance of coming out of it."

"How soon?"

"The doctors are telling me no more than a month or two."

Gina touched her hand. "I'm so sorry, Blair."

"All I can do is hope for a donor—stay optimistic that somebody else's tragedy will become my second chance at life."

"I'll be there right with you Blair … hoping as well." Gina eyed the monitors set up around her bed. "How's Gregory feeling today? He didn't seem to be doing too good the last time we talked."

"Not well. But he's also a lot more optimistic than I am. We're just so close as siblings… I just don't know how he's going to survive without me. I mean our mom died when we were young. I was a teenager at the time, but he was only ten and I've been almost like a mom to him ever since."

Gina brushed a tear away. "I had no idea."

Blair sighed. "Not many people do. But does it matter now?" She pointed to a piece of paper on her tray. "He keeps trying. Just this morning, he stopped by with an excited look on his face. He said he found a possible cure and then pushed this printout in front of me."

"Can I have a look?"

"Of course."

It was from an article describing a heart transplant center in Acapulco. As Gina read through it, she became more confused. "I don't get it. This says the center can do heart transplants without your body rejecting it and it's open to anybody. Where are they getting the organ donations from?"

"That's why Gregory's so excited. The center figured out a way to grow a new heart from stem cells that my body will accept. It'll be all mine with no possibility of rejection."

"Wow." It sounded too good to be true but Gina didn't want to deflate Blair's optimism. "Why only Acapulco? Why hasn't it been approved here?"

"It's the bureaucracy of the FDA. It's still experimental which is why they're doing it in Mexico away from the nose of the U.S. government." Blair paused, then said optimistically, "The success rate is around eighty-five percent. They want to get it up to ninety-five before they apply for FDA approval. It should pass through easily then. ... Of course, when people are desperate and there's no alternative and the government's moving too slow, anybody's willing to go anywhere."

Gina always admired Blair's intellect. She was a medical journalist who researched everything before writing about it but Gina could also sense the resentment. Blair knew story upon story of people dying because their government had let them down. Now she may be one of them. "If there's anything I can do, please let me know."

Blair took her hand. "There is one thing."

"Of course."

"If something happens to me, will you please take care of my brother?"

Gina closed her eyes and gritted her teeth. *Anything but that*, she thought.

Chapter 6

The sun slowly neared the horizon, signaling the end of the day for a small group of tourists.

But Sabrina's day was nowhere near finished. Squinting from the remnants of the sun, she trudged, camera in hand, along the Neskowin beachfront toward the Little Johnny statue. As it came into view just beyond one of the downtown sand dunes, she caught the greenish outline of the copper glistening in the late afternoon sun.

Sabrina stepped around its backside, startling a woman who had slumped against the foot of the statue. She eyed Sabrina with sadness, her apathetic eyes glossing casually over Sabrina's frame. An awkward minute passed. "I'm sorry … didn't mean to disturb you," Sabrina finally said.

The woman waved her off. "No, no," she replied softly. "I'm done." She took a small breath, and forced her crumpled body from her perch.

Sabrina moved closer. The woman was hunched over, but she still couldn't be more than five feet tall. "Can I help you get somewhere?" she asked, extending a hand.

The woman waved her off as she straightened. "I'm on my own now so I might as well get used to it."

Now that she was fully upright, Sabrina studied her features: She had wiry black hair that seemed forgotten—as if she usually kept it tied back but lost the desire. She was thin, almost unhealthily so, and her long narrow face was void of any emotion. But underneath it all, she still held the body of someone barely older than Sabrina—maybe thirty-five at the most.

Sabrina eyed an open bench just to the right of the statue. "Why don't you take a seat? You look like you have the weight of the world on your shoulders."

Compassion filled the woman's eyes, which in an ironic way, Sabrina wasn't all that used to. "Thank you," the woman replied.

"Is there anything I can do for you?" Sabrina asked as they both dropped onto the weathered bench wood.

The woman touched the base of the statue. "This boy—he seemed to grab my attention. And I don't know why. Maybe it's the look of innocence."

Sabrina eyed the five foot statue of the boy facing land, one hand over his eyes as if protecting them from the sun. The sculptor had molded him in knickers and a vest, perfectly suiting him for the wear of the day. Maybe it was his favorite outfit. "I think a lot of people feel that way, even today," Sabrina replied.

"Do you know what happened?"

A nod. "From what I could gather, a careless nun let a candle burn out of control in one of the reading rooms on the first floor. The house's wooden frame then went up in a flurry of flame. But, somehow, due to the bravery of the young man, fifteen of the twenty girls were saved."

The woman replied, "And did he make it?"

Sabrina shook her head. "He went in to save two more girls. They made it out, but he was never heard from again."

A sigh. "Such a sad story."

"I'm sorry. I didn't mean to strike a nerve."

The woman looked away. She opened her mouth but then decided against it.

Sabrina coaxed her. "It's okay. Tell me what you want. Maybe if I had properly introduced myself, you wouldn't feel like you were talking to a stranger." She let out a little grin. "My name's Sabrina Katz."

The woman looked down at her trembling hands. "I'm Carla Sanchez, although that may not be my last name for very much longer."

"Why?" Sabrina put her hand on Carla's hand.

"Why?" the woman repeated. "Because my husband died."

"I'm so sorry." Sabrina felt speechless. She didn't know what else to say.

Carla sat up straight and stared at the sun-drenched water lapping onto the white-brown sand. Sabrina could tell there was emotion behind her face, but she just couldn't release it.

"He was the one that washed up on the beach here," she stated in a monotone voice.

Sabrina's heart leaped. "You…you're…" Sabrina responded, stuttering. Suddenly, the floodgates to Sabrina's psyche opened and she had a dozen questions to ask. Problem was, this wasn't the time to be asking them.

"I am," Carla replied, seeming to understand her. "He was such a beautiful man. He was tall, blonde and oh so cute." She bunched her hands on her lap. "I'm not sure if we truly deserved to be together, but it was a match that seemed to work without the usual strife most marriages go through."

"What was his name?"

"Eric." She paused. "Eric Sanchez. We had met at the university—The Seattle Center of Bio Research—during our graduate work. I don't know … it just seemed so surreal." A pause. "We met in lecture, in the third week of class. He nervously came up to me and asked if I wanted to do a group study with some of his friends." Carla's eyes moved up, toward the clouds drifting overhead. "He had the eyes of a cat and the smarts of anybody on this Earth, and that just drove me to him." She looked down, at her hands. "After class, sometimes we would engage in small talk and he just captured my attention. Hard to believe."

"Why do you think that was?" For some reason, Sabrina was captivated by this woman's memory of her husband, regardless of the obvious fact that this would be a remarkable story for the Beacon.

Carla gazed over at Sabrina. "I was never the courting type. I just wanted to better myself academically. At least that was my goal going into grad school. It certainly wasn't to find love. But he was so sincere and hardworking … really wanted to make a name for himself … and compassionate. That was something I hadn't seen in a boy since, well, ever."

She started playing with her wedding ring. It was simple in design. The platinum band held just a hint of diamonds around a larger diamond set atop a circular base. Carla continued, "And then to have it stripped away, so brutally, so suddenly. I'm not sure I'll ever have the desire to love again."

Sabrina couldn't look away. She was drawn in by the story, even if love and courtship were beyond her own comprehension. "How long were you married?"

"Our ten-year was coming up this year. We always knew we were going to get married, but we also knew that our work in biochemistry was just as important. So we held off on marriage until our careers got off the ground."

"Did you both work for the same firm out of school?"

Carla nodded. "Yes. It was a company called BioHumanity. He was recruited heavily by them. They were investing in stem cell research and needed the best and brightest to do the research. And he was certainly all of that."

"How long were you both there?"

"I left after about three years and went to nonprofit. He stayed on. He got into a division where he excelled. The fast track as they say."

Sabrina noticed her eyes looked a bit brighter, maybe even a little warmer. "When did you see him last?" Maybe it wasn't the best time to ask this, but as a reporter, she had to.

Carla sighed, as if uncertain how much she wanted to tell Sabrina. "It's a day I'll never forget. It was a Sunday afternoon. He said he wanted to take his line down by one of the piers around the bay."

"Line?"

"In the Oceanside area we have all kinds of bays and hidden waterways that are just right for fishing. Eric was such an avid fisherman. That was one of his favorite hobbies—just to go out when he had a little time and relax. But that day was different."

"Why do you say it's different?"

"I don't know. He just didn't seem right when he had left that afternoon. He said he was going fishing and he had brought his usual fishing tackle with him, but the look in his eyes seemed to stray elsewhere. It was if he was shouldering a lot of stress. That wasn't Eric."

The late afternoon sun suddenly caught them in the eyes. It was a reminder that Sabrina needed to get a picture soon, before the sun dropped below the horizon.

"You probably didn't think much of it then, did you?"

Carla nodded. "No, I didn't. When he didn't come home, our conversation came back to me in a rush. That's when I really started to think something was wrong." Carla glanced at the statue. "I visited all of his favorite places, to see if there was any sign of him but I didn't see a thing, not even his fishing tackle. Then I heard about the body down here and my heart just skipped. I knew it was him. I just knew."

In a shallow tone, Sabrina replied, "I believe the coroner ruled it an accident. Coronary death."

Carla frowned at her.

"Don't you believe that?"

"I'm not sure what I believe. Yes, the authorities say it's an accident but to me—and I can't prove it by any means—I think it was the farthest thing from that."

"You mean murder?"

A slow nod.

Sabrina swallowed hard. She was never a hundred percent sure, but maybe her intuition was right. "Maybe I can help," Sabrina offered. Should she really go there?

"How?"

"I work in town as a reporter. Maybe I can look into it a bit more. I do have some connections."

Carla bolted to her feet. "You're a what?"

Sensing Carla thought she had been tricked, Sabrina hastily replied, "Look Carla, I came here just as a compassionate stranger —to listen to you."

"You came here to find out my story and to print it." She put her face in her hands. "God, that's the last thing I want."

Sabrina touched her arm. "Listen—"

The woman pulled away. "No. No! I don't want to say anything more."

"But—"

Carla wiggled a finger in Sabrina's face. "Don't you dare write anything I just told you," she barked before storming off.

Chapter 7

As Gina sat in the small waiting area, conversational chatter was replaced by an apprehensive silence whenever a woman walked in. Everyone sitting around her seemed to eye the woman with empathy, wondering what led to the decision to come to the clinic.

And Gina was no different.

It had only been twenty-four hours since she left the hospital with the news she was pregnant. After a night of restless sleep pondering her own morals, she came to the realization that having this baby would be for all the wrong reasons: She would be angry at the world, angry at herself, and especially angry at Gregory knowing he would always be in her life.

There was no way she could carry this baby to term knowing those emotions would always be there, regardless of how selfish it was or the dilemma she felt about her beliefs.

A muffled cry to Gina's left replaced her thoughts. She eyed the woman, covered in a bulky sweater from the day's chill, trying to hide the tears that were streaming down her face. A sense of compassion flooded Gina as she watched the woman struggle to hold back the tears. She placed a hand gently on the woman's knee. "Hey. It's going to be okay."

The woman peeked through her fingers at Gina and then wiped her eyes with the damp tissue she was holding in one hand. "I'm that loud, aren't I?"

"Does it matter? You have every right to get emotional. It's a huge decision for us—one that's not right or wrong ... and so stressful. I know we want the privilege, but it's still so hard."

A second wipe to her eyes. "I s'pose. I just thought I had a handle on my life, especially after I met my boyfriend. We were on a first date, everything was going all so well. And after a couple glasses of wine, one thing led to another.   I know I should've reminded him about a condom, but I just got lost in the moment."

"Hey, it happens," Gina replied softly.

"I was going to keep it, we were going to get married … do the right thing. And then he just left me, leaving me no way to afford the baby."

"I'm so sorry," Gina replied as she thought about her own story. "How far along are you?"

"Almost in the third trimester."

"Oh? Can you … still do this?"

"I was told the clinic would find a way to take care of me." The woman stuck her hand out. "I'm Helen by the way."

They shook hands. "Mine's Gina."

* * * * *

Tucked away in a small office near the back corner of the clinic, Melanie Li eyed her laptop and then tapped the mouse a few times. She browsed the names that splashed across the screen until she located her next two patients—Gina Hyde and Helen Mesona. After a click, a new screen popped with all the relevant information and videos. She hovered over the link to a video posted just below Gina's name and clicked it.

As the three minute ultrasound played on her computer, Melanie tapped the zoom controls and centered on the tiny muscle that, if born, would become the most vital organ in the body—the heart. She watched it flick back and forth as it raced to pump blood at a hundred seventy-five beats per minute. Even at this early stage, it was truly a remarkable feat of nature.

When the video ended Melanie leaned back in her chair and looked at the family photos scattered on her desk and shelves. There was her dad, fighting to keep a normal life after undergoing countless surgeries to keep him walking. There was her son: A boy born as normal as could be but quickly falling prey to autism. He was considered mild compared to others diagnosed with the same, tragic condition but the weekly sessions with the therapists—the sessions that tried to keep her outlook positive—wore on her both financially and emotionally.

What else was she supposed to do? She needed the money. Although her target patients always took a little coaxing, it generally wasn't hard to get them to select the option that would pay her the commission, or bounty she sometimes called it.

Gina would be her next target. She clicked over to Gina's personal information. A smirk worked its way across her face.

Teacher. Student loans outstanding.

A perfect candidate.

Melanie launched the Web browser on her computer and logged into BioHumanity—the global pharmaceutical giant that paid her commissions. Feeling confident she could get Gina to agree to the program, she spent five minutes typing in Gina's information before uploading her ultrasound. She wasn't quite sure why the ultrasound was required for admission into the program, but they required all the patient's data before she could get paid.

She hit the green *Submit* button at the bottom of the screen and then watched as the commission dollars for Gina—it was now up to five hundred dollars for each referral—rolled into her account … pending, of course, Gina's completion of the program. And Melanie knew, once they agreed to be in the program, the commission was virtually guaranteed.

Just then her voice of reason spoke up, which it periodically did, and wondered if she was doing the right thing. To comfort her decision, Melanie clicked a few more times. The screen showed she continued to be the highest paid sales agent in BioHumanity's referral program. But that didn't impress her anymore. What did impress her were the times BioHumanity's CEO, Steven Vua, personally called to congratulate her commission achievements.

The computer chimed reminding Melanie of Gina's appointment. She grabbed her red shoulder bag made of Spazzolato leather and slipped it into a desk drawer. It was going to be a good day: Gina would be her third referral, netting her fifteen hundred dollars in commissions.

* * * * *

An older Asian-looking woman, maybe in her early fifties, walked into the waiting area. "Ms. Hyde?" she warmly asked.

Gina stood. "Yes, that's me."

She stuck her hand out. "I'm Melanie, one of the counselors here. Won't you please come with me?"

"Of course."

As they headed into the back area of the clinic, Melanie said, "I understand you just finished the ultrasound from one of our assistants."

"Yes, I tried to tell her I just had one yesterday which is why I'm here in the first place, but she just said it was the rules of the center."

"I'm afraid that's right. Before we can determine a course of path, we needed to confirm how many weeks along you are."

The woman took her into a small, private office that was warmly decorated with pictures, plants, and volumes of books. Gina sat across from a faux oak desk as the woman casually seated herself behind a small computer screen.

Melanie eyed the paperwork Gina had filled out, and then lobbed a warm smile toward her. "I know this is your first time here," she said in a steady, motherly voice. "We'll make it as comfortable and relaxing for you as possible. Don't feel like you're the only one going through this. There are thousands of women who come through these doors every year and they all feel the same way you do."

Gina looked away. Guilt was pouring through her as she embarked on a decision that was the result of poor judgment. Then again, what other choice did she have?

She gathered her strength and turned back toward Melanie. "That's very kind of you to say. but there's nobody to blame except me. It shouldn't have happened the way it did … but it did." She touched her belly. "There's just no way I can go through with the pregnancy knowing I would be committed not only to the baby, but also to a father I want nothing to do with."

Melanie smiled as if she heard the story a hundred times. "I understand. We'll take care of everything, but we just need to make sure you're committed to the decision. If you're confident you are, then let's go ahead with what's available to you and see how you want to proceed."

"I am," Gina replied, "and the sooner the better."

Melanie raised an eyebrow, her smile widening. "Okay, let's move forward then."

"What are my options?"

Melanie handed her a short pamphlet describing the next steps. "Now that you've had the ultrasound, we can confirm that you're within the acceptable boundaries for an aborted pregnancy."

"My doctor just calculated it to be fourteen weeks. Is that what you have?"

"I'm afraid not."

Gina leaned forward. "What do you mean?"

"From the test and ultrasound, it's closer to sixteen."

Gina's jaw dropped. "Sixteen weeks? There's no way I wouldn't have noticed my period missing that many times."

"That's what many women say, but sometimes there's a bit of spotting that can be mistaken for a period and that's probably what happened to you."

"Impossible—"

"That's what we're here for," Melanie said in a soft voice. "Since you're within twenty, we'll be able to manage the procedure just fine—either through a medical abortion or a surgical one."

"A medical abortion?"

A nod. "It's medication-based. That is, it's a non-intrusive procedure that relies on the administration of two pills—one while you're at the office here, and the other twenty-four hours later while you're in the comfort and privacy of your home."

"How will I feel... I mean afterward?"

Melanie took a peak at Gina's files spread across her desk. "From reading your history, it sounds like you've never experienced a miscarriage before. Is that right?"

"It is."

"Well, the feeling will be a lot like that. You'll have some heavy bleeding and cramping, and it can last for several hours afterward."

Gina gulped. Her cycles had always been fairly light so she didn't know how she would take such pain. "And the other option?"

"It's a surgical procedure performed here at the clinic. You'll be with our doctors and nurses who will perform an aspiration abortion. We'll sedate you and provide numbing medication for your cervix. From there, the doctor will insert a tube through your cervix into the uterus and then a suction machine will gently empty your uterus. It's a very quick procedure, no more than ten minutes, and then you'll be in the recovery room for another thirty minutes, just to make sure everything is okay before you letting you go."

"What about the pain?"

"It's a bit less painful than the medical abortion. Women generally report milder cramping without prolonged stomach issues."

Gina's heart started beating more. She didn't like either option. One was way more intrusive than she liked and the other was going to be more painful. She bit her lip. How could she have put herself in a situation like this? She vowed never again.

Then there was the question of how she was going to pay for it. "Any chance the cost is under fifty dollars?"

A small smile. "I wish that were the case. It would make it so much easier for women to have the procedures they're entitled to. Unfortunately, honey, that's not the case."

Gina nodded. "I didn't think so."

Melanie pointed to the sheet she handed to Gina. "It's all on there. The medical is about four hundred dollars while the surgical is six hundred."

That stung. It wasn't a ton of money but she had already maxed out her credit cards and this was another expense she just didn't need right now.

Melanie studied her. "Is that too much?"

"Normally, I'd say no," Gina replied. "I'm a teacher just finishing my first year and I'm still paying off my loans. I'm already behind two payments."

"Well," Melanie said slowly, "we do have another option."

Gina could feel her face brighten. "Really?"

"Really."

"Do you mean financing?"

Melanie's eyes settled on Sabrina. In a calm voice, she said, "Not exactly. It's an option where we cover you."

"What's the catch?"

"All we ask is for your time and service in return."

Sabrina straightened in her chair. "Do you mean I have to volunteer my time at the clinic?"

"Heavens, no." A pause. "It's about our affiliation. The Humanity North Center, along with about fifty other clinics across the United States, is associated with a life sciences company called BioHumanity. We aren't owned by them but we do have a strategic partnership that allows our patients to enjoy the latest in technology and keep your costs down."

"How low?"

"Zero."

"Zero?"

Melanie leaned forward. "Let me explain why: BioHumanity, being a global life sciences company, is constantly doing studies and clinical trials. One of the most exciting things they've been working on are human organs generated from our very own cells."

"Wow ... okay. So how can I help?"

"One of the first organs BioHumanity has been able to regenerate is the human heart. With this breakthrough, they will save thousands of lives by transplanting these regenerated hearts into patients who otherwise would die waiting for a donor."

A warm feeling spread through Gina's body as she thought about Blair sitting in the hospital waiting for a donor. "So this bypasses the heart donor system?"

Melanie rubbed her hands together, as if washing them. "Completely."

"Where is it done?"

"That's where it gets very interesting. To recreate the organs, BioHumanity uses stem cells, which are extremely hard to mine from the human body. So they developed the technology to extract the cells from something else: the placenta." She paused. "Unfortunately, as you can imagine, the placenta isn't readily available for stem cell retrieval."

Gina was beginning to understand. "So my fetus will be used as the source for stem cells in return for a free abortion."

"No," Melanie replied quickly, "not exactly." She then said, "It's not about the fetus. It's about the placenta. The only way they can get to the placenta is through an aborted fetus or a live birth."

"I'm not getting it. Why not use the placenta from birth?"

"They'd love to, but there's just not enough available that birthing mothers provide."

"I think I'm starting to understand why the procedure is free."

"We do it for the inconvenience. Nothing else," Melanie said. "That's because the U.S. hasn't approved this lifesaving procedure yet. So BioHumanity funds it and performs it in Acapulco."

"Acapulco?" Gina thought back to her visit with Blair. Didn't she mention something about a heart center in Acapulco?

"Does BioHumanity also do the heart transplants there?"

"Very good. They do. The stem cells extracted from the placenta are cultured and incubated until it's a fully functioning heart."

So this was the place where Gregory wanted Blair to go. "What's ironic is I have a friend fighting for her life … who's considering a heart transplant in Acapulco."

"Really? Then there you go: You'd be helping not only yourself but also saving your friend's life."

That thought almost made it too easy not to say no. "How long would I have to be there?"

"I don't know all the details, but from what they tell me, no more than a week, possibly two. But you would have to leave on short notice—within the next few days."

"That's not a problem. As a teacher, I have the whole summer ahead of me."

"That makes it easy," Melanie responded. "Just remember you would not only be saving your friend's life but others as well."

Gina looked into her counselor's eyes as she thought about the conflict she felt about making this decision. As much as she didn't want the pregnancy, she knew having the baby would put her on a path that she could never recover from. On the other hand, to help other people who could live a fuller, richer life—one where the fetus's own kin could benefit seemed to make the decision that much easier. "Okay, I'll do it," Gina finally said.

Melanie's face lit up. "That's great. Let me get the paperwork started and your signature on a few documents."

"What do I need to do to prepare?" Gina asked.

"Just pack. Make sure your passport is up-to-date ... and get ready for Mexico. You'll receive a call from the Donor Center with all the travel arrangements."

"I can be ready this week."

Melanie reached over and they shook hands. "I guarantee it'll be an experience you won't soon forget."

Chapter 8

Mist fell intermittently as gray clouds moved swiftly off the Pacific. As much as the weather didn't cooperate with the tourists, it meant good business for the local shopkeepers of Neskowin. Along the corner of Breaker Boulevard and Amity Avenue, streams of people waded in and out of the various boutiques, looking for that perfect item to remind them of their time in the Northwest.

"Seems like you're getting a little more comfortable here," Blogg said as he and Sabrina ducked under an awning. They were on their way for a cup of coffee across the street from the paper. What made it palatable was that he had asked her to join him.

Sabrina looked at him. "Yeah, I am."

"Feeling like a local yet?"

A grin emerged. "I don't know if I'd go that far."

"You might be a New Yorker, no let me take that back, a brutal New Yorker, but I'd say you're a Pacific Northwest girl at heart."

"Why do you say that?"

"Because you're an enviro-urbanite."

"Enviro—what?"

"Love the city but love the outdoors even more."

She thought about it. "I suppose that's true." A pause. "What about Getty? Does he get me yet?"

He leaned a shoulder against the storefront. "I said you're feeling comfortable. That doesn't mean you've been welcomed with open arms—at least not yet."

"Does that mean Getty or you?"

He chuckled. "Maybe a little of both."

She smiled at the half-truth: It was probably all she was going to get out of him for the time being. At least he was being supportive. "I guess I'll take that." Her conversation with Carla entered her thoughts. "Can I ask a favor?"

"Of course."

Sabrina was momentarily distracted by a couple carrying a colorful vase down the sidewalk. *It must be nice living a normal life*, she thought. "You've heard the body's been identified?"

He nodded. "Getty's got an update coming out tomorrow."

"Did he meet her wife?"

A shoulder shrug. "Just looked at the coroner's report, from what I understand.

"So he didn't know she was in town yesterday?"

He looked confused. "Why? Did you see her?"

"When I was taking a picture of the statue. She was sitting there—we had a nice chat until…"

"Until what?"

"Until she found out I was a reporter."

He laughed. "Welcome to the club."

"It's disappointing because I really felt a connection to her," she replied seriously. "Carla really loved that man."

"Of course she did. They were married."

She shook her head. "It's something more. A bond you rarely see in a couple. I'd just …"

He raised an eyebrow. "Uh-oh. What are you thinking of now?"

"I'd like to do a follow up."

He threw his hands in the air. "Absolutely not."

"Why?" She raised her voice to match his. "Just because this is Getty's territory?"

He hedged. "That's part of it."

"What else is it?"

"It's been ruled an accident. The whole thing's really a non story."

"Are you kidding?" She was fuming. "You've got to have a heart. This woman is bleeding her husband. Besides, she believes her husband was murdered and I don't disagree with her."

Blogg turned and looked into her eyes. "On what grounds are you and … What did you say her name was?"

"Carla Sanchez," she replied distastefully. *He can't even remember her name.*

"On what grounds," he repeated, "does she and you make these accusations?"

Sabrina looked away. "It's a hunch. I can't explain it since you're a man, but it's my intuition. Carla just feels it and I do too."

Blogg sighed deeply. "This conversation is over."

She threw darts at him with her eyes. "Fine but I'm not over it." She stormed off down the sidewalk and around the corner. She found her convertible parked on a side street and threw herself inside.

What the hell was wrong with that man?

Was it really about reporting facts, and nothing more? She dug her fingernails into the steering wheel and took a deep breath.

Now what?

A thought struck her: *What if I write about him?* To get what she wanted, she would need Carla Sanchez's blessing. Unfortunately, the only place she knew Carla was going to be next was her husband's funeral.

She thought about it for a few minutes. It was the only way and yet it was scattered with land mines. Could she really bother Carla when she was trying to mourn his loss? Blogg would no doubt be pissed if she went through with it.

What other choice did she have? The more she thought about it, the more she knew she had to do it.

And maybe, just maybe, it would draw out the killer.

* * * * *

Sloan Mannheim, looking far younger than his forty-two years, eyed the tablet strategically placed in front of his face. Scanning the news, he settled on an article written by the local reporter David Getty. Swiping his finger, he continued onto the next page, and then the third.

The reporter had done a good job covering the facts of the Sanchez death. All the facts without any assumptions. It was exactly the way he liked it.

A man and woman began quarreling a mere ten yards from him, interrupting his train of thought. Placing the tablet quietly on the table, he took a sip of the double espresso and turned an ear toward the couple.

After the woman stormed off, he placed the cup delicately on the cafe table and pondered what she had yelled at the editor. He took another sip as he watched the fiery woman turn the corner down the street.

She would need to be dealt with. She was a loose end.

He hated loose ends.

Chapter 9

Everywhere Gina looked there was chaos.

Just outside the entrance to the Welcome Center near Playa del Secreto in the inner bay of Acapulco, twenty or thirty women were shouting in unison while holding signs. "Baby killers! No more murder! No more murder!" they chanted. Gina glanced at the pictures splashed across the signs and then pulled away, sickened by the vulgarity of it. Every sign showed graphic depictions of abortion including bloody fetuses.

To Gina, it was more than disgusting: It was unfair.

As the sea of demonstrators circled around her, Gina searched for the door. She finally locked eyes on one of the security guards who beckoned her with his hand.

Pushing forward, she was nearly knocked over by a woman running into her. "Excuse me," Gina said tersely. The woman gave her an accusatory stare before moving on.

Uncomfortable with the perceived accusation, guilt poured through Gina. She wasn't quite sure why she felt such guilt but she also wasn't sure why these women felt such hatred toward women wanting to save lives. Trying to forget the altercation, Gina moved on, keeping both hands in front until she reached the top step of the Welcome Center. The security guard opened the large glass door and pulled her inside. "Buenos tardes, senorita!" he said.

With her child's understanding of Spanish, Gina barely translated the welcome. "Gracias," she replied.

The guard, dressed in a white polo and black pants, nudged her down a small hallway toward a second set of glass doors. She had been told the Donor Center was a short ferry ride from the Welcome Center but they were required to come here first for orientation. He motioned with his hand. "Please head through the atrium and take a seat in the auditorium. Our CEO and the Center's director, Dr. Vua, will be there to welcome you," he said in broken English. "They will then take you across the bay to your dorm." A pause. "Any questions?"

Gina shook her head. It was all happening so fast. There just wasn't any time to think.

"Perdóname." He bowed his head slightly and headed back toward the front entrance.

With the commotion behind her, Gina took a deep breath and tried to brush off the unnerving welcome she received. While she wasn't quite sure who the women were, it was obvious they treated this place as a killing center for babies. It was a message Gina didn't need to be reminded of as she thought about the wrenching decision she made seven days ago.

I'm not going to be intimidated, she thought. Regardless of what those women believe, being here was the right decision. She was sure of it. Blair needed a chance to survive and the abortion would give her that. Besides, she needed the time away to start fresh, to cleanse her soul of the grief she felt.

Gina pushed through the door into a large, cathedral-like atrium. Her jaw dropped with awe: Bright colors were splashed everywhere—a nod to making the donors as comfortable as possible. Fresh displays of daffodils, irises, tulips, and roses of every imaginable color were splashed across the atrium, choreographed to music flowing throughout the room.

She remembered back to why BioHumanity chose this spot. "Acapulco offered a stress-free recluse for the patients and donors, and the Mexican government had offered the least resistance and the most tax incentives to lure BioHumanity into building here," a counselor had said.

"Gina?"

She tossed her eyes right. A hand waved near the auditorium entrance and then a woman in a muscular yet compact frame, with a small belly bump, approached.

"Helen!" Gina said excitedly. She wrapped her arms around her. "How have you been?"

"I'm good. I'm really glad I made the decision to come here but the demonstrators outside were a bit unnerving."

Gina rolled her eyes. "I know!"

"Seriously. I wish somebody would do something about it."

"Any idea why they're demonstrating here?"

Helen shrugged her shoulders. "Nobody seems to say much about it. It just may be that they don't like abortions being performed here."

"Maybe."

"Whatever it is, I wish they'd leave. They make a terrible first impression."

"That's probably the point. They're trying to discourage us and I'm sure it's working on some women, but not me."

Helen squeezed Gina's hand. "That's girl power, honey."

"Are you feeling better about the decision you made?"

Helen looked at Gina. "I was really confused when I first met you … and I don't know if I'll ever get over ending the pregnancy." She sighed. "It's just an awful decision to have to make. … I'm just so happy we'll be seeing this thing through together."

"I feel the same," Gina responded. "I'm becoming more comfortable with the decision knowing it might help someone close to me."

"Really?" Helen's eyes brightened. "Who's that?"

"My ex-boyfriend's sister. We became close over the years as I was dating her brother, Gregory. Then I found out last week she has a degenerative heart problem and needs a transplant. So I'm hoping the stem cells I'm donating to the Center will be a match for the new heart she needs."

"Does she know?"

"That I'm here?"

A nod. "I mean, your ex must be loving you for doing this, especially if he broke up with you."

Gina shook her head. "Maybe … but I definitely don't want that. Besides, I broke it off with him."

"Really?"

"He was an ass. Luckily his sister knows that. At least I think she does. I wrote her a little note and mailed it to her hospital room."

"Oh? What did it say?"

Gina looked up for a second before settling on Helen's face. "I wanted her to know that I was thinking of her, trying to do anything I could to help her—that I had decided to donate stem cells here in Acapulco from an abortion I was having and that I hoped it would lead to a regenerated heart for her."

"Your ex knows nothing about this?"

Gina sighed. "I hope not. I told Blair not to mention this to Gregory at all, because I didn't want him thinking I was doing it for him."

"I hope she gets all the help she needs," Helen replied softly.

"For her sake, I hope so too."

"I don't quite have the same motivation but if I could help save the life of a stranger that's enough for me." Helen took a step back and took in Gina's body. "You do look fabulous."

"You're too nice ... and likewise!"

A smile formed on Helen as she put her hands up in the air. "Can you believe this place?"

"I know. It's absolutely breathtaking."

A loudspeaker high above them crackled, telling them the presentation was about to begin in the auditorium.

Gina grabbed Helen's hand. "C'mon. It's time to hear what Dr. Vua has to say. I've heard so many good things about him since I signed up and I'm dying to see what he's like."

The small brown and beige colored auditorium filled quickly with not only the donors but members of the BioHumanity staff. Gina spun around as she admired the auditorium's eclectic circular design—huge glass panels adorned the building's perimeter, creating a seamless fusion of wall and ceiling. "This place is amazing," Gina whispered.

They stepped into an aisle near the middle, sitting next to a wiry man with black horn-rimmed glasses. She glanced at him and thought a white lab coat with pens hanging out of the pocket would complete the picture of a nerd perfectly. *Must be a researcher,* she thought. Helen jumped in right beside her, grabbing the aisle seat.

The man smiled at them. "Welcome to Acapulco."

Gina rolled her eyes. She hated it when men she had absolutely no attraction to wasted her time. "Thank you. I hope so, too" she replied with barely a glance in his direction.

"I'm Dr. Mason Guthrie."

She peered out the corner of her eye. "That's nice."

Helen nudged her. "That's Gina."

Gina shot her a glance.

"Pretty name," Guthrie said.

"Thanks," she replied flatly.

He continued, "We do appreciate your commitment to helping us save lives."

"Thank you. That's why I'm here."

"Have you ever seen Dr. Vua before?" Guthrie said. "He's legendary in these parts."

"No but I've heard impressive things about him," Helen interjected. "Even if my friend Gina isn't all that impressed."

Guthrie chuckled. "Well, I'm sure that will all change after you meet him." A pause. "To me, he's a rock star for what he's been able to accomplish."

Gina couldn't resist turning her head. "You can't be serious," she replied as she scanned him head to toe. She was right: He was a nerd.

"Completely serious. He's been able to accomplish so much for so many." Guthrie leaned in toward Gina and Helen. "Without him, hundreds would've died waiting for a traditional heart transplant."

Then he added, "He's a miracle worker."

Chapter 10

In the cemetery clearing Mannheim knelt behind a large oak, his high-powered field binoculars trained on a funeral gathering a couple hundred feet ahead of him. Mourners, most dressed in black, had circled the burial site and were somberly saying their last goodbyes. *Sanchez had been a fool*, he thought. Scanning right, he focused on the sky blue convertible, and its female driver, inching along the gravel path toward the funeral. He crouched even further, his black T-shirt dusting the ground, eyes trained on the woman's face. His mind was racing. As he stared at the young yet mature-looking face, and the closely cropped black hair, he thought for a moment about the mourners, and the fact that they were gathered here because of his work ten days ago.

The Sanchez operation was complete save one loose end—but it was a costly one. Evidence linking his contractor to the murder had leaked from the desk, and mind, of Sanchez. It was a little black book—a journal—that Sanchez had kept for months leading up to his death. His contractor found out about it after they started tracking Sanchez's movements. The contractor had relayed that information so Mannheim could interrogate Sanchez about it. When confronted, Sanchez refused to acknowledge its existence, even through his untimely death.

Mannheim smiled from behind the binoculars. Reliving the terror on Sanchez's face the moment he knew he was going to die made Mannheim fell tingly inside—probably as much from the rush of adrenaline watching someone die as to the six-figure payout he was promised after the kill. Sanchez's death would've been the fifth such payout this year. Most people would be shocked at the amount of money he made, given his thrifty lifestyle. That is, until they spent a weekend at his Spanish-style villa on the Mexican peninsula. It was his one single splurge that gave him a place to relax and recharge after high-stress kills. Besides, keeping his luxuries out of sight from the simple lifestyle he enjoyed in a middle-class Seattle suburb dampened any suspicion one conjured up. For the sake of his reputation and career, he preferred to keep it that way.

The Sanchez job really bothered him.

He was supposed to receive five hundred thousand for the kill but only received half that to date. Although Sanchez's death had been executed perfectly, his contractor refused to give him full payment until the journal was recovered. And just to emphasize how serious they were, they would give him a hefty bonus—double the original payout—if he eliminated the loose end. But there would be one catch: He would have to deliver the journal within the next five days to get the full payout. Otherwise, his contract called for splitting it with a partner—a woman with a long-standing relationship with the contractor.

A more pressing matter occupied his thoughts: What to do with the reporter? Mannheim zoomed in on the convertible as it pulled tentatively to a stop at the end of the funeral procession. The reporter was becoming more than just a nuisance. She was becoming a roadblock to his payout and that didn't sit well with him at all. The beauty of it was, as a trained sharpshooter from his days as an Army Ranger, he could easily put a bullet between her eyes, even from this distance. But it wasn't the right time. Today would be about gathering intelligence, trying to see what she knew and who she talked to.

So what was she up to?

She obviously sniffed something otherwise she wouldn't be at the funeral. Being here made it clear to him the reporter felt a story was there—either about Sanchez's murder, the journal, or both. He bit his lip. She was making things messy for him: messy to clean up, messy to explain, messy to his contractor.

He hated messy.

It was then he decided he would give her one warning: Get out of town or die. The reporter slipped out of the convertible and cautiously walked toward the gathering. Now was his moment. He pulled the binoculars away from his face and placed them back in their leather case. In a low crouch, Mannheim slithered toward the funeral procession.

He smiled. A huge payout was knocking on his door.
Life doesn't get any better than this.

Chapter 11

Dr. Steven Vua stood just off stage right and eyed the thirty-five sets of eyes awaiting his opening remarks. His left eye twitched rapidly, the only sign of nervousness he showed. He knew it was ridiculous, but stage fright was never something he fully conquered in all the years of being founder and CEO of BioHumanity.

The chatter of the audience within the Welcome Center floated toward him. What would he say? It was something he agonized over no matter how many times he delivered his speech. Of course he would tell the donors how dramatically their lives would change from the experience. And it wasn't just the audience that would change. It would be the lives saved through their generous donations.

Little by little, day by day, his dream was becoming a reality—like a skyscraper going up beam by beam. The business plan he had put together was working.

It was almost sick it was so easy.

He counted the revenue in his head. Every month brought in four million dollars, give or take a few hundred thousand. If he were able to increase the volume, to say, eight million a month, the Heart Center would be well on its way to becoming a hundred million dollar business unit. If he played his cards right, he should be able to increase that tenfold within five to seven years. That meant his dream of achieving a billion dollar business would be complete.

The lights dimmed, causing the audience's voices to fall into a shallow murmur.

"Dr. Vua? They're waiting for you," an event coordinator said from behind him.

The voice startled him. "I'll tell you when I'm ready," he hissed.

"I'm ... I'm sorry, sir," the shy, boyish voice replied—seemingly unsure of what to say next. "When ... when should I come back?"

"Just cue the intro," Vua demanded. "And leave me alone."

"Yes, of course." The coordinator held out his hand. "Here's the headset you'll be speaking into for your speech." He then quietly backed away.

The stage lights flipped on and focused on the empty podium. Another smile, this time more sly, crossed Vua's face.

It was time to mesmerize his audience.

A video montage introducing Vua began playing. "Ten years ago, a mission was born by Dr. Steven Vua," the narrator said. "It was a mission to find a lifesaving alternative to traditional heart transplants—one that would save thousands of patients who would otherwise die waiting for that precious organ to arrive. What he discovered was a true medical miracle—a way to mold stems cells from the placenta into heart-saving organs ... in a matter of weeks."

That was the cue. Vua moved briskly across the stage toward the podium as the audience erupted with applause. He looked up, toward the lights, his brother never far from his mind. *I owe all of this to you my brother,* he thought.

* * * * *

Any sibling would feel traumatized and utterly hopeless as they watched a dying brother or sister take their last breaths.

But Steven Vua wasn't one of them.

At that moment, while his brother lie powerless and clinging to life, all he could think about was his company: Somehow, somewhere, he needed revenue growth.

A doctor came in, interrupting Vua. In a low voice, the doctor told him that, unfortunately, a donor's heart had been found but it was the wrong match. And so the lifesaving heart would be given to the next in line.

As his shoulders slumped with despair, Vua turned back toward his brother, floating in and out of consciousness, and wondered if he already knew he wasn't going to make it. He leaned over the bed and waved a hand back and forth across his face. No reaction.

He eyed the defibrillator keeping him alive. As he watched the air compress in and out, an idea came to him. At first, he thought it was too far-fetched to seriously consider, but the more he thought about it, the more he realized the idea had the potential to be something big: What if he could reverse the fortunes of thousands of heart patients who would otherwise die?

He knew it would take investment and a lot of R&D to make it happen, but at that moment, it suddenly seemed plausible. It was simple economics: He would radically change, and control, the supply for heart transplants, driving the cost up. He would then become the financial beneficiary. Vua's thoughts were interrupted by an alarm screeching from his brother's heart monitor. Looking up, he saw nothing but a flat line.

He was dead.

Chapter 12

Soothing, new age music filled the small auditorium from the loudspeakers. "Here we go," Guthrie whispered to Helen and Gina.

Gradually, the music reached a crescendo. And then everything went quiet. "Ladies and gentlemen," an unseen announcer said through the speakers. "Welcome to the Acapulco Heart and Donor Center. Your commitment and time to helping save the lives of eventually thousands of heart patients does not go unnoticed to the patients themselves, the staff, or our founder, Dr. Steven Vua—the CEO and Founder of BioHumanity. To show his gratitude to you, the donors, he would like to say a few words as you begin your journey into saving the lives of those that are less fortunate as yours or mine." A pause. "Ladies and gentlemen, I introduce Dr. Steven Vua."

The audience began applauding. Gina and Helen looked around and then joined in. Everybody rose to their feet as Vua entered the brightly lit stage from stage right. He waved briefly to the audience as he walked toward the podium. He then motioned with his hands for everybody to sit. The room quickly quieted down with everybody settling back into their chairs, their attention focused on what Vua was going to say.

"Let me be the first to welcome you to Acapulco," he began.

Gina leaned back in her chair and studied his features, wondering why people thought he was a rock star. He wore a black suit over a gray shirt; he was medium-built, dark-skinned, with a hint of Asian influence. As he spoke, his eyebrows creased downward, as if he was determined to instill his thoughts into the audience.

"Your donation to the forefront of science is allowing you and BioHumanity to save hundreds and eventually thousands of lives. I am proud of your commitment and look forward to meeting every one of you as we embark on this journey together." Suddenly the lights dimmed and a batter of drums echoed throughout the auditorium. The sacrifice you are making will not go unnoticed. The placenta from your aborted fetus contains some of the richest stem cells available anywhere. It is this rich biology that will save the lives of heart patients who normally wouldn't get a second chance at life, one they surely deserve."

The tempo of the drumbeat picked up. Vua took a breath. "It's hard to envision a genetically focused heart center being successful without its greatest resource: its donors. People like you, who are sacrificing your time and your own genetic future, in the name of helping others. You are the ones that deserve the applause." Vua started clapping and his staff quickly joined in.

"That's what I mean. … He's the real deal," Guthrie whispered.

Motioning with his hands, the crowd quieted and Vua continued, "We are at the crossroads of revolutionizing how we regenerate our own organs. It is your volunteerism that we're laying the groundwork for saving lives who ordinarily wouldn't be saved with traditional procedures."

"How are you doing it?" someone yelled from audience.

A chuckle rolled through the crowd as Vua put up his hand. "That is a very good question, my friend." Gina rolled her eyes, as it seemed to be a planted question from one of his staff, and a cue to the next part of his speech. But to his credit, she was interested in what he had to say.

"As I mentioned before, each one of you is carrying a valuable resource for the regeneration of the heart. The placenta that your fetus is using for nutrients and protection contains one of nature's richest sources of mesenchymal stem cells, or MSCs as we like to call them. These MSCs are normally used to repair damaged cartilage, heart muscle and other damage to the heart organ, which allow it to reconstruct into a normal functioning heart."

"We will be using the placenta from your aborted fetus to save lives by building new hearts from the very same stem cells inside the placenta. We have discovered a revolutionary new way to use these MSCs to develop new hearts. The beauty of it is, because of the MSCs we'll be using, there will be no chance of rejection by the heart recipient—a complication more traditional procedures have never been able to solve."

A murmur of excitement rippled through the audience.

"This is going to save lives, by the hundreds today and the thousands tomorrow!" Vua said, raising his voice with each word. "And it is all because of you!" he shouted as he pointed to the audience.

The lights then went down and the music stopped.

Chapter 13

Sabrina tapped lightly on the brake as she crept along the gravel path in her convertible. With every crunch of the stone beneath the tires, she gritted her teeth a little tighter. She needed to slip in—make a quiet entrance, not be a distraction.

A hundred yards behind the procession, she stopped and pulled the rearview mirror toward her. She eyed her outfit. *The top would work with the gray pencil skirt and knee-high boots*, she thought. Not bad, considering how quickly she pulled it together. She pushed herself out of the car and clicked the door shut. A towering oak nearby seemed to offer some cover so she slid into its shadow.

Five couples stood arm in arm gathered in a circle around a decorated urn that sat on a nickel and gold pedestal near the gravesite. In the center of the circle, a pastor, fully cloaked in a rose-colored robe, was giving the final prayers.

A raindrop fell on Sabrina's head. She looked up at the gray, churning clouds. *Perfect*, she thought, *just what I need*. She then started second-guessing herself. Being here was a brash move. Carla would feel it was tacky at best and offensive at worst. But how else could she find Carla in such short order? Eric Sanchez's funeral was the only way, she kept telling herself.

The pastor's words floated toward her: "Oh, Father, how art that we can go on, given this enormous burden we feel without our loved ones?" Sabrina spotted Carla weeping silently as she placed a hand on the urn. After a few more words, the pastor said, "Let us now have a moment of silence."

The mourners' circle grew tighter as they wrapped their arms around each other. After standing motionless for a minute, Carla stepped away from the group, knelt on her knees, and with her hand trembling, placed a single red rose on the urn's pedestal. She then pushed her face into hands and started weeping. A man standing behind her began rubbing her back, gently comforting her.   After a moment, clearly still struggling with her emotions, Carla wiped her face and slowly stood.   The pastor closed his Bible. He nodded toward the small gathering, affirming the service was over.

Friends and family melted away, leaving Carla alone with her lifeless husband as she shared one last moment together.   Sabrina eyed Carla nervously as she gathered the courage to walk up to her. *This isn't going to be easy*, she thought.   But now was the time get more information about Eric Sanchez's death, she kept telling herself, even if there was little chance Carla would give it.

Sabrina took a breath and started walking along the line of trees.   Carla stared at the urn for a few more minutes and then turned toward her waiting car.   Jumping on the opportunity, Sabrina bolted from the darkness of the trees.   When she was within a few yards of Carla, she said, "I offer my sincere condolences to you."   Sabrina intentionally tried to keep her voice as somber and caring as she could.

Carla opened a swollen eye and turned toward the voice.   Her sad demeanor quickly morphed into anger.   "How dare you come to my husband's funeral?" she hissed beneath her breath.

Sabrina swallowed hard.   "I completely understand what you may be thinking ... but I'm only here to help and that's it."

Ignoring her, Carla wrapped the black shawl she was wearing tight around her shoulders and walked away.

"The other day ... It wasn't my intent to coerce anything from you," Sabrina called after her.   "I was there taking pictures for an article on the statue.   That's it."

Carla stopped but didn't turn around.   "Then why are you here?   Just to apologize?   Then apology accepted.   Now leave me alone."   She then continued walking up a berm, in the direction of her ride.

Sabrina trotted after her.   "I think your husband got a horrible sendoff in the paper ... and after listening to your story, I just think ... well ... that the life of Eric Sanchez should be told and celebrated."

"This isn't some reality TV series.   This is my life," she barked over her shoulder.

"It would be a feature celebrating his life.   Nothing more."

Carla stopped and turned. Smudged, black makeup had run down her face. "I'm not interested in publicizing my husband's death anymore than it already has," she replied, but this time her voice was calmer. A single tear slid down an eye. She dabbed at it with her handkerchief. "That's the last thing I want."

Sabrina reached out to her, hesitated, and then touched her arm. "I know. But think about our readers. All they know is what's been published—that a body was discovered. They read it. They feel terrible. They move on with their lives. Don't you think your husband deserves an honor more than that? He's positively affected so many in his life that he deserves more."

Carla's eyes danced with every word, as if she were pondering what to do. Finally, in a jerk reaction, she pulled away. "Why are you bothering me? The last week and a half has been absolute hell, and now I have to relive that through some reporter that happened to stumble upon me while I'm grieving?"

"I just thought it would be something that we could … you know … do together. You could help me focus the feature on your husband's life. We would write about it and—"

"What don't you get?" Carla interrupted. "I will never see my husband again for the rest of my life." She started sobbing. "I won't be able to sit down and have romantic dinners, talk about our days at work … do anything with him that I loved to do. That life is gone forever."

"Don't you want people to understand your loss?"

"The last thing I need is for people to feel sorry for me. Do you honestly think I want the pity of email and telephone calls raining down on me every day? Everybody has their own way of dealing with loss, and acknowledging that to the outside world is not how I do it."

Sabrina was losing her. "I completely understand that but—"

"I don't mean to be rude but I think this conversation is over. Have a good day." Carla then turned and opened the door to her ride.

Sabrina let out a sigh of disgust as she trudged back to her own car. If she was going to survive as a reporter she would need to learn how to negotiate with her subjects. Otherwise, this job wasn't going to last very long. She started up the engine and began rolling through the cemetery, and then headed toward the highway. She eyed the dashboard clock and sighed again. She had wasted her whole day chasing something Blogg would blow a fuse if … no … when he found out. And for all the hours spent on this, she had nothing to show for it. A small piece of folded-over paper caught her eye as it rested on the passenger seat. She glanced at it and then again. That's weird. She didn't remember putting anything on the seat. She reached over and flipped it open. In bold, all caps lettering, eighteen haunting words stared back at her:

YOU WILL DIE UNLESS YOU STOP INVESTIGATING. CONSIDER THIS THE FIRST WARNING. YOU WILL SOON EXPERIENCE THE SECOND.

She tossed the paper onto the floor as her stomach started churning. Suddenly, something ahead caught her eye. The headlights of an oncoming car were in her lane, heading straight for her. She instinctively slammed on the breaks but applied too much pressure. The car veered from side to side as she tried to regain control of the steering. She turned the wheel hard in the other direction, but she overcorrected. The car's tires squealed in desperation as they tried to save the driver from injury.

No matter what she did she couldn't change the inevitable.

The convertible spun through the intersection and plowed into a guardrail, causing the car's cockpit to wrap around her. She felt her body twitch and then a sheering pain shot through her.

Before she could reach for her arm, everything went black.

Chapter 14

The ferry was nothing like Gina had ever been on before. Built more like a luxury cruiser, the donors sat in comfortable recliners inside an air-conditioned cabin as they cruised across Playa del Secreto.

Extravagant as it was, Gina certainly didn't mind it. She cupped her hands against the oval window and stared out at the vast ocean. Sunlight glistened off the water, shooting rays in every direction. It reminded her of high school prom when the DJ trained a light on the dance globe. Gina leaned back in her seat and closed her eyes. It was the first time she had a moment to herself after such a whirlwind week.

"I think I see the lights," Helen suggested from the seat behind her.

Gina opened her eyes and eyed the overhead display. They were five minutes from arrival. She had fallen asleep, even if it was for only fifteen minutes. The ferry slowed to a few knots as Gina looked out the window. A sun-drenched, all-glass building drifted into view just on the other side of the pier.

The architecture was impressive. Eight or nine floors of exposed beams, painted royal blue, held large diamond-shaped glass panels in place. Along the bay side, each floor sported large floor to ceiling windows that extended beyond the frame of the building—with glass wrapping all sides.

"Wow," Helen said. "This place is amazing."

"I guess they want us to be comfortable," Gina replied, her nose still firmly planted against the window.

The ferry hung for a few seconds in the water and then jolted forward as it hitched to the pier. A moment later, a metal docking pier dropped with a clang onto the boat. "Welcome to BioHumanity's Acapulco Donor Center," a staff member said as they filed off the ferry and into the covered walkway that led to their new home for the next few weeks. They followed the staff into a large atrium, this one more airy than the Welcome Center, every inch lit by its massive windows.

Gina turned toward the bay, marveling that the windows were the only barricade to the outside world. "Amazing … feels like there's nothing between us and the outside," Gina said to Helen.

"I think we made the right decision coming here," Helen replied, all smiles.

"No doubt."

Chapter 15

"You okay?"

Sabrina opened her eyes. The flash of the accident ran through her head before giving way to an intense, throbbing pain on her right side. "I don't know," she gasped as the smell of fuel circled them. The Samaritan yanked on the driver's door but it wouldn't give.

"We need to get you out of here ... good thing you're in a convertible." He reached in and tugged at her belt. After a second tug, the belt released and recoiled sharply into its holder.

"Whatever you need to do," she replied halfheartedly. "Are the police coming?"

"Don't worry about that. They're on their way." As if on cue, the sounds of sirens could be heard in the distance. The Samaritan reached in with both hands. "You think you can grab my arms as I pull you out?"

She shook her head. "Maybe with my left but I can't move my right."

He rolled up the sleeve of her top and looked at the bulging bruise that ran from her elbow toward the shoulder. "I see why."

She saw him nod toward the passenger's side. "Maybe we can try the other door," he said. "You'll just have to find a way to drag yourself over the gearbox."

"I'll try," she muttered. Everything was in a fog but her fifth sense caught the stench of gas and it seemed to be getting stronger. "I think you better hurry," she said as loud as she could but it was probably no more than a whisper.

He ran to the other side and pulled hard on the door handle. The car shook but then the door popped open. He knelt inside and wrapped his hands around her midsection.

"I'm going to give you a quick pull to nudge you loose, okay?"

She nodded. What he didn't have to say but that they both understood was that it was going to hurt. He pulled her as gently as he could, but her arm banged against the dashboard and stick shift. "Oh," she groaned as the pain ricocheted through her arm and chest.

"Okay. The worst is over. Now we gotta keep moving."

Her legs dropped from the car and she was dragged quickly across the highway. They couldn't have been more than thirty feet away when her car exploded in a fusion of fire and gasoline. The thrust of the impact launched them onto the asphalt. A shirring pain ripped through her arm. "Augh!" she cried as tears flowed from her eyes.

She rolled onto her back and looked on helplessly as the intense heat flooded her face—her convertible now a heap of smoldering metal, rubber, and plastic. The Samaritan stumbled awkwardly back to his feet and wrapped his hands around her shoulders, yanking her toward a light pole. The sirens seemed to surround them and then an unfamiliar voice said, "We can take it from here."

"Yes, of course," the Samaritan replied as he loosened his grip on her.

Sabrina looked into the eyes of a police officer kneeling before her. "Ma'am? You all right?"

"It's her arm. The right one," she heard the Samaritan say behind her.

"Just stay calm, ma'am. We'll have a paramedic look you over in a minute."

The accident flashed through her mind again: She had looked straight ahead just as the oncoming car was going to hit her, and for a second, saw the driver's face. It may have only been for a moment but she would never forget the cold stare he gave her. "What about the driver who hit me?" she stammered.

He shook his head. "Hit and run. We don't have much to go on right now but we'll get 'em."

Another siren wailed in the distance. Before she knew it, a paramedic was at her side. "What do we have?" he asked the officer as he went to work on her.

"She was the driver of the convertible. Possible broken arm, bruising along the face."

The paramedic eyed her warmly. "Let's get your arm set and then how 'bout a little ride to the hospital?" he asked in a calming voice.

She nodded before muttering, "That would be fine."

Chapter 16

Vua eyed the candidate curiously from behind the lobby doors.

The man looked anxious as he entered the seventh floor lobby —his long hair flowing with a mix of blonde and brown— matching the persona of an urban professional in his thirties. *Must be here for a family member,* Vua immediately thought. It was exactly the situation he wanted the candidate to be in—desperation—they would be willing to overpay for the transplant. For a moment the man took in his surroundings and then headed to the receptionist. After a short conversation, she nodded politely and then waved him over to a group of orange and tan couches positioned in the center of the atrium.

A second later, Vua's cell buzzed with a text message from the receptionist announcing the third visitor of the day had arrived. Vua pushed opened the stainless-steel door from which he had been eyeing his prospect, drew a smile, and stepped into the lobby. He pulled the lapels of his sport coat tight to make sure it fit evenly across his narrow chest and strolled over to the candidate. "Mr. Archer?" Vua asked as he extended his hand. "I'm Dr. Vua."

The man awkwardly jumped to his feet and grabbed the man's hand. "Yes, hello." He wiped his brow as a bit of sweat dripped down. "Thank you for meeting me on such short notice."

"Of course, Mr. Archer."

"Please call me Gregory."

Vua's smile widened a bit. To him, it was obvious the prospect was trying hard to be polite—something that didn't come easy given his demeanor. "Welcome to Acapulco, Mr. Archer. I hope it wasn't too much trouble making it here."

"No problems, even though it was last minute … especially since I came in from San Diego."

Vua eyed the flyer Gregory held in his hand. It was a printout from one of the ad campaigns he had run just a few weeks ago. He already had fifty leads from that promotion. *Money well spent*, he thought. He pointed to the ad. "Is that how you became aware of us?"

"It was my sister. She found it online and showed it to me when I visited her in the hospital. It just seems like our only option."

A nod. "Given your sister's urgency, I don't want to keep you waiting any longer. Won't you please follow me?"

"I'd be happy to."

Vua led him through the door from which he had just come and into a sunlight-drenched walkway that led to another stainless-steel door. He placed his thumb in the security sensor. When the door unlocked, he pushed through into a similar looking walkway, with doors lining both sides of the hallway. He stopped at the third door one on the left and knocked twice. "I always think it's important for our potential clients to experience how we're creating the extraordinary technology we use in our patients. To us, it provides both a sense of comfort and confidence for the patient's family." The door clicked and Vua pushed it open. He waved his hand across the room. "This is one of the five donor incubation laboratories that make up the heart of the center, so to speak," Vua said. "In rooms such as these, we generate the organ your sister so desperately needs."

Gregory became visibly more relaxed as he eyed the room and the rows of small black containers. "Unbelievable," he said under his breath.

Vua continued, "I read your application." He enjoyed getting right to the point. It made the visitor uncomfortably aware of the urgency of their visit. "The doctors believe your sister has a severe form of cardiomyopathy and needs an immediate transplant."

Gregory's frame stiffened. "Yes, she doesn't have much time … the doctor says weeks at the most." He paused, then said, "Honestly, I'm out of options with traditional medicine. She's just not high enough on the donor list and your approach seems to have great results."

Vua smirked. "Correction. I'd say it has the best results." Vua felt ecstatic inside. He loved prospects that felt they had run out of options, and Gregory was a bulls' eye. Besides, he had already tipped his hand and didn't even know it. Vua could easily charge prospects like him an extra thirty thousand and they would still do it—because they knew what the alternative meant.

Desperation. It was capitalism at its best.

"Every one of the hundred incubators you see here contains a live beating heart that is growing hour by hour, day by day until it reaches the size needed for transplant into the patient." Vua beckoned with his hand. "Please … feel free to have a look."

Gregory stepped forward, toward one of the small incubators and peered through a small window inset into the black, molded capsule that made up the incubator. What looked like a mesh of human tissue was beating rapidly, more so than any adult heart. "These are live, human hearts growing?"

"Yes, every one of them," Vua replied proudly. "And not only that, the one that's selected for transplant into your sister will have an exact cell match to your sister's genetic makeup. That's important because it means the heart will never have a chance to be rejected by her body."

Gregory's face lit up. "How do you do that?"

"It's both simple and complex at the same time. Every person is part of a segmented group that shares a similar cell makeup. What we do is secure hundreds of donors that are willing to spare stem cells for each of these segments."

"You mean directly from the donor?"

Vua laughed, almost rudely. "No. Impossible. What we draw the stem cells from might surprise you."

"How so?"

"A mother's placenta contains the richest set of stem cells available. That's the fuel we need to grow these hearts from … literary nothing … to what you see here today."

Gregory shook his head. "Unbelievable … but how do you get the women to undergo such a procedure?

"You would be surprised how many women sign up to do this. It's really quite a long list. If the incentive is there, most women are happy to take our terms."

"You're saving lives, but isn't it … " He stopped as if searching for the right word.

"You mean unethical?" Vua asked.

"Yes."

Vua stroked his chin, a mischievous grin forming on his face. "What's your definition of unethical? If it's using cells from an aborted life to save another, then guilty—and mind you that decision was made before the donor arrived here. But I prefer to look at it differently: You have no idea how many people come up to me and shake my hand, thanking me for saving a loved one they couldn't imagine living without—it's a situation just like yours. And you know what? Every one of those lives I saved just makes me more motivated than ever. I'll continue doing this as long as there's a demand for it."

Gregory stopped at an incubator halfway across the room. He again looked through the small window at the growing organ. "All I care about is Blair." He then turned and stared at Vua. "If you're able to save her, to me, you'll be a miracle worker."

A chuckle. "I've been called many things, Mr. Archer, but it'll be the first time I'm called a miracle worker."

Gregory lowered a brow. "I'm confused about one thing, though."

"What is that?"

"If you're so successful, then why the demonstration outside?"

Vua's demeanor turned serious. "I'm sorry you had to experience that. That's a sad reminder of abortion foes who would rather a woman keep an unwanted baby than provide life for somebody else."

"What you're doing is completely legal?"

Vua sighed. "I'll be blunt with you. Not in the States, but it is here … and that's fine with me and my staff. If the United States doesn't want to reap the benefits of an industry leader that provides jobs for a local economy and saves thousands of lives, then certainly Acapulco will."

Gregory turned back to the incubators lining the room. "You sound like someone holding a grudge."

"Let me show you something." Vua said, ignoring Gregory's comment. He led Gregory out of the lab and down the hall to another room. Vua stopped at the door and peered through the small six by six window. "Good. They're working today." He knocked twice and then opened door, waving Gregory to follow.

The room was filled with black-surfaced counters, like the ones found in college labs. Spread across the lab, six men and four women seemed captivated as they peered through microscopes at petri dishes.

"You see these people? They are extracting cells from the fetus's placenta and then multiplying them to create the organ we are targeting.

"In this case, a human heart?"

"Exactly … just like what you saw in the other room. I know it's hard to imagine, but look at it this way—hearts are an organ in your body, like your kidneys and liver. And organs, like the heart, are made of tissues that perform a specialized function. These tissues are built from cells, and it's these cells where we can manipulate the genetic switches. So once we have the right switches flipped, we incubate it, causing the cells to multiply into the organ we want.

"Why the heart?"

"Because it has the largest effect on saving lives." *And my wallet,* he thought.

Gregory started pacing back and forth. "I have to admit, I'm floored," he finally said. "I mean, I know zero about science, but to be able to do what you're doing … is brilliant."

Vua nodded a few times. He never tired of people telling him how brilliant he was. "I'm glad you understand the value of what we're doing." He eyed his watch. "If you're comfortable with our operation, then let's step in my office and see what we can do to help your sister."

"I'd like that very much," Gregory replied without hesitation.

With Gregory ahead of him, Vua gave a nod to the team in the lab, and then closed the door. They continued down the hall and pushed open a stainless-steel door with a nameplate bearing Vua's full name. As the door widened, they were bathed in sunlight from the floor to ceiling windows lining the large, semicircular room.

Gregory stepped inside and looked out the windows. "Is that Acapulco Bay?"

"It is—it's the inner bay off of Playa del Secreto."

He turned toward Vua. "Unbelievable."

"To me, the unbelievable part is the hundreds of donors and patients who have had their lives profoundly impacted by what we do."

"One that I hope continues with my sister."

"I'm confident it will." He pointed to the round table near the windows. "Please, have a seat while I get the paperwork ready."

Vua picked up one of ten folders neatly stacked on a corner of his desk. He sat down and spread three pages in front of Gregory.

"This is a very simple document—another positive about being in Acapulco."

"You mean the legal language?"

"Yes, we aren't required to have you sign the many consent documents U.S. law requires. I do suggest, however, you look over the third page—it lists the terms and conditions along with the payment schedule." He looked down at the page. "To lock in the procedure, I need a twenty percent down payment today, fifty percent will be due when you arrive at the Center with your sister, and the remaining thirty when she's released. So that will be twenty-six thousand, sixty-five thousand, and thirty-nine thousand dollars."

Gregory's eyes bulged as he swallowed hard. "If my math's right, that's a hundred thirty grand. From what we discussed on the phone, the procedure would be a hundred thousand."

Vua's face turned dead serious as he stared at Gregory. After a few seconds of silence, he started gathering up his papers. "I'm sorry. I thought you were serious about saving your sister's life. Maybe I was mistaken."

"I absolutely am," Gregory replied quickly. "I also don't like to be overcharged because of the position I'm in. That's all."

"The bottom line is costs vary based on availability of donors and the incubation period of the hearts. And right now, the demand is high and the supply low." Vua looked at Gregory, before adding, "Besides, I don't know how you put a price tag on your sister's life. I know I certainly couldn't."

Gregory crossed his arms and stared, angered by being misled because of his predicament.

"So you're ready to continue?" Vua asked sternly.

Gregory continued staring, then abruptly said, "Not so fast." He jumped to his feet and walked out.

"I'll give you thirty minutes to reconsider," Vua bellowed. "And then the deal is off the table."

Chapter 17

Gregory burst through the Heart Center's revolving door and into the blazing sun. He reached into his jacket and grabbed the vodka bottle he always carried with him. After unscrewing the cap, he swigged until the alcohol dripped on his shirt.

Now what?

He glanced at his watch. Three hours before his flight back to San Diego. He eyed a pier that extended into the bay and headed that way. He collapsed onto a bench and finished off the bottle. When he was done, he let the bottle slip between his fingers and clank against the wooden pier. As the buzz of the alcohol hit him, he put his head between his legs and started weeping. The truth was as plain as it was simple: He didn't have the hundred thirty grand Vua wanted. Besides, where was he going to get it?

His thoughts turned to Gina. He had really blown it with her, pushing her over the edge.

Why was I such a prick? he wondered.

He needed to change. Otherwise, he would never amount to anything if he kept doing the same thing over and over: Self-pity. Drink. Hangover. Self-pity. Drink. Hangover.

Seagulls squawked nearby. Gregory picked up his head and watched them prance and frolic along the pier, pecking at their feathers, enjoying the simple life they had. He eyed the empty vodka bottle lying next to his feet and stared at the white label that seemed to spin round and round. Something dawned on him.

It was at that moment he decided to embark on a journey that would forever change his life. He grabbed the bottle and flung it as far as he could into the ocean. He watched it splash into the afternoon water and then sink below the surface.

He then walked back toward the Heart Center.

Chapter 18

The massive glass sculpture, spiraling fifty feet upward, owned the attention of every visitor to the Donor Center. For a moment, Gina couldn't take her eyes off it. She then gazed at Helen who didn't seem to be at all impressed by the art as she chatted with two other donors near the entrance.

Wondering if it was really made of glass, Gina inched forward and gazed more closely at the sculpture. The snake's glass twisted and distorted the sunlight coming through the skylights, creating bursts of color that made it seem more vivid than it already was. Shaped as some sort of snake, maybe a python, it was obvious the sculptor had paid painstaking attention to the smallest detail—from the ripples in the glass skin to the multilayered eyes near the statue's top. He had used the atrium's architecture to produce a piece that seemed to be in perfect harmony with its surroundings.

"Ms. Hyde?" a woman said as she approached. "Can you direct me to Ms. Helen Mesona? I'd like to show both of you to your room."

"Over here!" Helen said, overhearing them as she walked over.

"I just can't get my mind off this sculpture," Gina said. "It's absolutely stunning."

"I think you'll find every detail of this research center was paid special attention. We want our guests to not be just comfortable, but mesmerized by their experience," the guide replied. "Dr. Vua's dream has always been about the people. If donors are willing to volunteer their time for the good of mankind then he believes the least he can do is make sure the time spent here is as special as possible."

Gina eyed the guide. "When you see Dr. Vua you can tell him he's already made it special."

"I'll be happy to do that." The woman beckoned with a hand. "Let me show you both to your room." She led them to a bank of elevators outfitted in stainless steel. An elevator chimed and the doors opened. "Fifth floor," she stated.

"Confirmed," a computerized female voice replied.

When the doors opened, the guide said excitedly, "Welcome to the SV wing. Please follow me to your room."

"S ... V?" Helen asked.

"Yes, you're in the SV, or South View wing of the Center—with one of the best views of the harbor, I might add."

Gina couldn't take her eyes off the floor as backlit glass caused the corridor to glow a pale blue hue. "I'm in dreamland," she mustered.

"Seriously." Helen responded.

The guide walked them down the hall toward a closed door with 565 stamped on it. "Here we are. Room SV-565. To get in you'll need to use the palm reader. And don't worry, only you will have access."

Helen put her hand on the reader. It clicked green and the door slid open.

Gina gasped. The room was enormous—enough to fill her apartment twice over. Along the left wall, water floated down a black brick wall. On the opposite side, a bank of LED TVs stood ready to entertain them. In the main living space, a black and white diamond-shaped area rug covered the floor—accented by two loungers and a coffee table. Altogether, it was warm, and inviting.

Helen grabbed Gina's hand. "You're coming with me. We've got to check this place out."

"It's really a suite," the guide explained. "This is the living area while your bedroom is there against the windows."

"There's a full bedroom?"

"As I said, BioHumanity didn't spare any expense."

Helen pulled Gina through another doorway that emptied into the shared bedroom.

"Seriously?" Gina said.

A bank of windows wrapped around the room, giving them a hundred eighty degree view of Acapulco Bay. Gina walked up and stared at the dark horizon. "I bet you can see for miles." She then turned and eyed the rest of the bedroom: Two king-sized beds, decked in satin linens, occupied one wall while a garden of mixed flowers and vegetation covered the opposite wall. "Wow," Gina said.

"I know you're both probably exhausted from the long day and would love to get some rest," the guide said. "I'll leave you both alone until the morning. Till then …" She then left them alone in the bedroom.

Gina grabbed one of the beds and collapsed on it. Helen quickly followed. "You know what I find humorous?" Gina said as she stretched her arms and legs.

"No, what?"

"I had no idea you were going to be my roommate."

Helen laughed. "Neither did I. The last time we saw each other was, what, a week ago?"

"I think you're right."

"Do you think they knew we were friends?

"You mean the people at the clinic?" Gina replied.

"Yeah."

A shrug. "Dunno." Gina's eyes suddenly felt heavy. "I think I might get some sleep. I hardly ever say this but I'm exhausted."

Helen slipped beneath the satin cover, not bothering to undress. "Me too."

Gina rolled over. "Sweet dreams."

No answer.

Fighting the urge to sleep, Gina opened them wider. She put a hand under her head and focused on the bay window, squinting. She couldn't see anything save for a few bright stars but it didn't matter. She was two thousand miles away from home and loving every minute of it: No pressure from teaching. No pressure from her friends and family. And no Gregory. She bit her lip. Why did she have to think about him? She thought about the fetus she was carrying with his sperm. While he had been nothing but an asshole to her, their fetus would help save his sister—and he would never know a thing about it. She closed her eyes knowing she was doing the right thing.

Something caused her to stir. Was it the door? "Helen?" she whispered lightly as she turned toward her roommate's bed.

No answer.

"Helen." Her voice had more authority.
Nothing.
Hmm, she thought. *That's weird.*

Chapter 19

"What brings you to Oceanside?" the doctor asked as he immobilized her right arm and shoulder in a sling.

Sabrina stared at his gorgeous brown eyes. "Unfortunately, a funeral. I was on the way back to my house when I was hit."

"I guess you didn't quite make it."

"And neither did my car," she replied. "I loved that car. It was a gift from my dad."

"How did he end up buying it for you?"

"I came home sobbing one night after getting yelled at in culinary school. I told him I was going to quit … I just couldn't take it anymore. He sat me down and said he'd buy me a car if I completed school."

"Who was yelling at you?"

"'The instructor. He kept saying, 'The meat's too dry, the vegetables don't have any flavor!' I had had enough and stormed out."

"So I guess your dad's offer worked—you ended up with the car."

"More than that. I graduated with honors."

"So what do you think?" He pointed to her arm.

Sabrina looked at the off-white sling covering her upper arm and shoulder. "I guess it's as fashionable as it's going to get."

"You were lucky. You had an anterior dislocation. All you'll need is to immobilize the shoulder to allow the inflammation and swelling to subside. After a few weeks, you should be out of the woods. Otherwise, everything else checked out okay. Lot better than a break."

She looked at his shaggy mop and casual dress. Beyond the seductive eyes, the warmness of his smile and the comfort of his voice seemed real—not the phony empathy she sometimes felt from people. For some reason, his gentleness and compassion seemed beyond the standard medical attention.

He flipped through her chart. "You're from Pacific City. That right?"

"Right. I work at the Beacon and came to Oceanside to follow up on a story."

"The Neskowin Beacon?"

A nod.

"The funeral you spoke of—were you following up on the Sanchez story?"

She sported a quick smile. "I was. Not hard to figure out, I guess. Not a lot goes on in Neskowin."

"Wouldn't think so."

"Did you know him?"

"Not particularly. From what I know, he and his wife kept to themselves." He paused. "I don't know if it's a coincidence, but I did treat Eric Sanchez a few days before they found him."

"Really?" Her attention perked. "What for?"

"Can't really divulge that. Doctor-patient privilege you know."

Her face dropped in disappointment. "I guess I can understand."

A nurse came in and set down a cup of ginger ale. She looked at Sabrina. "For your stomach—just in case the pain medications cause a bit of nausea. "Do you need anything else?"

"I'm fine, thank you." Sabrina took a sip as the nurse left. She turned to the doctor, kicking herself for not asking who he was. "You know, I'm not sure I ever got your name."

The doctor straightened. "I'm not sure I ever told you. He stuck a hand out. "Scott Brieman … I'm part of the ER staff."

She grabbed the hand with her left. "Kind of awkward."

"You'll get used to it."

"So what do you know about me?"

"Sabrina Katz. Age twenty-nine. Lives in Pacific City but your ID says New York City."

"That's right. I just got here a little more than a month ago after deciding working for a small-town newspaper might be the change I needed." She sighed. "I just didn't expect to end up here."

"At least it's a good way to meet someone new."

"Like whom?"

"Like me."

She studied him. Was he being more than just charming? It had been so long since another man showed interest, she wasn't sure if her brain was believing what her ears were telling her. He was attractive—there was no mistake about that. The natural curls hovering over his forehead added to the sense of mystique she felt for him. It made her wonder if he was truly interested or just a player.

She looked at his left hand. No wedding band. "Don't you have a girlfriend?" She blushed. Did she really say that out loud? "I mean ..."

He chuckled. "Don't worry about it. And no would be the answer." He bent over and peered into her eyes. "Look, Oceanside isn't exactly a hotbed for single men. Once somebody attractive comes along, even if it is by accident, I take notice."

Her breasts started tingling. It made her red with embarrassment. Then again, she couldn't remember the last time she felt that. "About Sanchez," she quickly said, changing the subject.

He propped his hands on the gurney, his eyes still trained on hers. "Maybe if you tell me what you're looking for, I can help you out."

"Well," she replied. "For starters, I met his wife the day she came to Neskowin."

"To identify him?"

A nod. "One of the saddest moments I'll ever remember."

"That must've been tough."

"It was."

"Did you get her name?"

"Carla Sanchez."

"How's she faring?" There was a genuine look of concern on his face.

"Not well. It was probably one of the hardest conversations I've had in a long time and it wasn't just because of Carla."

"How so?"

"I'd been following this story since the day Eric's body washed ashore, which also happened to be my first day with the paper. Then I got into a fight with my boss." She stopped. "I can't believe I'm telling you this," she gushed. "I don't even know you."

"Hey, it's all right. I'm just here to listen. You can tell me whatever you want."

She smiled. For some reason, that simple response calmed her. "You don't mind?"

"Not at all. So why the fight with the boss?"

"Because the paper refused to investigate Sanchez's death. I mean, is that wrong for me to think that way?"

He shook his head. "Not at all."

"The coroner said it was an accidental death so they closed the case." She sighed. "I mean, the paper could've cared less what the reason was. All I wanted was to write an article about him, to honor his life. You know, to be more than just a statistic in the paper."

"I can see your point but I'm not surprised. They probably deal with more stories day to day than they can handle. They could be overworked, understaffed, and feel the facts are as they are. So they publish what they have and move on."

She thought about that. "Maybe that's why they resent me."

"Why do you say that?"

"Because the editor, James Blogg, didn't hire me. One of their top investors felt the paper needed a softer side to bring in more women readers."

Brieman chuckled. "Then you may be on to something. They probably don't like anybody intruding in their boys club." He stood straight. "How did you get to know the investor?"

"My mom knew her from when they were kids back in NYC. When I decided to leave, I made a call to her and she was willing to hire me." A sigh. "So here I am, all by myself."

"Then why push it?"

"Why push what?"

"The story. I mean, why push something on your editor if you know it's going to rub them the wrong way?"

"Because it's a story that moved me. And I figured if I felt that way, then maybe others would too."

"You mean your female demographic?"

She nodded.

Brieman turned toward the laptop sitting on the small desk. "Can I tell you something?"

"Sure."

"You seem to empathize with others."

She didn't think she was that way but maybe there be a bit of truth to it.

"Are you convinced it was an accident?" Brieman added.

Without hesitation, Sabrina replied, "No, I don't. Why do you ask that?"

"Because I don't think it was an accident either."

Her heart started pounding. Could she be right after all? "How do you know?"

Brieman paused. "How about a deal? I'll tell you what I know but it has to be off the record. You know, just don't publish who told you."

"That's fair. I'll take anything at this point." *How exciting*, she thought—her first anonymous source.

"Thanks," Brieman replied sarcastically. He spun back around and faced her. "This was the second time I had treated him. The first was for a bad case of influenza, but this time was different. He came to me complaining of some dizziness."

"How did you treat him?"

He gazed out the window. "There wasn't really much I could do. Physically, I checked everything out and he seemed okay. So I gave him a sedative to relax and told him to call me in a week. Who would've known he'd be dead just a day later?"

"What did you think after you heard?"

"Honestly, I racked my brain thinking there was something I could've done differently."

"But how could've what you did or didn't do keep him from dying, especially if it wasn't an accident?"

"Nothing, I s'pose.

"Especially if it was murder."

He thought for a second. "Honestly, I can't rule that out. Not after seeing him a day before he died."

"Did he say anything odd that caught your attention?"

Brieman leaned back on the stool and looked over the shoulder. "You know, to this day, I've been trying to make sense of a comment he made after I asked him when he started to feel sick."

"What did he say?"

"He said he felt dizzy at work the day before. He had been working late. That's nothing out of the ordinary—stress could've caused that. But then he muttered something about organ donations."

"Organ donations?" Sabrina opened her notebook and looked at the quick notes she had made about Eric Sanchez. "He worked for a pharmaceuticals company. What could he possibly know about that?" she asked, almost rhetorically.

He shook his head. "Don't know. But he also muttered something about finding something. I think he used the word 'disturbing'."

She forced her bad hand onto the page and scribbled a note to herself. She looked at the handwriting. First graders would've been more pleased.

"It was almost as if he had caught himself saying something he shouldn't have," Brieman added.

"Did he mention anything else?" Sabrina asked as she looked into his deep blue eyes. *They could melt the coldest butter,* she thought.

"No. At the time, I chalked it off as a slight case of delirium from the stress he was probably under at work."

"What makes you believe it couldn't be an accident? Was it his behavior?"

He took a deep breath. "I barely knew the guy. I don't know what his past was like … or how he deals with stress."

"What does your gut say?"

He leaned forward and stared into her eyes. "That it wasn't an accident. It just wasn't in the cards."

Suddenly, the cellphone rattled on the bed tray next to Sabrina. She struggled but managed to grab it with her one good hand. "Hello?"

"You okay?" the voice said at the other end.

She looked at Brieman and rolled her eyes. Although she hadn't been with him long, she instantly recognized Blogg's voice. "I think so … but I'm going to be in a sling for a few weeks."

"I heard the message you left me and figured I'd see how you're doing." A pause. "I hope it doesn't interfere with your writing."

Sabrina smiled. "I'll be fine." *No matter the circumstance, Blogg would always be Blogg,* she thought.

"What the hell are you doing in Oceanside, anyway?"

"To see a friend." It really wasn't that far off base. She just needed to get to know Dr. Brieman.

"Fine, but you need to get your sweet ass back here. We've got a paper to run."

That wasn't going to happen. After speaking with Dr. Brieman she knew there was only one thing she needed to do—talk to Carla and make her aware of what she just found out. "That's what I need to talk to you about."

"You got an issue with your assignment?"

"How about something better."

Blogg paused. "Keep talking."

"What about a series on Oceanside?" She bit her lip.

There was a deep sigh. "What's wrong with Neskowin? Don't you have enough to cover here? Or do I need to load you up some more?"

"Look, I've just spent the entire weekend here and I've gotten to know some of the folks fairly well."

"You mean the medical profession, don't you?"

She ignored him. "I just think this is a beautiful place to write about. The readers would love it. I know the tourists would, and I'm sure the Neskowin locals would like to know more about their neighbor."

Without hesitating, he replied, "I have to ask again—what's wrong with Neskowin?"

She didn't really have a good answer, or at least one she wanted to tell him. "Nothing. It's just that I'm already here and I think I owe this town something for their kindness the past twenty-four hours."

The other end drew silence.

"Blogg?"

"You're killing me, Sabrina. Look, I'm not going to say I'm thrilled with you showing interest in something outside of Neskowin—I don't know what I'm going to tell our investor. But you're there already and you need to rest up. I'll give you one article and that's it."

She was sure he could see her brimming smile. "You won't regret it."

"I already have."

Chapter 20

"Gina?"

She grudgingly rolled on her back.

"Good morning," a cheery woman's voice said in a thick Mexican accent.

Gina stretched her arms and yawned and then opened her eyes. The woman, maybe in her forties, smiled softly at her.

"Buen día!"

Gina eyed the short, plump, dark-skinned woman. An orange and brown scarf was wrapped around her shoulders, hiding the collar of her gray uniform. "Buen día to you," she replied.

Her mind raced to last night. She looked over at Helen's bed.

"Señorita. What is wrong?"

She eyed the crumpled figure of Helen. "Last night ... I felt like somebody was in our room."

A chuckle by the Mexican woman. "Ah, a case of the nerves. I'm sure of it. Your mind is playing tricks on you."

Gina sat up. "It just seemed so real. What time is it anyway?"

"Six o'clock in the morning. It's a special day for you. It's time to have your procedure done."

"Really?" A shudder rolled through her. "I ... I'm not sure I'm ready."

"No worries, my dear. You won't remember a thing."

"Why the rush?"

"That's for Dr. Vua to answer. He'll be here in a—"

Suddenly there was a faint knock on the door. "Please come in," the assistant called out.

The door opened and Vua, dressed in black, sauntered in. He had a bright smile about him, something Gina hadn't seen earlier. "Did Ms. Yana give you the good news?"

"Yes ... I'm just not sure I'm ready."

He put a hand on her knee. "I'm sure you're a little nervous, but everything will be fine. Just remember a life is going to be saved because of you."

Gina remembered back to the orientation. "You mean through my baby's placenta?"

"Yes, the placenta is the fountain of life, and now is the time to give the miracle."

A shot of adrenaline pushed through her. "Do you have someone in mind? I mean, who's going to be the recipient?"

He shook his head. "I'm sorry, I can't tell you. But it's someone—a woman—who needs this miracle soon; otherwise we'll be too late."

"Do you know what's wrong with her?"

"She's dying from cardiomyopathy," Vua said matter-of-factly.

Gina's thought back to her visit with Blair. Could it really be her? Just the thought of saving Blair, or someone like her, made her feel a lot better about what she was going to do. "Okay. I'm ready."

Vua looked at her and gave a quick smile. "You don't know what this means to the patient." He turned toward the assistant. "Ms. Yana, can you make sure she's ready?"

"Sí. Of course."

Vua's cellphone buzzed. He looked at the caller ID. "I need to go." He walked out without saying another word.

Chapter 21

As Sabrina tapped the brake on her newly rented car, she eyed her phone, making sure she had Carla's address right. "Five four two seven," she whispered to herself as she scanned both sides of the road. Set against a backdrop of mountains, the rural community just outside Oceanside was dotted with farmhouses, bungalows, and A-frames, each set on an acre or more of land. The sparse community seemed just right for those wanting to forget the grind of the big city.

She squinted at the half-painted numbers on the house to her left: *5427*. There it was. She gazed at the off-white cedar exterior and its front bay window. Peaking from behind the windows were a set of clumsily laid curtains showing no sign of activity. As she pushed her car into park, she wondered if coming here was the right thing to do. *Maybe it will backfire*, she thought. Things certainly didn't go well in their last conversation and this could make things even worse.

But now she was aware of new information Carla had to at least listen to.

Sabrina stepped clumsily out of the car, her shoulder throbbing with every move. Taking a nervous breath, she eyed the house, unsure what she was going to say or how she would say it. Deciding now was as good a time as any, she walked up to the porch and knocked lightly on the door frame. A moment went by. No response. She knocked more forcefully this time and again waited. No answer. Sabrina turned and looked up and down the street to see if Carla might be outside. Around a curve in the road, she caught sight of a woman strolling toward a pasture of trees. *Maybe it's Carla*, she thought.

Sabrina jogged toward her but lost sight when she slid into the cover of the trees. Running into the pasture, Sabrina spotted her about a hundred yards ahead, admiring the neatly kept wildflowers just off the gravel path. Sabrina eyed the sign to her right: *Welcome to Oceanside Lookout Park.* She hurried up to her and smiled: It was Carla.

She was dressed in a long dark casual skirt and a pastel long-sleeve top. Although her face suggested interest in the nearby nature, her body language hinted she labored from the shock of her husband's death—possibly more so than at the funeral.

"Carla?" Sabrina asked cheerfully.

Carla whipped around and stared menacingly at Sabrina. "How dare you track me down in my own neighborhood? How many times do I have to tell you to leave me alone?"

"I'm only trying to help you," Sabrina pleaded. "I just came here to see if you'd be willing to give me a chance."

"Well, you've run out of chances. Now I have to insist that you please leave me alone," Carla said in a raised voice. She then turned and headed farther into the park.

Shit. She was blowing it. "I have evidence Eric's death may not be an accident." She knew it wasn't confirmed—at least not yet—but she had to say something.

Carla's frame froze. She slowly turned and motioned to a nearby boulder.

Sabrina understood. Carla wanted her to share what she knew. "Thank you, Mrs. Sanchez," she replied. "I promise I won't take up too much of your time."

Carla fell onto the boulder in a clump of exhaustion as Sabrina sat beside her. "I want to make one thing clear," Carla whispered. "I've decided to listen to you only to explain yourself further."

Sabrina nodded. Time would not be on her side.

"What do you know?" Carla asked.

Sabrina caught a look of anticipation in Carla's eyes. "Are you sure you want to relive those last couple of days?"

Carla nodded slowly. "I already am. I'm talking to you, aren't I?"

Sabrina took a breath and pointed to her sling. "It all started with this."

Carla's eyes met where Sabrina pointed but she didn't say anything.

"I know showing up at your funeral on Saturday upset you, but I was there as a compassionate human being ... not a reporter."

Carla rolled her eyes. "Please! Are you expecting to get on my good side so I'll tell you my most personal thoughts? There's not a chance of that happening."

Sabrina looked into Carla's sad eyes, which didn't seem to match the venom in her voice.

Carla continued the verbal assault: "Really. What is wrong with you? Are you some sort've L.A. celebrity blogger out to get me?

"No. ... It's not like that at all," Sabrina responded defensively. "I came to the funeral to tell you Eric Sanchez's life was worth more than a blurb in the paper—that his life deserved to be celebrated. Now I believe there's more to it. ... I know there's more to it."

Carla looked at Sabrina's arm. "Why do you say that? And where does the sling fit in?"

Her questions were fair, but her accusing tone made it difficult for Sabrina to concentrate on what she was going to say. "After I left the funeral, I got into an accident which sent me to the ER," she replied.

"I'm sorry to hear that, but how does that relate to me?" Her voice was calmer.

"Because it was deliberate."

"How do you know?"

"Somebody left a note in my car warning me to stay away. And then the accident happened—too much of a coincidence for my taste."

"Well, maybe that person is right," Carla said flatly.

You bitch, Sabrina thought. But she couldn't let Carla see her anger otherwise she'd never get a chance to explore Eric's past. Sabrina took a deep breath. "I ended up in the hospital."

"You must've ended up at Oceanside Community—over on Sunset Avenue."

Sabrina tapped her arm. "While I was there getting my shoulder reset, I got into a conversation with the ER doctor. He wanted to know what brought me to Oceanside in the first place. That's when I told him about your terrible loss."

Sadness colored Carla's face.

"He knew the name right away—said he had treated him on a Friday just before he was last seen."

"I don't understand." Carla seemed puzzled. "Friday? He was at work. He never told me about a doctor's visit."

"That may be true … for most of the day. But in the evening he came to the hospital complaining of dizziness."

"Are you sure the doctor was talking about my husband?"

"Yes. He knew the name. He had even been in once before."

"Now that is true. He did go to the ER about two months ago. He was a bit dehydrated from having the flu. I guess I just don't understand how he could have been at the hospital on that Friday. If I remember correctly, he was working late and he told me as much."

"Not to be impolite, but maybe he really didn't want to tell you what was going on."

"I can't believe that." Carla looked away as a tear worked its way down her face. "He told me everything."

Sabrina sat quietly and watched Carla's movements. Remarkably, they were still talking. Even more remarkable was she seemed to be warming to Sabrina. That's when she decided to keep pushing. "What about organ donations? Did he ever say anything to you about that?"

Carla pondered the question. "Not sure why he would be involved in that. We both worked in pharmaceutical research."

She seems engrossed, Sabrina thought. "That's what I find s interesting. The ER doctor seemed to remember him saying something about organ donations."

"During the visit to the hospital?"

"Apparently."

Carla was thinking hard back to those last days. "I just don't have any recollection of Eric being involved in organ donation or transplant research. It just wouldn't make sense."

"Did he work with anybody?"

"He did. He worked every day with someone he had known since college."

"What happened to him?"

"He apparently left BioHumanity to take a job in Europe. It was a huge loss for the research they had been working on. But Eric was determined to carry on—until it was complete. He was working on a new drug to fight breast cancer."

"Breast cancer?" A jolt of emotion brewed within her.

A nod. "He felt what he was doing could save lives and he poured his heart into it."

"My mother was diagnosed five years ago," Sabrina replied

"I'm sorry to hear that." Her demeanor suggested honest concern.

"It was a harrowing time for my sister and me. But," Sabrina said optimistically, "she beat it, and has been in remission for three years now." Then she added, "I don't know what I would've done without her."

But that wasn't the full story: Sabrina had no intention of telling Carla her mother had to fend for herself the day Sabrina left for New York. It was a selfish move, Sabrina knew, but she needed a new beginning otherwise she would never survive. As hard as she tried, that terrible memory two months ago was never far from her—day after day. Sabrina had told her mother she would be back: Back to New York City, back from the depression that almost cost her own sanity. But only when she was ready. *Maybe that's why,* she pondered, *I need to write about him.* It was the only way she could right a wrong after her sister was murdered. She couldn't force Carla to understand her motive. That would take time. And now wasn't it, so she changed the subject. "I thought the ceremony was lovely."

"Thank you. It was a very emotional day but I thought Pastor Creighton did a wonderful job presiding over the funeral." Carla stopped and looked away. And then she said, "I just wish they hadn't …"

Sabrina narrowed her eyebrows as she put a hand on Carla's arm. She didn't pull away. "Hadn't what?"

"Cremated him," Carla barely replied. "That was never his wish or mine."

"If that was against your wishes, then why do it?"

"I didn't. After the autopsy, he was cremated. When I found out, I couldn't believe that happened, especially after everything else. So I called the funeral home, assuming it was them. They said it had been authorized by the coroner's office. Of course, I demanded answers from them but all they said was that it had been authorized by the family."

"By the family? But you just said—"

"I know," Carla said, interrupting her. "When I protested, they acted as if it were an administrative error."

"Not even an apology?"

"Nothing. The coroner—I think her name is Yori Wainer. She was absolutely unapologetic."

"I can't believe someone could be so callous."

Carla bit her lip. "What can I do? I can't bring his body or his life back."

Sabrina was losing her but she still needed to find out about Eric's last days. "Can you take me back to that Friday? What was his work schedule like?"

"I can remember him coming home late from work that day, which really isn't all that odd. On occasion, he had been known to work long hours."

"So he tended to bury himself in his work?"

"Sometimes. But he was also very aware of the time apart from me. He would bring something on the days he worked late to show how guilty he was. God, he was such a sweetheart." Carla's voice seemed more upbeat.

"What did he do on Saturday? Anything out of the ordinary?"

"That is what's so puzzling. It was normal. It was like any other weekend day when he worked a late Friday."

"You say he did things for you. What did he do on that Saturday?"

"He made me breakfast in bed. He was such a romantic."

A certain jealousy fell on Sabrina. A man with those kinds of thoughts never entered her life, let alone being married to one.

Carla leaned toward Sabrina. "We talked a bit about his work. I do remember him saying they were approaching a deadline and it was making him nervous. But that's about it."

"So nothing too peculiar?"

"No. Not really. We spent the weekend cleaning the house, like we do most of the time. We had a nice quiet dinner Saturday night."

"Very ordinary."

"Yes, mundane was all the rage with us." There was a peek of a smile under the layers of sorrow.

"And Sunday?"

"You know … as I talk about it today, that's the only day he wasn't really himself. At the time, I figured he was thinking about the workweek ahead."

"Stress?"

She nodded. "Every time he heard about another woman dying from breast cancer, it made him that much more motivated to complete the research. So he went fishing that day, which in itself was not a big deal, but he usually planned for it—you know, made his own bait—that sort of thing. On that day, we had breakfast and then he abruptly left for the lake."

"Does seem impromptu."

"Yes. And like I said, not like him. He gathered his gear, kissed me on the way out and said he would be back in a few hours. How could I have known I would never see him again?" Carla's shoulders slumped.

Sabrina sat motionless. Every answer seemed to draw new questions, yet she knew it was taking a toll on Carla. What was surprising was she had been more open than Sabrina ever thought possible. There was one last thing she needed to find out and then she'd leave her alone. "You say your husband worked at BioHumanity?"

A nod.

"Do you think you can get me in there?"

"I'm not sure I understand."

"I'd like to find out what happened to your husband and BioHumanity would be a great place to start."

A tear slipped down her face. The sun hit it just right causing her cheek to shimmer. And then it was gone.

"Carla?"

She focused on Sabrina. "I'm getting there. I'm just trying to figure out if this is worth it. You know, unraveling the last few days of my husband's life."

"If there's another truth, I'll do everything I can to find it."

Carla took a deep breath and eyed the setting sun. "I don't know what it means, but Eric wasn't himself the last few weeks of his life."

"Do you think it could've been work related?"

"I think so. About a week before his death, he opened up over a cup of coffee."

"What did he say?"

"That the company was thinking about cutting funding for the research. To him, that didn't make sense and he intended to find out why."

"Did he give you any more details?"

Carla shook her head. "No."

"Maybe it contributed to his death?"

Carla stayed silent for a few seconds, then replied, "It's been weighing on my mind ever since his death."

Sabrina sighed. She had more questions than answers. And she still hadn't secured what she wanted—Carla's help in getting Sabrina into BioHumanity. "Carla?"

Carla gazed at her wearily.

"It's really important I see where Eric worked. Will you help me?"

An awkward silence followed as Carla pondered the question. Her eyes gazed toward a flock of birds circling just above them.

Sabrina winced. She could tell Carla was withdrawing emotionally.

Carla reached out and put a hand on Sabrina's arm. "I'm afraid I have to leave."

"But Carla—"

"To answer your question," Carla replied calmly, interrupting her, "yes, I will." A small smile appeared on her lips and then she vanished into the darkening horizon.

Chapter 22

Vua sat in his chair, peering through the spacious penthouse office window toward the Acapulco Bay. *Breathtaking*, he thought.

He sighed.

He was spending too much time in his office. Normally, he would've taken the time to stroll around Acapulco's Harbor with this much sun bleaching the sandy beaches. But not today. Especially not today. A small security lapse was interrupting his day, causing his patience to run thin. And it still wasn't resolved.

Vua's thoughts wandered to his brother. What would he say about the success his younger brother had achieved? It was his brother who had made this all possible. It was his brother who had given Vua the idea for the Acapulco Heart Center, and because of that, Vua reasoned, he was well on his way to growing a hundred million dollar company into a billion dollar powerhouse if things stayed at this pace. Besides saving lives, he was becoming richer than he ever thought possible.

What could be better?

A knock on the door made him anxious. He was waiting for the all-clear on the security breach and this had better be it. "Yes?" he almost shouted at the door.

The head of security, Rico Salarez, walked in, his gentle frame and demeanor a direct contrast to the type of work he did for a living.

"Do I have anything to be worried about?" Vua quizzed Rico when he closed the door.

A quick shake of the head. "No. After the woman in the protest was identified as a former donor, we reran the video to see if she contacted or conversed with anyone. Nothing could be interpreted that she did."

A sigh and then Vua banged the desk with a fist. "So what you're telling me is it's inconclusive. That right?"

A pause as if unsure how to respond and then, "That's right, Dr. Vua," Rico repeated calmly.

"Well, I want her out of my sight. Have the authorities deport her immediately." Vua was well acquainted with the local politicians and authorities given the amount of money he had donated over the years. All Rico had to do was say Vua's name and the request would be handled immediately, without any questions.

Rico nodded curtly. "Consider it done." He turned and opened the door.

"One more thing," Vua called after him. "Have your staff run an analysis again on that footage. I want to make sure every piece of that video is cleared not once but twice."

"Yes. Of course," Rico responded. He then closed the door.

"Shit," Vua muttered to himself as he spun his chair to face the massive windows. He didn't like cracks in security. If any of them broke through, that could be the end of his dream.

Chapter 23

Sabrina winced as the high sun poured through the driver's window. Fumbling for her sunglasses, she suddenly wished she was still driving her convertible. *It had such a feeling of freedom,* she thought, *especially on warm afternoons like this.*

She eased up on the gas pedal. The rental labored as she reached the end of Maxwell Mountain Road, just north of the Oceanside foothills. A mixture of brownstone and granite came into view on the left announcing the corporate headquarters of BioHumanity. She stopped at the security gate where an older man with shaggy hair and droopy eyes inquired about her visit. After announcing whom she was visiting, the man checked his list and nodded his approval.

Good. Carla had done her part.

She found a parking spot in the visitor lot, just a few steps from the glass atrium entrance. She gathered her black backpack and headed for the revolving door centered among large, triangular glass panels that numbered in the hundreds. She smiled to herself. BioHumanity was a corporation that liked to flaunt its riches.

Inside, an energetic buzz seemed to lift the atrium into a purr of activity as twin escalators carried its employees to and from a lofty second floor.

"Can I help you?" Sabrina turned toward a guard near the security desk staring at her closely. He was wearing a dark turtleneck under a company-issued gold sport coat and, although he was bald, he had a striking look given his black eyeglasses, chiseled face, and muscular frame.

She made sure to keep her voice steady and perky. "I'm here to see Joseph Batton," she replied. It was the only name Carla knew inside of BioHumanity. He was Eric's manager, but as Carla noted at the end of their last phone conversation, Batton tended to work in isolation, so may not be the best person to glean anything from.

He typed the name into a small laptop hidden under the long, black marble counter. "You must be Sabrina Katz?"

"I am."

He handed her a visitor's pass. "Please wear this while you're on company grounds and return it to the front desk when you're visit is over." She took the plastic badge and took a seat on one of the leather couches occupying the center of the atrium. It couldn't have been more than a minute when a voice interrupted her.

"Sabrina?"

She looked up expecting the deep, burly voice to belong to a man of similar physique. Instead, a small boyish-looking man with round spectacles and very fine sandy brown hair stood before her. She almost wanted to classify him as a nerd but for the fine choice of clothing.

He pushed a hand toward her. "Joseph Batton."

"Glad to meet you. I'm Sabrina Katz," she replied as he compressed his hand forcefully into her only good one.

Batton eyed her sling. "What happened?"

"A bit of a mishap on the road."

"That's unfortunate," he replied without a hint of compassion. He turned and waved her on. "Won't you please follow me up the grand staircase." He led her down a long stretch of hallway where large opulent sconces made of aluminum projected hazy diamond-shaped figures on the wall. Doorway after doorway they passed, all framed in natural maple, until they stopped at a stainless steel door with just a hint of glass at eye level.

He placed a thumb in the scanner next to the door. The security light flashed green and the door clicked open.

"After you, Ms. Katz," he said, holding the door open.

"Sabrina will do just fine," she replied softly.

They entered a lab flooded with maple-colored lab counters. A subtle hum layered the room as, everywhere she turned, LED lights and digital numbers flashed in what seemed like random order. A researcher stood on the other side of the room, staring at flat screens popping with lines and numbers. Batton led her to a cluster of offices near the back of the lab. "Feel free to get comfortable in my office," he said. Sabrina grabbed a leather upright while Batton plunked down in a heavily padded office chair facing her.

He eyed her for a few seconds then reached into one of his drawers. A second later, his hands reappeared with a rubber band and quarter-sized rubber ball covered in the same rubber bands. "Ever know why golf balls bounce?"

She eyed the ball as he juggled it lightly in his hand. "Because it's made of rubber?"

He smirked as he wrapped the band around the ball, joining what seemed like a hundred others. "Rubber's only part of the story, my dear. The golf ball gets its bounce from the tightly wound core bound with everyday rubber bands."

She frowned at the awkward exchange. "I'm afraid I don't follow."

He reached across his desk and grabbed a white golf ball sitting near the edge. He tossed it to her. "Look at its gleaming outer shell."

She wasn't in the mood for any games. "It's white and has dimples," she replied. "So what?"

"That's right. From the outside, you know nothing of the inside. … All you see is the pretty white shell."

She looked away. He was telling her something but she wasn't getting it. "I don't play golf … so I'm not sure what you're getting at."

He smirked a bit more, revealing yellowing teeth between his lips. He put the ball down and watched as it rolled a few inches away. "Mrs. Sanchez asked if I would help you. Out of respect for Eric, I told her it was the least I could do." He focused on her eyes.

"Thank you." Ignoring their exchange about the golf ball, she asked, "What can you tell me about Eric?"

"He was an A+ researcher … had the drive and the knowledge needed to rapidly develop a drug in less time than any others I've worked with in my career."

"What about him as an individual?"

"You mean his personality?"

"Right."

He shrugged. "Didn't get to know him very well. We were busy doing research."

"Was that the breast cancer drug?"

He looked confused. "Oh, yes. Of course."

She eyed him. It was a peculiar response. "Can you tell me anything about how it was going? Was he close to a breakthrough?"

He grabbed the arms of his chair as he tried to get a bit more comfortable. "He was in the midst of researching a clinical trial. We were just about ready to get the FDA involved."

"Must've been going well then."

"It was."

"How close do you think he was to finding the answer?"

He shifted uncomfortably. "Company policy says we can't disclose research projects to the outside world." He lowered his voice. "I'm sure you can understand that." An underbelly of anger grabbed her attention and it made her instantly feisty.

"I get that, but … I'm not sure what the policy is on a dead person. I would assume you've already checked into that?"

The brittle smile returned. "Don't get smart with me, Ms. Katz. I'm only doing Carla, and you, a favor. Do you know how hard it is see one of our best pass away?"

"Hold on—"

He moved briskly from his chair. "I think our time is up. I want to thank you—"

"Do you know why Eric might be involved in organ donations?" Sabrina interjected.

Batton had just opened the office door but the question froze his intentions. He purposely shut the door and spun around. "Why would you think that?"

"Because he complained to a friend a few days before he disappeared."

"What friend?"

No way she was going to involve Brieman. "Can't disclose that."

He grinned. "Then there's nothing to it."

"Judging by your body language, I'd say there is something to it."

He stared for a second at her, as if trying to figure out a way to dismiss the comment. He shrugged. "Many of our researchers get involved in pet projects. Maybe it was just a random comment on somebody else's work. That's common around here."

"I'm not sure—"

He again opened the door. "I have another appointment. I'll have my assistant, Mona, stop by and walk you out. If you have further questions, leave them with her and I'll be glad to answer them when I can."

Sabrina didn't believe the sincerity one bit. She grabbed her things and walked passed him, not bothering to thank him for his time. She met a woman standing just outside Batton's office.

"Sabrina?" the woman asked, holding out her hand.

"Yes, that's me," Sabrina replied, before giving the woman a quick handshake. She appeared to be in her twenties, but that may have been because of the way she dressed. A tight-fitting, low-cut top was wrapped around her petite torso, matched with black capris.

"I'm Mona Frederick."

"Nice to meet you. Mr. Batton mentioned you would be meeting me."

"Of course," Mona replied with a curt smile. "I'll help you get back to the lobby and on your way." She then turned and said, "Please follow me."

As they walked back to the lobby, Sabrina was still burning from the confrontation with Batton. "Are all the men here like that here?" she blurted out.

Mona stole a glance at Sabrina and then laughed nervously.

"Are you referring to Joe Batton's coarse personality?"

Sabrina smiled back. "I like you already. You get right to the point."

"Yes, well, don't worry about him. He's not very important here. He's what we call a program manager. They don't do anything except push paper and make asses out of themselves. Everybody knows it's the researchers that drive the company."

Sabrina smiled. "I don't suppose that's much different than a lot of companies. Let the program managers think they're in charge."

"Seriously … but we know who's really in charge." Mona reached the bottom of the grand staircase and then headed toward the glass atrium. "The admins."

Sabrina giggled. "Now I really like you."

They reached the revolving doors. Mona turned to Sabrina. "You were discussing Mr. Sanchez, is that right?" she asked. Her voice seemed more serious.

Sabrina captured Mona's blue eyes darting from side to side, as if she wanted to keep the conversation going. "I was."

"And the breast cancer research Eric was doing?"

A nod. "Seems like a noble cause."

"Let me guess … he didn't tell you anything."

A small laugh. "How did you guess? I must be wearing my disappointment on my sleeve."

"I'm not surprised."

"How so?"

"Because about three months ago, Batton moved him off the project to focus on a confidential priority one project."

"Something more important than breast cancer. What could —"

"Let's just say it was for the benefit of the company and certainly not for the women's lives that would be saved."

"How do you know?"

"Because Eric told me. He was absolutely beside himself. He wanted to tell his wife but he couldn't because of the shroud of secrecy the company placed on it. It absolutely ate him alive inside."

"Then why do it?"

"Because they told him it would be only temporary and he was their top researcher. Three months tops, they kept saying, and then they were going to increase the funding for the cancer research. It was an offer he felt worth taking."

"What was so urgent?"

She hesitated and then replied, "I shouldn't tell you this but it had something to do with stem cells. And it wasn't any coincidence that once his three months were done, he ended up at the bottom of the ocean."

"Really?" Sabrina reached into her backpack for her notebook and jotted a few things down.

"Yes. They also abruptly canceled the breast cancer research."

"Which was around the time he drowned?"

"Within two weeks."

"Is there any proof of a connection? I mean … if what you're telling me is true it seems too much of a coincidence."

"That's what I think too."

"Is there any proof?" Sabrina pleaded.

Mona eyed her and then looked away. "There is something," she finally said.

"Like what?"

Mona shook her head. "I've already said too much." She took Sabrina's arm. "You must go."

Sabrina bit her lip. There was something there and she had to find out what it was. "Wait a minute. Can we talk later?"

Mona looked into her eyes. She nodded quickly.

"Here's my number." Sabrina quickly jotted her number on a piece of paper and handed it to her. "Please call me."

"I will." Mona crumpled the paper and jammed it into a pocket. "Enjoy the afternoon," she said and then turned toward the staircase.

Sabrina pushed through the revolving doors, excited at the turn of events. She slipped her sunglasses over her eyes and headed back to the car, confident this could be a huge breakthrough.

What she didn't notice were the security cameras tracking her every move.

Chapter 24

As his partner finished scrubbing, Vua hunched over the unconscious body and looked into her eyes. *What a beautiful woman,* he thought. He was dressed in gray scrubs and matching black apron that tried to hide the stain of blood and other bodily fluids from previous surgeries but it failed miserably. "Are you about ready for the extraction, Marta?" he said out of the corner of his mouth.

"Just about there," Marta replied. She snapped the latex over both hands and then placed the disposable drape over the patient's abdomen. She eyed the laptop computer on a table just to her left and started reading aloud, "Gina Hyde. Age thirty-one. Beginning of second trimester … the fetus is seventeen weeks." A pause and then she said, "I don't know how you do it sometimes but you always seems to find the perfect patients."

Vua smiled. He loved always being right. "Is she dilated?"

A nod. "Ten millimeters."

"Good," Vua replied. He felt her abdomen. "We'll need to roll her a bit to get the fetus in a better position … and then let the imaging take it from there."

"Yes. Of course." Marta rotated the woman onto her side and placed the ultrasound on her abdomen.

Vua yanked on his latex and then turned to his left, toward the surgical tray. He selected the smallest forceps available and moved them through the vagina into the dilated cervix.

Marta stood over the monitor and eyed the ultrasound. "It looks like the head is tilted a little to the left, toward his momma's hip."

Vua leaned in and nodded. "I'll rotate the fetus a bit to the right … but I'll need a bigger instrument. That should help line up the lower extremities with the vaginal opening." He grabbed a larger set of forceps and worked his way into the uterus. "I think

I've got it." He pulled his hand back a bit, drawing the fetus from the uterus. "That's as far as it'll go." Vua flipped the forceps onto the tray and reached in with his left hand, searching for the baby's head. "I need a bit of pressure on the uterus."

Marta pushed lightly with both hands on the abdomen.

"Now it'll fit through." He grabbed the suction and pulled the rest of the fetus through the vaginal opening.

"It's a boy," Marta announced as she grabbed a new set of forceps. "I'll take the placenta."

Vua walked the fetus over to another surgical table, this one half the size of the others. He paused as he looked at the dead fetus. "This is like finding a hundred thousand dollar diamond at the bottom of a mine," he murmured. "And it's the first of three today." Reaching with one free hand, he selected a small scalpel and dug deep into the fetus's chest and drew an incision vertically between the breastplates. Using both index fingers, he pulled at the breastbone, snapping it like a chicken leg. Vua gazed at the exposed heart in the underdeveloped body cavity. *It's a shame this child will never experience the joys of life*, he thought. *But then again, it wouldn't have to experience the cruelties either.* "Marta, I need the ice packs and cooler," he hollered over his shoulder.

She rushed over the supplies as Vua snipped the blood vessels that fed the tiny heart with his surgical scissors. He then reached in with a tool that looked like a small ice cream scoop and pulled the heart out of the cavity. Wrapping it in surgical plastic, he placed it in the tiny cooler.

Marta delicately placed the ice packs around the newly harvested heart and then screwed the cap on the cooler. She pulled off her gloves and threw them on the table. Looking at her watch, she said, "Not bad. Twenty minutes start to finish."

Vua's cellphone buzzed in his pocket. Yes, of course. A new customer had arrived.

It was time to give them his best sales pitch.

Chapter 25

It was just before daybreak as the paid assassin made his way to the farmhouse set deep in rural Tillamook County. Mannheim casually glanced at the white exterior and wondered why they picked this particular house but then his thoughts quickly moved to his objective—the murder that was about to take place.

He walked quietly across the front yard and placed a small package at the base of a shrub. *The reporter should enjoy the contents,* he mused. He then slipped around back, toward a gray porch that acted as a gateway to the house's backdoor. Stopping, he scanned the yard, as any good assassin did, looking for anything out of the ordinary.

He didn't want any surprises.

Mannheim again went through the details. Every plan needed to be meticulously analyzed from every *what if* angle. If something were to go wrong, he wanted to be quick with a resolution, especially given the high stakes. When he was satisfied everything had been thought through, the adrenaline buzz kicked in—the same high he always felt when the fate of another human rested with him.

Such power he felt.

He also knew there was no alternative. The Sanchez widow had become a nuisance in the last few days, providing help and details that only fueled the reporter's quest for an answer. It had to be dealt with quickly and harshly. To him, the blame for the widow's pending death squarely fell on the reporter. She had been given ample warning to stop pursuing Sanchez but refused. And now the bitch would pay a heavy price—something he was convinced would end her pursuit of the truth.

He eyed his watch. Now was the time. It was almost daybreak, meaning the moon was at its dimmest and the sun had not reached the horizon. Mannheim tugged on his black leather gloves and pulled his black cap low across his forehead, matching perfectly the black shirt, pants, and shoes he chose to complete the camouflage.

Carrying a bag of tools over his back, Mannheim made his away up the porch toward the back door. He peered in through the door's glass insert, and scanned the room before him. It was the kitchen and the dim light above the stove provided just enough glow for him to get his bearings: Straight ahead was a hallway that led to the second floor, and the widow's bedroom.

Peering down, his eyes stopped at the doormat covering the kitchen floor. *Excellent,* he thought. That will help deaden the sound of glass breaking.

He wrapped his right fist in a small towel and smashed one of the glass panels, creating a muffled shatter as the glass sprinkled on the mat below. Reaching in with his good hand, he unbolted the door and pushed himself carefully in. Grabbing his flashlight, he scanned the room for any alarms or sensors, but there were none. He then waited for footsteps in case the break-in had been heard.

After a minute, he smiled. Nothing.

Moving forward, he found the staircase and walked up gingerly, taking care in case of a floor groan. When he reached the second floor, he spun his flashlight low on the floor, in a circle, and counted the number of doors. There were four. That meant two bedrooms, a closet, and a bathroom. He knew from experience the master bedroom was always the farthest from the hall bath given it usually had its own.

After finding his target, he walked quietly up to the closed door and turned the handle slowly. *Good,* he thought. *No squeaks.* Now that the sun was starting to rise above the horizon, it provided just enough light to make out the contents of the room. The bed was straight ahead, underneath a high window. To the left was a simple white dresser. To the right, a matching nightstand. Peering ahead, he saw the still figure of the widow crumpled into a ball under several blankets.

Everything was going to plan.

He removed the lighter fluid from his toolkit and started soaking the floor around the bed. When he came to the window near the foot of her bed, he doused the last few inches of the curtain in the fluid as well. Then, without hesitating, he grabbed his lighter and lit the bottom of the curtain. Within seconds, fire shot upward. Quickly retracing his steps, he locked the bedroom door and closed it from the hall. Mannheim glided down the steps and pushed his way into the kitchen and through the back door. Once off the porch, he ran straight for woods. For a second, he turned and admired his work. Already, flames were shooting from the bedroom window as smoke billowed into the air.

He then turned and hit the trail that would guide him back to his Jeep.

Chapter 26

"Let me get this straight," Blogg's voice boomed from Sabrina's phone. "You think Sanchez was murdered after seeing an E.R. doctor? And his company has something to do with it?"

She was sitting on the couch in a motel in Oceanside. On her lap was perched her laptop with a pile of unorganized notes spread around her. "That's right. I'm going to prove it too."

"What the hell you still doing in Oceanside, anyway? I said one story ... that's it."

"I know ... I know. I stayed over because of Carla Sanchez. She finally agreed to meet with me. And not only that, she helped me get an interview at BioHumanity—you know, where Eric Sanchez worked." She took a breath, excited about what she was able to accomplish. "That was a huge coup. It's all because of Carla." A pause. "I'm sorry Mr. Blogg, but I just couldn't let the opportunity slip away." She bit her lip, expecting the blowup.

"You've got to be kidding me, Sabrina." His voice was full of irritation. "I want—" He was interrupted by another call coming in. "I've got to go ... but you need to promise me one thing."

"What's that?"

"That your ass is going to back here in Neskowin by tomorrow." She shook her head. It wasn't enough time. But if she didn't, he'd cut her from the paper. That was the unspoken truth. "Fine," she replied meekly.

"Don't make me regret this," Blogg replied. And then the line went dead.

Sabrina threw the phone on the couch and sighed. He was such ... a male.

She eyed her watch. Her date! Brieman was going to be by at seven. He had called yesterday and she said yes without any hesitation.

Could her life finally be on track?

Her cellphone buzzed. She eyed the caller ID and rolled her eyes. What did he want now?

She picked it up. "Yes, Mr. Blogg?"

"Sabrina." His voice seemed rattled. "You've got to get over to Carla Sanchez's. It's … her house."

"What are you talking about?"

"It's her damn house. That's all I know."

"What about her house?"

"I don't know. I don't know. Just get there. I'm gonna drive up right now."

Shaking, Sabrina bolted for the door. Carla was being targeted because she was helping her. She was sure of it. She hurried into her car and started the engine. The tires screeched against the soft pavement as she gunned the car forward. She found the highway and pushed the car as fast as it would go. Tears flowed down but she quickly wiped them away. More tears came. This time, she didn't bother. She found her way to Baughman Creek and sped across the bridge to the farmhouse she had seen only days ago. As she approached, flashing reds flooded the road, easily illuminating the normally dark countryside.

Sabrina gasped at the destruction before her.

Carla's house was awash in a fiery blaze that had already lopped off the roof. The fire was now working its way down the front like a baby crawling on all fours. Three ladder trucks were there, battling the sickening blaze as much as their strength allowed. Two squad cars and an ambulance sat on the front lawn, but with nothing to do. Sabrina pushed her way past the web of fire hoses and the growing crowd. She stopped and put a hand over her mouth as she tried to contain the emotion spilling out. Her eyes welled with tears as she watched the house burn into obliteration—a house seemingly so peaceful just days before.

The sound of shattering glass ricocheted through the yard as the firefighters were losing miserably in the fight to save any part of the house. More glass disintegrated as a once-beautiful bay window became another exit for the angry flames. Fire hissed everywhere, as if beckoning with a fiery finger to join the party. The crew captain screamed at his men to step back as the brittle wood started cracking under the weight of trauma. Firefighters continued dousing the flames with high arcs of water—but their actions seemed frustratingly pointless. The captain brushed passed her, talking animatedly on his walkie-talkie. "The woman is embedded deep inside—looks like her bedroom," he spat at the black plastic.

Sabrina froze in terror. Up to this point, she had just assumed that they were treating Carla in the ambulance, maybe even for minor burns. She had never once thought that she might still be inside the house. She looked toward the driveway as a new set of car headlights distracted her.

It better be Blogg.

It was. He jumped out of the car and headed toward a paramedic pacing back and forth near a grove of pines. As a red light passed Blogg, she caught the horror plastered on his face. Sabrina ran up to him. Grabbing his arm, she shrieked, "What do you know?"

He turned toward her, quickly looking into her eyes before shying away. "She's trapped inside."

She spun back toward the fire but he grabbed her arm before she could move. "Don't even think about going in there—you'll cook yourself in a second."

"But she's the key to everything," Sabrina screamed. She peeled his fingers away and bolted toward the torrent flames.

"Sabrina!" Blogg yelled after her.

She got within twenty feet of the house before a firefighter grabbed her and pulled her over to one of the squad cars. Sabrina crumbled into the man's arms before sitting her down in the backseat.

The captain screamed for his crew to move back again. A moment later, the complete second floor collapsed onto the first.

"No!" Sabrina yelled.

It would be a miracle if Carla survived.

Chapter 27

A little before ten in the morning, four emergency workers exited the charred two-story house with a stretcher. On it, a white sheet was draped over the remains. An onlooker turned away, sickened by the ghastly sight. Carla Sanchez had been reduced to a charred, lifeless body and it was more than any person could handle.

Sabrina buried her face into Blogg's wide chest. He didn't shy away from the awkward intimacy; instead, wrapping his burly arms around her shoulders for comfort. He, too, felt the pain—squeezing her as hard as he could. They got off on the wrong foot but their body language proved a mutual understanding of the anguish they both felt.

She pulled away and looked into Blogg's reddened face, and silently thanked him. Without her even asking, he had driven up to meet her, without Getty. And she knew in the deepest part of her heart he had done it to comfort her, even if he refused to acknowledge it. A simple thought trickled into her head: Maybe he wasn't an ass after all.

Scanning the yard, something caught Sabrina's attention. Near a barely disturbed flower garden, the late morning sun caught the reflection of a small picture frame. She walked over and wiped away the smattering of mud that covered the front. It was a honeymoon photo, taken maybe twenty years earlier, showing a strikingly beautiful and fresh Carla Sanchez with another man. She was sitting in an armchair next to the gentleman of fascinating taste, his blondish hair tossed effortlessly straight back. He was dressed in a dark suit, his hands cupped together in a charming pose.

Eric Sanchez.

A random thought passed through her: *Who would claim their possessions?* From what she knew of them, they had no immediate family. She surveyed the disaster tossed around her. Then again, there was nothing left to even consider a possession.

The hum of an engine pulled her back into reality. A red pickup crawled up the drive and braked within a few yards of her. A plump looking man worked his way from behind the wheel. He was similarly dressed as the firefighters, but wore a white shirt instead of the standard navy blue.

"Good morning, ma'am," he started, tipping his head as he held a folder of paper. She eyed the patch on his shoulder—it was the insignia of Pacific City. "I'm the fire marshal overseeing this case."

"Morning," she whispered back, her voice barely able to project anything remotely intelligent.

"You related to the deceased?" he asked gingerly as he approached the corner of the house where a set of windows once stood.

"Me?" She shook her head. "Just a stunned reporter. I was doing a story on her murdered husband when I found out about the fire."

"Alleged murder," corrected Blogg, walking up to the pair. "The homeowner was recently widowed."

"In the last two weeks," Sabrina interjected.

"Hmm," the fire marshal said. He opened the folder and made some notations on a yellow pad.

Sabrina watched him for a moment. She dearly wanted to ask the one question that would answer why he was here. "I didn't realize this was part of Pacific City jurisdiction," she blurted.

He stopped writing and looked at her with puppy dog eyes. "It's being investigated for arson, ma'am ... and I'm 'fraid Tillamook County doesn't have the resources to handle it."

The thought of an arsonist made her swallow hard—first Eric and now this? "Why do you think that?"

"The captain on the scene reported it as such. It's in the initial report I just received. That's why I'm here. Let me tell you, it's always a rush to get out here before the place gets too disturbed." He glanced at the house. "Although it looks like there's not much someone could muss up."

"Did the captain say why it might be arson?"

"Let's see here." He flipped through a couple of pages. "Path of fire was accelerated due to unknown additive. Source appears to be inside wall of master bedroom. … Discovered broken window in backdoor when first arrived."

She moved closer to him. "I don't understand who would want to murder a reclusive widow. She seemed to just want to keep to herself."

"That's if it's not related to her husband," Blogg blurted.

The fire marshal shook his head. "I'm 'fraid I didn't really know her. But when I'm done here this morning, I'm convinced her house is gonna leave quite a few clues what happened—maybe enough to catch the bastard."

The revelations made her mind churn. Why? Who? If connected to Eric's death, it was making her crazy she was no closer to an answer than two weeks ago. "Do you mind if I give you my email address? I would love to see a copy of the final report—you know, anything I can maybe make into an article."

"No problem, ma'am." He handed her his notepad.

Struggling with her one good hand, she scribbled on it and gave it back. "Could I use you in a follow up story?

"Damn it, Sabrina." Blogg interjected. "Aren't you seeing a problem here? Someone tried to run you off the road. And now, after you persuaded Carla to help you with her story, someone burned her house down and took her with it. Isn't enough, enough?

The realization of what he was saying sliced through her. "Really? Are you suggesting this is my fault?"

"No, but somebody sure as hell doesn't like what you're up to."

Sabrina threw imaginary knifes at Blogg with her eyes and then stormed off, toward the house. She got within twenty yards when she noticed a vanilla-colored envelope tucked away in a nearby shrub. She was about to call the fire marshal over when she noticed her name typewritten on the front of it.

Wondering if Carla had left it for only her to see, Sabrina decided to have a peek before alerting anyone. There was no name written on the envelope indicating who it was from, only that it was clearly intended for Sabrina—both her full name and address had been typed on the envelope.

She looked over at the fire marshal and Blogg, who were in a deep conversation and ignoring what she was up to. She looked back at the envelope, turning it over several times, debating if she really should open it.

After one more look at the fire marshal, she was convinced it was the right thing to do. She slid a fingernail under the envelope's flap and then reached inside. She felt a few pieces of paper, maybe one thicker than the other, and pulled them out.

A color photo came into view. Her eyebrow creased as she turned the photo sideways. *What am I looking at?* Then it registered. Gasping, she dropped the envelope and backed away as if it was poison.

How did they know?

Chapter 28

Mannheim sat in his black Jeep and smiled. Watching the smoldering house just a few hundred yards away provided the perfect ending to his objective.

If only his contractor could've seen the look on the reporter's face.

Mannheim had promised to take care of the situation and it was going exactly as planned. He put the binoculars back up to his eyes and tracked the reporter as she stumbled toward her car. Mannheim then turned the binoculars on Blogg: He was calling to the reporter, obviously noticing her bizarre behavior. She was ignoring him, slamming the car door just as he was within a few feet of her. She then backed out of the driveway, not caring she was half on the lawn.

Shit. He hadn't prepared for such a sudden departure. He threw the binoculars on the seat and slid down. As she sped by, he eyed the horror on her face. She was looking straight ahead, her face ghost white, unaware that she just passed Carla Sanchez's murderer.

Mannheim moved back into an upright position and started his car. Giddy at what he had accomplished, he knew the threat to his employer was just about over. While he relished the opportunity to eliminate the reporter, that would be too messy—besides, she was clearly shocked by the package and should be long gone by tomorrow.

Now he just needed to take care of one more piece of business: Mona Frederick.

His contacts at BioHumanity alerted him to the conversation Mona had with Sabrina. They were monitoring all of Sanchez's colleagues and recorded what Mona had said to the reporter. That conversation persuaded him Mona needed to be addressed.

The unfortunate part was he was going to have to finish the job with an accomplice—the deadline to act alone had passed and he still didn't have possession of the journal. As far as how the bonus would be split, he would work all of that out with his contractor once the job was finished.

He smiled.   *Wouldn't it be coincidental if the accomplice met an untimely death?*

Then the bonus would be all his.

Chapter 29

On the other side of the Heart Center, in the administrative wing, Rico hovered over his assistant, Vale.

"See here," Vale said, pointing at an LED monitor.

"No, I'm not seeing it," Rico replied.

Vale rewound the video a few frames. "It's hard to catch because she's quick, but it's definitely there."

"Can you blow it up?"

Vale drew a box around the woman's hand with his finger and clicked a few keys on the computer. The screen zoomed, showing her hand near another woman's jacket.

"Now rerun the frames ... in slo-mo."

The woman pushed her clenched hand into another woman's pocket and then pulled it back, but this time, her hand was open.

"Damn it!" Rico shouted. "You're right." He jumped from his chair. "I'm gonna need a lockdown on Gina Hodgkin's room now!"

Rico bolted out of the security wing and into the stairwell. Taking two steps at a time, he jumped to the next floor's landing. Slamming the stairwell door opened, he sprinted down the hall to Vua's office, bursting in without knocking.

"I'm sorry to bother you, Steven ... but it's urgent," Rico said, interrupting a client meeting.

A look of disgust crossed Vua's face until he realized the urgency in Rico's voice. "Can you excuse me for a moment, Ms. Cho. I promise I'll be right back."

Vua directed Rico toward the hallway. He closed the door when they were both outside. "This had better be good."

Rico nodded. "You asked me to take another look at the video from the woman we deported. Well, we just analyzed it. There's definitely been a breech. She gave something to Gina Hyde."

"Are you sure?"

A nod. "Hundred percent."

"Then get down to her room and find out what it is."

"And if Gina found it?"

Vua looked away. "I pray for her sake that's not the case."

"But if it is?" Rico pressed.

Vua thought for a moment. "Then we'll simply have to see if Ms. Hyde is willing to become an evangelist for BioHumanity."

"I see," Rico responded.

Chapter 30

The Beacon's front door groaned as Sabrina pushed her way into the office. All around her, empty desks were scattered with paper and pencils. The writers were out scurrying for their next story, well aware that a big story is always hard to come by in Neskowin. That is, every writer except two.

In the far corner, near the reporters' makeshift kitchen, Getty was at a table hunched over his laptop, pounding the keys with two index fingers. Just to the left stood the only interior door in the whole office—the entrance to Blogg's office. The blinds were drawn shut over the window inset in the door but Sabrina could still make out the heavyset figure of Blogg making a point on his cellphone.

Disrupted by the visitor, Getty casually turned to see who it was. Realizing it was Sabrina, he grunted, then quickly returned to taking out his aggression on the keyboard.

You're an ass, Sabrina thought. She pushed her way past him and gave two quick knocks on Blogg's door. He had called her an hour earlier saying he needed to talk … urgently.

Blogg squinted toward the blinds then gestured her in with two quick waves. She popped in and slid comfortably into the old leather chair that sat across from his desk.

"We've got to get to the bottom of this. Now!" Blogg hollered into his cellphone. He let the caller talk for a minute and then replied, "Fine. Let's get it done then." He flipped the phone onto his desk and gazed over at his visitor. "I appreciate you coming in on such short notice, especially after what you've been through the past few days."

"It hasn't been easy," Sabrina said softly.

"I understand that. I really do." His voice was mellower. "It hasn't been easy for me either." A pause. "But I want to know what the hell is going on here. ... There's too many people dying ... too many to be considered an aberration."

"No argument from me."

Blogg breathed heavily and then said, "And that's what I want to talk to you about."

Sabrina looked away. She didn't like where this was going.

"You're way too close to this thing. You're going to get seriously hurt." He crossed his arms. "And I think you know that."

"Look ... it's not about me. It's about finding the truth. That's all I'm trying to do."

"And you think the best way to do that is to stay one step ahead of what the killer is doing, to be smarter than him or her. And hope he doesn't kill you in the process. Is that right?"

"No," she pleaded. "It's not that at all. I just know he's going to make a mistake, and that'll be my big break."

"That's the problem I have with this." He leaned forward. "Look, you are one of the most passionate reporters I've ever met but also the most stubborn. It's clear you care about your subjects and your writing is really showing promise." A pause. "Hell, I'll just say it. You're turning into one helluva reporter ... I'll tell you that. You've still got a lot to learn but you've grown leaps and bounds since we first met."

Sabrina's eyes opened wide. "I don't know what to say. I mean, I wouldn't expect such a compliment."

He leaned further over the desk. "We've been through a lot in the short time we've been together, and because of that, I've developed a bit of affection for you."

"Thank you," she said embarrassingly. He let his guard down, which he had never done in their previous conversations, and she didn't know how to respond.

He waved her off. "There's no need for that."

"No, really. Thanks for the vote of confidence. I never thought, after our rough start, that I'd ... like ... ever hear such things. But can I also say ... I haven't quite developed the same level of affection for you," she said, half-smiling.

Blogg smirked. "That's what I like about you. You never mince words ... that's for sure. And boy, you say what you're thinking. Those are great attributes of a reporter, especially a first-time one." But there was an undertone to his voice that suggested he wasn't taking this time just to praise her.

"So why do I have this feeling you're going to give me some bad news?"

He reached behind and grabbed a stack of papers sitting on a shelf. After rifling through them for a few seconds, he pulled a photo and pushed it across the desk. "I found this on Carla's front lawn. I think you saw it too, and were quite disturbed over it."

Sabrina grabbed the photo and, without looking at it, pushed it into her handbag. "I'm sorry you had to see that," she said, knowing her face was beat red from embarrassment.

He pointed toward her bag. "Is that why you left New York?"

She looked away. "I don't really want to talk about it." Then she said, "But it's a past I'm trying to forget, if that's what you're asking."

He nodded. "I don't suppose you know who left it there for you?"

She shook her head. "No doubt it was whoever killed Carla, trying to scare me off." She took a deep breath and then her voice became louder, stronger. "But if he thinks he's gotten the best of me, he's dead wrong … it's only made me more determined."

"That's what worries me."

A lump formed in her throat. "So what are you saying?"

He stood and started pacing. "I don't think there's any way for this to end good. It's headed for a very bad ending and I can't have that on my watch."

"So what do you want me to do?" Her voice quivered with emotion she hadn't felt in weeks.

"I want you to stop putting yourself in danger … to be safe. Look, I get it. You're trying to do the right thing … to help people who have had an injustice handed to them. You had a hunch, and you were right. And I admit, we didn't think there was a chance in hell you'd be right. But you were."

"That seems like a small consolation now," Sabrina replied.

"But being right doesn't mean there aren't consequences. The fact is we now have a killer out there who's most likely killed Eric and Carla Sanchez. And now he's on to you. That scares the hell out of me."

She stood. There just wasn't any possible way she was going to give this up. She just needed a little more time. "It was just a picture. That's not putting me in harm's way," she pleaded.

"Maybe so." He pointed to her sling. "And what do you think that was—an accident?"

Her shoulders wilted. She hadn't thought about the car accident in a week. "So you're firing me?" she asked half-jokingly.

Blogg looked away. And then he nodded as his eyes welled with tears.

It was the first time she had ever seen him emotional but her anger suppressed any empathy she might've felt.

"Oh my God, it's so unfair." She grabbed a copy of the Beacon stacked next to the door and threw it at him. "How's this for news. You've just made the biggest mistake of your life!"

She whipped open the door and stomped out, the blinds clattering in response.

"Sabrina!"

She turned.

"Just go back home to New York. It's the safest thing for you right now."

She shook her head. "I can't do that."

Chapter 31

As the Acapulco sun poured through the large window, Gina rolled over in bed, trying to shield her eyes from the brightness. She flipped on her side, her nose an inch from the wall, and then turned the other way. Nothing seemed to worked.

Why was she so tired?

She looked around the room, disoriented at first, and then realized where she was. She tried pushing herself up but her abdomen still felt swollen. Sighing, she eyed the bedside clock thinking she should've felt better by now. After all, it had been three days since Vua's procedure.

Why did she agree to do this?

And then she thought about Blair and her death sentence. If nothing were done to help her, she would die. It was as simple as that. For Blair's sake, it was worth the heart-wrenching decision she had to make. Blair was Gina's friend and she would do whatever it took to save her, no matter how much Gregory was an asshole.

Across the room, her roommate's bed remained a motionless clump. *She should be awake by now*, she thought. "Helen?" Gina whispered, not sure whether she wanted to wake her or not, but feeling lonely at the same time.

She didn't budge.

"Helen!" Gina repeated.

The clump stirred and then Helen's face popped out from beneath the sheets. "Ohhh," she muttered.

Feeling bad about waking her, Gina whispered back, "Go back to sleep. It's not important."

A sigh. "No. No. It's okay. I feel like I've been hit by a bus. What time is it anyway?"

"Six."

"In the morning?"

"Yeah, you've been out since yesterday."

Helen rubbed her eyes. "Seriously? I must've been asleep twelve hours."

"They took you in yesterday. Don't you remember?"

"Yes, of course." She felt her stomach. "What a strange feeling. Almost like my body still feels like there's something inside." She turned toward the sliders that led to the small, outdoor deck. "I need to get my body going. You up for a little sun?"

"Definitely." Gina tried moving upright but the throbbing pain surged through her abdomen.

"C'mon, old lady. Let me help you up," Helen said as she reached out a hand. Gina grabbed it and they walked on to the sun deck to take in the warm morning. A touch of a breeze was blowing off the harbor, a single cloud hiding the sun.

"You know, I never had a chance to tell you this, but I had the weirdest dream a few nights ago," Gina said after settling into one of two matching loungers.

"Really? Like how?"

"I mean, it must've been a dream but it seemed so real. I woke up and felt as if someone was in our room."

Helen chuckled. "I'd definitely call that a dream. Maybe it was your nerves playing with you."

"That's the thing ... I didn't have time to be nervous. I thought the procedure would be done a few days later but I guess they had other plans."

"Nice surprise ... They must've pushed it up for a reason."

"I wonder why."

"Have no idea."

The sun finally escaped from behind the cloud. Gina covered her eyes. "I need to get my sunglasses."

"Do you mind getting mine?" Helen asked. "They're in the top drawer."

"Sure." Gina pushed through the slider back into their bedroom. Pulling open a drawer near Helen's desk, Gina found them—a pair of amber colored oversized sunglasses—just where she said they were. *Nice*, she thought. *Now where are mine?*

She opened and closed her drawers then realized they were still in her jacket. She pulled the jacket from her closet and reached into the side pocket, wrapping her hand around a tiny plastic object. Confused what it might be, she pulled it out and stared at a ruby red USB drive.

She flipped it over, wondering whose it was. Mulling over what to do next, Gina decided the best way to stir a memory was to have a look. She pulled the cap off and plugged it into her laptop. The drive window popped on the screen with only one file showing—an MPEG called *Watch-Me-Now*. She looked out the slider at her roommate resting effortlessly in the lounger, oblivious to why Gina was taking so long. She returned her attention to the file and decided she needed to have a look.

A grainy video started playing, taken with a cheap camera phone in some sort of operating room. The camera was facing two women but was far enough away that she couldn't quite make out their faces. The two were talking but all she could hear were muffled voices. She reached for the laptop and turned the volume up.

"I think I feel it!" the women to the left said.

"The patient is doing fine," the second woman replied, after glancing at the vital signs.

Gina's eyes widened as she realized it was a video of childbirth.

"Suction," the first woman said.

The second woman reached in with a device while the first woman—her hands hidden from the camera's view—struggled to complete the birth.

"Ah, I've got 'em," the first woman finally said as she pulled her hands, bloodied from the effort, toward her chest.

The second woman applied forceps to the placenta while the baby, no more the size of the woman's hand, dangled motionless in her hand.

Something wasn't right. That baby … why were they taking him out so early? Then it struck her: It wasn't a baby but a fetus—much the same age as the one she gave up. And it wasn't a delivery but an abortion.

The first woman took the fetus over to another table and set him down. Taking a scalpel from the tray next to her, she started pressing on the chest. Gina cupped a hand around her mouth and closed her eyes. Her body started shaking violently.

Oh my God, what are they doing? And then it started making sense.

A hand grabbed her shoulder. Startled, she opened her eyes. "I'm sorry it's taken me so long," she said, thinking it was Helen.

"You just put your nose where you shouldn't have," a man's voice said from behind.

"What are you—" A hand wrapped around her mouth, muffling any screams she tried to muster. The other hand, holding a rag drenched in a foul-smelling liquid, smothered her nose and mouth.

Her survival senses kicked in, trying to hold her breath as long as she could.

"Don't fight it," the man stated.

But she kept fighting until she could do it no more. *They've won,* she suddenly thought. She took the dreaded breath, feeling helpless as the rag's vapors swirled through her nostrils.

And then darkness collapsed around her.

Chapter 32
Three weeks later

A rare windstorm rolled through the bay, causing Gregory to grasp the wheelchair tighter than he intended. With the sky a swirl of gray and white, he pushed his sister up the ramp of the building and into the protection of the patient atrium. Waiting for his arrival were two women—one dressed in black scrubs, the other in teal.

"Welcome to the Heart Center," one of the women gently said.

"Thank you," Blair whispered back with all the strength she had.

Gregory added, "We're ecstatic this is finally going to happen." He put a hand on Blair's shoulder. "It's not a moment too soon."

The woman dressed in teal smiled. "Sometimes the stars align. We found a donor match right when your application was processed."

Blair looked at her brother. "I'm glad you met with Dr. Vua when you did."

Gregory rubbed her shoulders. "I am too. And as much as I'm happy now, I'll be that much happier when you have your normal life back." He then eyed the women. "We rushed down here as soon as I heard the news. I take it everything is still a go?"

"Of course, Mr. Archer. Our facility has an incredible success rate and we expect your sister to fully recover … and be as healthy as ever."

Gregory smiled. That comforted him.

"We don't have any time to waste," the woman dressed in black said. "We'd like to get started right away."

"Of course," Gregory replied.

"But as we tell all our incoming patients, please take a few moments for family time. We'll wait over by the patient wing. When you're ready, we'll take Blair in."

Gregory nodded.

The women backed away while Gregory knelt down next to his sister's wheelchair. He took her hand. "I don't want you to be afraid at all. Everything's going to work out just fine."

Blair looked at her brother's hand and nodded. "But I'm concerned how you're going to be able to pay for this," she whispered back.

He shook his head. "Don't worry about that. I'm gonna get it taken care of. The important thing is you need to get well and everything will be okay from there."

She reached over and grabbed his hand with her free one. "Gina—" she started.

Gregory looked away. "I don't want to talk about her. I know you loved her like a sister, and I loved her too, but she wants nothing to do with me."

She shook her head, struggling to get the energy to speak. "No. No. It's not about that. She's here."

Gregory looked confused. "What do you mean she's here?"

She nodded. "Here at the Center."

"How do you know that?"

"Because she told me in an email. She visited me in the hospital a month ago, saw the ad for the Acapulco Heart Center, and decided she would become a donor."

Gregory jumped to his feet. "A donor? But that's impossible. That means—"

Blair nodded. "Since they use the stem cells from the placenta, she must've been pregnant."

His body slumped with the thought that maybe he was the father. "But she wouldn't do this without telling me. Would she?"

"If she did, would you have let her come here and have the abortion?"

He pondered the dilemma his sister proposed. In truth, he probably wouldn't want her to but then what would've happened to Blair's transplant?

Blair added, "She didn't want me to tell you but I needed to. She's here for me, not you, and I just want you to know that ... no matter what happens."

He turned away, his eyes welling with tears. "She's an angel," he whispered.

"I'm glad you finally realize that."

Gregory knelt back down. Looking into her eyes, he said, "You're right."

"Then you know what to do."

A nod. "I'm gonna change, Blair. That's my commitment to you. And my commitment to Gina is to do whatever it takes to win her back."

She reached over and touched his lips with two fingers. "Don't do it for me," she whispered. "Do you it for yourself."

"Mr. Archer?" the woman dressed in black asked, interrupting their conversation. "We should get going."

Gregory nodded. "She's ready."

One of the women grabbed the wheelchair and began rolling Blair toward the patient ward. As they pushed through the doors, Blair gave one last look back and smiled, and then the doors swung closed behind her.

Another staff member, a man dressed in business attire, stepped up to him. "Mr. Archer?"

"Yes?" he replied, standing.

"Your appointment with the financing department is now … to talk through the remaining terms."

"Yes," he said somberly. "Of course."

"Excellent. Let it be said, we're happy to be working with you."

"I don't doubt it."

* * * * *

Gregory wiped the sweat accumulating on his forehead as he exited the Heart Center's administrative offices.

Paying off a hundred thirty thousand dollars was going to be a problem.

To get Blair admitted, he gave the Center his complete life savings, which only amounted to thirty thousand. But for the operation to go forward, he had to take out a high interest loan for another sixty grand.

Where was he going to get the rest when she was discharged?

He looked around the Center's expansive lobby—at the people passing him, blindly unaware of his circumstances. What was he going to do? Emotionally, he was a wreck and there was absolutely nobody in his life he could lean on.

The receptionist nodded warmly as he walked by. A thought occurred: Maybe he could see Gina—at least thank her, even if she wasn't interested in talking to him. He walked over to the receptionist's desk, wrapped in aluminum with a black granite top. "Excuse me," he said to her.

The young, dark-skinned woman smiled from behind her laptop. "Hola! How can I help you?"

"I was wondering if you could tell me what room Gina Hyde is in."

"Is she a patient or a donor?"

A pause. "Donor."

The woman moved to her laptop and started typing. After a few seconds, she replied, "Are you sure of the last name?"

"Yes. It's spelled *H-Y-D-E*."

She shook her head. "I'm not finding anybody with that last name, or first name for that matter. Are you sure she's checked in? Could she not have arrived yet?"

"I'm told she's supposed to be here. She talked to my sister about coming." A pause. "I don't think she'd lie about it."

"Maybe she checked out already." The woman fired her fingers at the keyboard a few more seconds. "Hmm."

"Did you find something?"

"No, not exactly. I did finally find her name in our records, but it's been archived."

"What does that mean?"

"It means she did have an appointment here, or even could've been here, but the visit was cancelled."

"Cancelled?"

She nodded.

"Can you tell if she at least arrived?"

"No, her data isn't available anymore." She looked at him with sympathetic eyes. "Sorry I couldn't be more help."

Gregory nodded and walked toward the entrance. He slammed his body into the door, causing it to bang against the building. "Damn it," he murmured to himself. "Where is she?"

Chapter 33

Gina opened her eyes and focused on a white ceiling fan twirling slowly around.

Where am I?

She tried to move her arms and legs, but they wouldn't budge. She was strapped to a narrow, dark vinyl chair—with a high back and tilted at a forty-five degree angle. Her eyes darted left and right, but again were drawn to the fan blades. A glimmer of sunlight flickered between the blades, reminding her of Dad's old movie projector when the film ran out. Sighing, she closed her eyes. She was just too tired.

"Tsk-tsk, Ms. Hyde. There's no sleeping yet," the soft male voice said behind her.

She grudgingly reopened them, heavily swollen from sleep deprivation. "What do you want?" she replied, barely comprehending him.

"I only want the truth."

"And what is that?" she whispered, rolling in and out of consciousness.

"What do you know about the Heart Hospital?"

"It's a place to abort your unborn child, like I did, for the benefit of others."

"And what is that benefit?"

"To cure terminally ill heart patients."

"Yes. But it's not only to cure them but to give them a new beginning. And of course the benefit to us is they become an evangelist for BioHumanity." He paused and then said, "Are you ready to become an evangelist?"

She stayed silent, thinking hard about whether she could muster anything other than the truth. "I'm ready to expose your crimes," she finally said. "That's what I'm ready to do."

A sigh blew behind her. "I see, Ms. Hyde. It seems we still have quite a bit more work to do before we can release you on our staff. I would've thought the three-week training you've been through would've helped. You must, after all, conform to our approach."

The chair creaked behind her. Was he leaving? An echo of footsteps followed, each one growing softer and softer, before she heard the groan of the door—a heavy, metal door.

"Good day, Ms. Hyde. I look forward to resuming our conversation tomorrow. Until then, enjoy the solitary use of our studio apartment. Just beware the sensors on your body will pick up any sleep, and make sure to stir you awake with a bit of a shock. But of course you already know this. We've been doing this for days now." And then the echo of the door slamming shut ricocheted around the barren, white room.

Gina closed her eyes and instantly felt the shock to her arm. She cried in pain as her eyes shot open. *I can't keep this up much longer,* she thought. And then through the blurry, uncontrollable world she was living, a moment of reason came to her. Gina smiled, nodding her head slightly.

She had an idea of how to escape this nightmare with her dignity, and soul, intact.

Chapter 34

Sabrina's cellphone chimed her favorite ringtone as it lay on the kitchen counter. But she refused to answer it. It rang again.

Who was bothering her?

The phone rang a third time. She opened her eyes as sunlight splashed across her face, blinding her. She quickly closed them, burying her head in the couch's cushion. Her phone rang a fourth time. *Leave me alone*, she thought. Sighing, she slowly slid her legs straight after being in a fetal position for what seemed like hours, and kicked the armrest. "Why?" she screamed to the empty house. "Why are you bothering me?" *Then again, why would anybody give a damn about me?*

She thought about the question.

It was true. Nobody did care. How else could she explain the attempt on her life or the cruel way a widow died just for helping a reporter? She shook her head. No, it wasn't that anybody didn't care—it was the fact that she lived in a world run by savages. She glanced toward the floor. The envelope she had found at Carla's house was strewn, half-ripped, across the room, along with the three photos found inside. She shuddered at the terrifying memory it stirred.

Those pictures.

She sighed deeply, burying her head into the cushion. Why didn't Brieman return her messages? Yes, she had stood him up but she apologized three times to his stupid voicemail. He, of all people should ... no, would understand.

A stench of body odor rose from an outstretched arm. *I really need to shower*, she thought. But what did it matter? She hadn't left her apartment in days and nobody seemed to notice ... until the phone call today. Deciding to forget the shower, she picked up her head and sighed at the food spread all over the coffee table: melted ice cream, half-eaten tortilla chips, Chinese carryout, and a pile of diet soda cans.

Mentally and physically, she was exhausted, and she just didn't have the energy for anything anymore. Thoughts drifted from the photos to her former life in NYC. *No*, she thought. *I'm not going there. I can't.*

But the wave of thoughts kept coming, over and over, until they swarmed her: her lucrative job, a great Manhattan apartment, her career. Some would have given their right arm to be a culinary instructor for the world's top aspiring chefs. It was a career that had been completely architected by her mother; yet she comfortably had followed along for nearly fifteen years. She had been successful, popular, and just a phone call away from the stars.

And then it all came crashing down in one solitary moment—

A knock at the door scattered her thoughts. Who was bothering her? She rubbed her eyes, unaware she had fallen back asleep. She looked down at her soiled clothes. She was a mess. The guest knocked again—this time on the door's glass. She turned toward the door, squinting to see who it was. Why so relentless?

One way or the other, she was going to have to deal with it. Sighing loudly, she warily pushed herself from the couch and staggered over to the window. She peeled back the blinds and caught the impatient figure of Brieman pacing back and forth. Her heart jumped. *What a nice surprise*, she thought. Without giving it a second thought, she pushed back the lock and opened the door. A fresh breeze pushed into the house. "Hi," she murmured as she used a free hand to push a mess of hair to one side.

"I don't suppose you recognize me," he asked playfully.

"How could I not?" It was hard not to forget the chiseled look of a man she sorely liked.

An awkward silence followed.

Brieman's eyes dropped to her shoulder. "Where's the sling?"

"It feels a lot better," she replied feebly, hoping he didn't notice the lie in her voice.

He shook his head as if he knew. "Do you mind if I come in?"

"Only if you promise to tell me you got my message."

He pulled a bag from his jacket. He waved it in front of her. "Yes, I did … and I'm sorry I didn't respond sooner. That's why I got you this."

Her eyes widened. "Really?" And then she said, "This is so not getting you off the hook, Dr. Brieman." She opened the bag and laughed. "A pager?"

"Yeah, remember the days before texting? I figured I'd give you my old one—it would be a good way to get a hold of me."

She laughed. "Although kinda corny, this might just be enough for me to forgive you."

He stepped toward her. "Look. I'm sorry. Rounds at the hospital were killing me." He eyed her clothes and then snuck a peek inside the house. "But then again, had I known you were in this bad of shape, I would've gotten here sooner."

"I'm okay. Just feeling a little down."

"About me?"

She shook her head. "It's not just you. It's something else."

He nodded toward the door. "So can I come in?"

The man apologized, she thought. That was good enough for her. She opened the door further. "Hope you don't mind messes."

"I didn't think you would ever answer that door," he said as he stepped inside.

"Something bothering you?"

"How long since you ventured out?"

She shrugged. "I don't know. A couple of weeks."

"Don't you have stories to cover?"

How was she going to answer this one? She moved past him, into the kitchen. "I'm not employed anymore."

"Does this have anything to do with Carla Sanchez?"

Very intuitive of him. "You could say that," she replied.

He looked at the empty wine bottles scattered on the counter. "Been drinking too, eh?"

"Not the last day."

"Great. You're on the rebound."

"Would you like some?"

He shrugged. "Better me than you."

Sabrina reached into the refrigerator and grabbed an open bottle of Chardonnay. "Don't expect to get hammered. It's all I have."

He eyed her. "I've been worried about you." There was seriousness in his voice.

She looked out the kitchen window. "Life always seems to throw a curveball at me."

"What's going on?"

"Nothing." She framed her eyes on his body. There was attraction but now wasn't the time.

"C'mon Sabrina. Don't lie to me."

"Ok. Fine. It's just that I'm thinking my short life as a reporter is a complete bust."

"Hey," he said softly. "It's only one job."

"Maybe so. But I've decided to go home."

"Home? You're not a native? I never would've guessed."

His attempt at sarcasm wasn't working. "That's not the least bit funny."

"I'm sorry. I was just trying to get you to loosen up."

He apologized twice in one hour, she thought. *That's a trait that would never get old.*

"So where is home anyway? East Coast?"

"Nice guess. New York. Manhattan. But then again, is there really any other part of the state worth visiting?"

"I hope there is. I'm from Rochester."

"Oh." Embarrassment crossed her face. "Apart from Rochester, of course."

"And my parents are from Buffalo."

"And Buffalo."

"My brother lives in Niagara."

A smiled worked its way out. "Okay. You got me."

He chuckled. "What did you do back there, anyway?"

"Taught school." She kept her answers simple. If he were really interested in her, he would have to work harder.

"A school teacher? That's a bit of a change from a reporter."

She laughed. "Nothing like that."

"Oh?"

"For budding chefs. I was an instructor in a culinary school ... a very established one."

"Really? I never would've guessed by looking at this place."

"Funny."

"No. Really."

"It was a huge passion with me. Besides, I got to work with some of the most well-known chefs in New York, not to mention the Eastern Seaboard."

"Did you have a specialty?"

"I did ... fresh from the ocean pan-seared Chilean Sea Bass. Try to slide by with a farm-raised broiled version and you will flunk."

He put a hand on the kitchen counter. A smile curled along his lips. "So you're a badass in the kitchen?"

She was enjoying the volley. "Nope ... just passionate about cooking. Besides, good food equals good company. Maybe I can show you sometime." She bit her lip. Did that just come out of her mouth?

"I just might take you up on that." He paused. She could see he was thinking about something. "Then why'd you throw all that away? I mean to come here and start over?"

Game over. "Can we talk about something else?"

He put his hands up. "Okay. Maybe another time then."

The two stared awkwardly at each other. It was wrenching it came to this after the friendly banter they just had. Why did she have to be so defensive? *Just tell him everything,* she thought. *Get on with your life.*

"All this talk of food is making me hungry," Brieman finally said. He hesitated, unsure whether to continue. "C'mon, let's get some dinner and figure this thing out." He reached out and put an arm around her shoulders.

She didn't move away. He had made a decision to stick with her and that made her all that more attracted to him. "Don't you need to get back?"

"I do. But there's this great little romantic place hidden deep within the hospital—light barely gets there, which makes it that much more eclectic. It's not crowded. Plus you get to clean your own table before you sit down and, now this will definitely be the selling point, you get to pick whatever food you want from a glorious buffet without having to sift through a menu."

Sabrina cozied up to him. "Hmm, sounds enticing."

"So what do you say?" Brieman asked as he placed the half-finished wine on the counter.

She looked into his eyes with a broad smile. For more than ten minutes, she was actually happy. And then she looked down at herself. "Look at me. I'm a complete mess. I need to take a quick shower. Do I need to think about bringing anything?"

"Just your clean self. That's it."

He worked another smile out of her. For a moment, she thought about packing an overnight bag, but that might've seen a bit assertive. No, she would let him take the first step. "Great. Make yourself at home and I'll be back in ten minutes. I promise."

"No rush."

As she headed toward the bedroom, she was distracted by her cellphone buzzing twice, signaling a voicemail. The vague memory of her phone ringing nonstop a half hour ago came back to her. "Is that you on my voicemail?" she called to Brieman. "You tried to call me before you pushed your way into my apartment, didn't you?"

"Now that's where we're going to have to work on our reporting skills," he replied. "You assume way too much."

She picked up the phone. "Let's see what message the good doctor left for me," she replied, ignoring him.

He laughed.

She hit the green voicemail button. It was Mona. As she listened, she suddenly regretted not paying attention to it sooner. Her voice sounded urgent. She needed to see Sabrina right away … so much so that she had already decided on a time and place that evening. Sabrina stopped the message and noted the time. "We've got to go."

"Anything wrong?"

"I don't know. It's Mona."

"Who?"

"She's a woman I met at BioHumanity. She's beside herself right now and wants to talk, but wants to do it in person." She pointed to the clock. "In twenty minutes at an old shuttered restaurant along Highway 131."

Brieman shook his head. "There's no way that's going to happen. We're too far out."

She dialed the number Mona called from. Maybe she could back it up fifteen minutes. The phone rang ten times and then Mona's voicemail picked up.

"No luck?"

She shook her head.

"Look, why don't I drive? There may be a chance with some back roads."

"You have to get back to the hospital. How is that going to work?"

"Like this." He grabbed his cellphone and punched a few keys. "I just made myself unavailable."

"What power you have."

He pulled her toward the door. "C'mon. Time's a wasting." A convertible Porsche sat just outside her house. It was midnight black but looked like it had never been driven.

"New?"

Brieman started the car with his key fob. "Nope … just too many hours at the hospital to enjoy it. Hop in. We've got some time to make up."

Chapter 35

Mona rubbed her shoulders. It was a chilly night as the sun slid behind the hills. Standing in the weed-infested parking lot, a hand on her car, she gazed at the abandoned restaurant before spinning around and eyeing the gravel road that led back to the highway. Where were they?

It was a mistake leaving a message and assuming Sabrina would come. She should have waited until Sabrina called back. But that was the problem: There wasn't any more time. She needed to let somebody know what was going on and Sabrina walked into her life at just the right moment. And she was the perfect person to tell.

Tires crackling against the gravel stole her attention.

Finally.

She looked at her watch. Ten minutes late. But they were here. She shielded her eyes against the oncoming headlights. The car, no, it was a Jeep—a black one—pulled alongside her Honda.

Her heart beat more rapidly. Why didn't this feel right?

Both doors opened and then shut with a firm thump. The crunch of gravel could be heard as two sets of footsteps gravitated closer. She backed up, stumbling along the abandoned building. A man and a woman suddenly appeared in the dim light.

"Can I help you?" was all she could muster. She had no idea who they were.

"I think you can," the woman replied.

"Are you lost?"

The woman laughed. "Hardly."

"Then what is it?" Mona's heart beat faster.

"We've been tracking your every move the last few weeks. We know what you've been up to."

She kept a hand on the building. "Who are you?"

Another laugh. "Let's just say we've been retained to find you."

She relaxed. Retaining was much better than hurting. "By whom? BioHumanity?"

"Not exactly."

"Then whom?" Mona pressed.

"Somebody who's very concerned about you."

A quick breath. "Tell whomever sent you that I'm fine." She took a step toward her car.

The man held out a hand. "Not so fast."

Mona looked at it then at his eyes. "What right do you have to say that?"

"Like we said …"

"You're not making sense." She brushed past his hand. He grabbed her arm and ran it behind her back. "You're hurting me," she shrieked.

"We need to have a little talk," he whispered into her ear.

"Please let me go," Mona pleaded.

He handed Mona to the woman. "We need a little more privacy." He knelt by the boarded up door and pulled with both hands. The decaying wood splintered with little force. He repeated for two more boards and then slipped through the opening. His head popped back out. "Hand her to me."

The woman pushed Mona through. The abandoned restaurant didn't stand the test of time. Aqua-blue booths littered the floor while chairs were randomly scattered across broken tile. It was probably five years since the fast food joint served a customer and yet there were still a few napkin dispensers and plastic spoons strewn across the tables. The man grabbed a nearby chair and righted it. He pushed her into it. Her body started trembling as she tried to follow his eyes. He grabbed two more and they all sat.

"What are you doing?" she spat at them.

"It seems you've been doing some things behind your company's back."

"What?" She was confused.

"Tell us about Eric Sanchez."

"There's nothing to tell. He was my boss. He died trying to save his reputation." A gulp of air. "I'm sure you know that."

"I think there's more you're not telling us."

She looked over his head. "No."

He stood up. In one fluid motion, he flipped open a switchblade and jammed it into her thigh. Mona screamed as the pain burst from her leg. She grabbed her leg and slumped over as blood oozed from the hole.

"Now let me ask again: What do you know about Eric Sanchez?"

"Ohhh," Mona cried. She put a hand up. "Please! What do you want to know?"

"Let's start with his research."

"He found something in his stem cell research that disturbed him." Her voice was filled with agony.

"We know that."

She held the leg tighter. "He recorded it in a journal."

"Did you read it?"

She closed her eyes, hoping that would lessen the pain. She nodded slowly.

"What did it say?"

"I didn't understand most of it, but he mentioned harvesting hearts," she whispered.

The man leaned back. "I see."

"How did you end up with it?" the woman asked.

Mona's eyes opened. "It fell into my lap."

"Explain."

She hedged.

"I don't have time for this." He reached forward and slammed the tip into her stomach.

She looked down in horror as her pink top stained red. No!" she cried as she doubled over. "Please. I don't want to die." Tears were spilling uncontrollably, almost allowing her to forget about the shearing pain. "He left it in my house."

The woman's eyebrows narrowed. "How did it end up there?"

"We shared everything," she blurted.

The woman laughed. "Really. An affair? That's a nice little bit of gossip."

"There's a woman you've been talking to. Tell me about her," the man demanded.

"She's just a reporter. She wanted to learn about Eric's life, that's all." Mona groaned as the pain swirled inside.

"Did you tell her anything?"

"No. Nothing. I swear."

"Then why are you here?"

"To tell her all I knew." She shook uncontrollably. She put her head into her hands, not caring they were covered in blood.

"What were you going to tell her?"

"The journal. And his hunch …"

"Which was?"

Tears flowed down her face. "That he was going to be murdered."

"Is that why he left it with you?"

She nodded, barely able to hear them through her sobbing.

He stood. "Then you know what you have to do."

Mona stared blankly at him.

He nodded with a cruel smile. "I think you know what I mean."

She struggled to her feet, but collapsed. "No. I can't give it to you. I don't have it."

"Wrong answer."

He moved forward.

She tried protecting herself, but she collapsed onto the floor, the chair falling to one side. He grabbed her and spun her onto her back. The knife was pointed at her throat.

"I'll give you one last chance," he hissed. He was so close she could feel the warmth of his sweat.

"I swear, on my father's grave."

Chapter 36

Chunks of asphalt, some big as a brick, blocked their path as Sabrina and Brieman pulled slowly into the vacant parking lot. "At the intersection of 101 and 130?" Brieman asked.

They were just north of Neskowin, along the Oregon Coast Highway. She looked at the map on her phone. "That's right. This is it."

Brieman jockeyed the Porsche into neutral and let it coast into a row of thistles. They took a peek at the boards tacked at every angle across the abandoned restaurant's windows.

"Any idea what this was?" Sabrina asked as she stepped into the clear, dark sky.

Brieman walked around to her side of the car. "Not sure. In the five years I've been here, I don't recall anybody ever mentioning this place."

They walked toward the worn and bruised colors of the abandoned building. Sabrina kicked back a few broadleaf weed stalks, revealing the branding of a long-abandoned restaurant chain.

"Drive-through, eh?" Brieman asked

"I'd say so." But there was no sign of Mona or her car. She checked her watch. "She should've been here by now."

She peered through one of the boarded up windows. Brieman took a step off the path and did the same. Paper cups, branded with a Chihuahua wearing a lime green sombrero, were scattered about.

"I guess the Chihuahua died a stray." Brieman said.

Sabrina rolled her eyes. It was a bad joke but for some reason it calmed how nervous and worried she felt—both for their lives and Mona. "I'll try to forget that one," she casually replied.

"My bad," he added.

She turned around and buzzed the parking lot with her eyes, swatting a few mid-season flies along the away. "We're only twenty-five minutes late, but there's no sign of Mona." Something just didn't feel right. "Could she have left?"

Brieman shrugged his shoulders. "Don't know. Let's plan on staying another fifteen minutes or so. Can you call her again?"

She redialed the number. Two rings and then voicemail. "Nothing," she said. Brieman didn't respond. Sabrina pulled her hair back and again looked around the lot, squinting to see against the dark sky. "Scott?"

"Yeah, over here." He was on the opposite side of the restaurant." A pause. "You gotta see this."

She jogged around the building. "What is it?"

"Take a look at the entrance."

She eyed the boards covering the doorway and shrugged. "I don't see anything. Looks boarded up to me."

"Look at the screws. They're new."

"Maybe they replaced them because of vandals."

"Maybe." The headlights of his car bounced off the glossy screw heads. "But they look brand new, like they were replaced today."

"You think it has something to do with Mona?"

"Maybe it's just a coincidence," he replied. "But how many times do people patch up a boarded up joint?"

"We should look inside. You have a screwdriver?" Sabrina blurted. Not knowing where Mona was made her feel wretched.

He nodded. "I like your thinking. I think there might be one in the hatch." He ran back to his car.

"Hurry," she yelled after him. "I just want to make sure nothing's wrong."

He returned a minute later. "Got it," he said—a screwdriver in one hand, a black flashlight in the other. He gave the flashlight to Sabrina. She flipped it on as he started loosening four screws holding the wood in place. The board dropped onto the cracked concrete. She kicked it to the side as he placed the screwdriver and screws on the weathered window sill. "Throw the light inside. Let's see what we have here."

Sabrina scanned the restaurant. A small animal scurried under a swinging door—most likely the kitchen. "Ugh." She shuddered and grabbed Brieman's arm. "Doesn't exactly make me want to eat," she whispered. They moved through the door and stood just inside, by the counter. Sabrina's grip tightened around Brieman's arm as she looked around.

The restaurant looked like it had been abandoned without notice. Cups still filled the dispenser. Advertising signs, containing long-forgotten slogans and motifs, littered the empty booths, while condiment packages were still in their holding trays. "When a fast food chain goes belly up, I guess they don't waste any time," Brieman muttered under his breath.

Sabrina's eye caught something unexpected with her sweep of the floor. It was around the corner from the counter, toward the bathrooms and a side galley that contained a few more booths. It wasn't necessarily something resting on the floor, but rather a shimmer that didn't exist elsewhere on the faux brick tile.

"Over there," she whispered, pointing her flashlight toward the floor in the distance.

"I don't see—"

She tugged Brieman toward the spot—her flashlight never straying from the focus of her attention. They stopped a foot from the round puddle.

"I don't believe it," Sabrina muttered.

Brieman broke from her and bent toward the circle of bright red liquid. He dipped a finger in it and rubbed it between his forefinger and thumb. "It's blood all right. And it can't be more than a few hours old. The consistency is still holding."

Only one thing came to mind. "You don't think it's hers, do you?" Sabrina asked.

He shook his head. "I don't know, but look at that." She followed his finger with the flashlight toward a trail of smeared blood that snaked its way toward a rear exit. "It has the look of somebody dragging a body, either dead or alive out the door." He walked along the path of the blood. "We've got to get the police here now."

"But what about Mona? If she's still alive, she needs our help now." She could only imagine the horror she must be going through. *I've got to do something,* she thought. She headed for the entrance.

He grabbed her. "There's no way we can leave. We've got to stay until the police arrive."

"Then give me the keys."

"We have to stay."

"Mona needs our help. The police aren't going to react in time. Look, they won't even think she's missing for twenty-four hours."

Indecisiveness crossed his face, his eyes darting every which way within the restaurant. He then reached into his pocket and flipped her the keys. "At least tell me where you're going."

She caught them with both hands. "Her house."

He shook his head. "I need to go with you."

"No. You're right. Someone needs to stay." She grabbed his forearm before heading back toward the door.

"Be careful," she heard him yell.

Chapter 37

"Detective Sam Urbina, please," Sabrina said to the police operator. She had thought about calling 911, but she needed somebody she could trust.

A click followed and then she heard the gravelly voice of the man she had only met once but felt immediate comfort with. "Who's this?" Urbina demanded.

"It's Sabrina Katz. I don't know if you remember me from Neskowin? I was the reporter ..." Her voice trailed off.

"Katz, eh?" The voice lightened. "How could I forget? I was your first interview. You're lucky you caught me here. Usually I'm at the bar tipping a few by now. What's up?"

"I need your help."

"Ah, the New Yorker needs help. With what?"

She took a deep breath. "Possible homicide. We were at an abandoned restaurant—"

"Hold on there, rookie." His voice was demanding again. "What do you mean we? Who were you with and what were you doing there?"

"Look, I don't have time to explain." Sabrina responded impatiently. "I think somebody's in grave danger, if not dead, and I need your help."

"You gotta give me something more."

"Her name's Mona Frederick. She worked with Eric Sanchez."

"Ah, there's the connection. I had a feeling you were still trailing that scent ... however stale it may be."

"She was supposed to meet us at an abandoned fast food restaurant north of town but never showed. We went inside and found blood. I was with a doctor who thinks it's recent." Her words became jittery. "And I think it's Mona's."

A pause. "As much as I want to help, you really need to contact the county—it's their jurisdiction."

She shook her head. "I can't. I need someone I can trust. Please," she pleaded, "you gotta help me."

A sigh. "Okay, Sabrina. Calm down. Where you headed?"

"Mona's house." She looked down at the address she found for Mona. "She's at five four five eight Chinook in Oceanside. It's just off Iris Street. A small white ranch," she said.

"Okay. Just stay put where you are. I'll take care of it."

"But I'm already here … at her house. Sitting in the driveway." *God, somebody needed to come.* She was afraid to turn off her headlights it was so dark.

"Shit. Okay, don't do a damn thing. I'm coming. And I'll send County to the fast food joint. Just …" A pause. "Just sit tight and don't do anything stupid. "I'll be there as soon as I can."

"I won't."

The phone clicked dead.

She threw the cellphone on the passenger seat. She stared at her hands. They were trembling worse than she ever remembered. What was she going to do? Urbina was at least forty-five minutes out and Mona could be bleeding to death.

Sabrina sighed deeply: Mona didn't have forty-five minutes.

She looked through the windshield at Mona's house number written in script above the door. It was definitely her home. She lowered her eyes and focused on the drawn blinds across the small front window. Time was not on Mona's side.

Maybe I should go in, Sabrina pondered. She admitted she was strong-headed. And most of the time it got her into trouble but just now it might save someone's life. She said a prayer and dragged herself from the car, making sure the headlights were trained on the front door. The closer she got the more lifeless it seemed.

Mona should've come out by now.

The faux arch doorway crept up to her. She stepped on a shard of wood, causing it to helicopter into the grass. A hand went up to her mouth as she gasped at the mess around her. Splintered wood was scattered up and down the walkway. She stepped onto the stoop and stared at the door. It had been violently chopped into thirds.

Oh Mona, she thought.

The perennial rhythm of a Pacific Northwest rain fell behind her. She turned and watched the water run across the headlights. Could she feel any more alone? *I should've stayed with Brieman,* she thought.

Mona could be minutes from dying and there was nobody else that could save her. She looked toward the gray-black sky. What should she do? The rain fell harder and the wind changed, causing her nylon pullover to whip around like a flag. She turned back around. The decision was made: Anger would win over fear. She moved carefully around the wood shards and walked up to the colonial-style white door. She peered with one eye through a gap the size of a brick. It was dark, save for few speckles of light working its way in from her headlights.

"Mona?" she screeched. She cleared her throat and began again: "Mona?" This time she was calm and deliberate.

No response.

She moved her eye around the room, trying to catch anything that may have been disturbed by her voice. "Hello?" Another few seconds whisked by. She looked at her watch. There was no other choice but to go in. Sam was still miles away. Thinking she needed to preserve the scene, she reached into her windbreaker pocket and used the fabric to hide her fingerprints. She pushed the door open, allowing the fading headlamps to work their way into the room.

Chaos was everywhere. Everything in sight had been torn to shreds or thrown carelessly around. She stepped inside, being careful not to step on any evidence, and moved toward a small kitchen. All the cabinets were open—silverware, dishes, and food were scattered across the tiled floor and counters. The refrigerator was half open—its light the only glow against the stark surroundings. Now she knew: The intruders were looking for something of value.

She peered into a bedroom just off the kitchen. The room was trashed—Mona's clothes had been tossed as if they were a salad. The nightstand and simple dresser were turned on their side. The mattress and box spring had been hacked with some sort of knife. She closed her eyes and then opened them, trying to comprehend what her eyes were telling her. The room started spinning, her mind unable to grasp the gravity of the moment. A nauseating feeling blew through her. Covering her mouth, she ran out the front door and into the grass. As if on cue, her stomach churned and vomited the only thing she had in her—chips and soda.

The realization that she hadn't eaten anything substantial all day buzzed through her. She coughed up the remaining fluids and then stayed there, kneeling on the wet blades of grass. It might've been still raining but she didn't care. A flood of tears welled around her eyes and then let loose down both sides of her cheeks. Everything that had happened in the past month seemed to bubble to the surface: Eric and Carla Sanchez, the car accident, those pictures, Mona's voicemail, the blood in the restaurant. She starting crying, shedding tears like she hadn't cried in decades. She had fought so hard to stay composed but her body had had enough. It was all coming out in one enormous purge.

Oh, God. What is happening to me?

Finally, the tears flowed no more. Her face was a certain wreck but she didn't care. She fumbled in a pocket and retrieved a damp tissue. It would have to do. She wiped her face, focusing on her nose and eyes. She sniffled a few more times and then slowly pushed away from her own mess. Her back ached as she strained to stand up straight for the first time in what must've been ten minutes.

"You okay?" a voice said behind her.

She turned to see Detective Urbina standing there, an ID badge dangling from his neck.

"She's not here!" she cried. "It's a mess in there."

"Don't worry, I'm on it." Urbina grabbed a radio from his pocket. "We've got a ten thirty-one here at five four five eight Chinook. We need backups, and forensics, now!"

"The door was hit and they just waltzed in," Sabrina added.

He nodded toward the grass. "Is that from you?"

"My emotions got the best of me," she responded sheepishly. The sound of braking cars spun her around.

Urbina turned and whistled with his teeth. "Francona. Over here."

Sabrina followed his gaze. Barging through the shrubs was a tall, skinny-looking guy, wearing narrow glasses, and fine brownish hair bouncing every which way. Behind him was a team of officers. And behind them was Brieman.

"We got a crime scene," Urbina announced to Francona

 Francona whistled to his team. "I need everybody to move through the house as quickly as possible. And don't touch a damn thing. I want the evidence preserved."

When Brieman walked up, Sabrina pushed herself into his arms. "I'm so glad you're here."

His expression seemed haunted.

She pulled back. "What? What is it?"

"It's Mona," he stated solemnly. "They found her off of Route 130, about a quarter mile in the woods."

Sabrina covered her mouth as the nauseating feeling returned. "How?"

"I don't want to get into that."

"Tell me!" she shrieked.

Hesitation. "Her throat … it was slashed," he finally replied.

She shook as the shock of what he said rippled through her.

Chapter 38

Gregory eyed the bourbon resting on the seat next to him, his mouth salivating for the taste, his brain craving the alcohol. He was parked across the street from Gina's home. He had been there for hours, waiting to see her beautiful smile and he didn't give a damn if anybody noticed. He moved a hand toward the bottle before swatting it onto the floor. *No*, he thought. He had promised Blair. No more. He stared at the drawn window shades showing no sign of life. *C'mon 'Gin*, he thought. *Where are you?* He slammed the steering wheel. *Damn it.*

For so many years, she had been the rock, and he desperately needed her intuition and advice now. She always knew what to do. But then the alcohol would always get in the way of them having the relationship they both wanted.

Always.

She'd smell the booze on his breath and that would be it—she'd refuse any interaction with him. If it meant slamming the door in his face, she'd do it. And she had every right to. He abused her. He knew that. When he was drinking, something just raged inside that he couldn't stop.

His childhood was where it all started.

His father would come home after a day's work as a public defender, smelling of his favorite gin from the local watering hole. It wouldn't take him long to find a family member to take the day's anger out on. The weird thing was he never touched his sister no matter how angry he became. But if Gregory was the first one his father spotted, it usually started with a couple of slaps across the face and then the belt came out, with fifteen or twenty lashings across his bottom. His mom tried desperately to intervene but it only made him angrier—he would slap her until her cheeks were cherry red. Gregory would cry hysterically as he knew there was nothing he could do … at least until he was old enough.

When he was a seventeen, he caught his dad abusing his mom and he just snapped. He jumped on his dad, and at even his age, was able to slam his dad to the floor and beat him until his face gushed blood. Gregory took out a life's worth of beatings in those fifteen minutes. After he was too tired to hit him any more, his dad just got up, wiped himself off and left. He never returned.

His mom didn't fare much better. For a year, she tried keeping her composure and the family together—but it was just too much. She ended up admitting herself to a psychiatric hospital. With both parents gone, Gregory became a surrogate father to his sister, teaching her everything he had learned to survive. He loved every minute of it. It gave him purpose in life that he didn't get his first eighteen years. But to know Blair was on the brink of dying, it tore at his heart. He needed help—admittedly most of it financial—if she was going to make it. If she was to die, his life would … be over.

He stepped out of the car, not caring it was still running, and stumbled to the front door. Cupping his hands around the front window, he tried to make out any sign of life but everything seemed disturbingly still. He opened the screen and knocked twice —hard—on the oak door. Nobody came. He knocked three more times. Silence. Slamming the screen shut, he looked around the porch. The red wood was littered with newspapers. A worried, sickening feeling filled him. It was obvious Gina hadn't been here for weeks. He grabbed one of the papers and pulled it from its plastic sleeve. He eyed the date. It was a month old. His eyes floated down to a headline that for some reason caught his eye: *Little Johnny Still a Hero to Women He Saved.*

He read the first few paragraphs, finding the writer to be remarkably savvy in grabbing the reader's attention. He sighed. This was getting him nowhere. Gina needed to be found. He thew the paper down and leaped from the porch. An idea hit him. He snatched the same newspaper and scanned for the reporter's name. There it was, tucked just under the headline: *By Sabrina Katz, Neskowin Beacon Reporter.* He read the folio under the newspaper's name: *Published in Neskowin, Oregon.*

Something bothered him: What was Gina doing with a newspaper from up the coast? Then he remembered she and her brother grew up in Oregon. Maybe this was a way to stay in touch with their childhood years. A sense of urgency rushed through him: He needed to find the reporter. If she can write a compelling story about an eighty-year-old statue, why not one that announces a fundraiser for his sister's heart surgery? The more he thought about it, the more he liked the idea. But there wasn't much time. The Center would need final payment within the week.

Chapter 39

Sabrina fidgeted nervously on the stool. The pint of beer sat untouched while a little black notebook lay on the table—a hand firmly on top of it. Her attention turned to a couple having a heated exchange near the bathrooms. *What are they fighting about?*

She took a sip and looked around the Irish tavern. She thought about Brieman. After leaving him an urgent message, he called back and said he'd leave his rounds early and meet her. *So where is he?*

Eyes seemed to focus on her. *What are they staring at?* She sighed. Maybe she was being overly skittish. But how could she not be? Three deaths in the last month would be enough to put anybody on edge; and in her mind, they were all connected. Plus, someone was obsessed with getting her out of the picture—that was clear from the photos someone left for her at Carla's house.

Public places. It would be the key to her survival.

The tavern door swung open, revealing the outline of a man she had befriended only a month ago but grown to adore. She stared at his confident figure, suddenly feeling her breasts come alive—something she hadn't felt in years. She took a sip of beer. *Snap out of it,* she thought. A lover would have to wait until Sanchez's death was answered.

Brieman saw her immediately. He walked over and gave her a quick hug. "Sorry about that. I really wish I could've gotten here sooner but we were shorthanded at the hospital." He took off his raincoat and shook it before placing it on a nearby hook.

No matter how short, she savored the hug. "No reason to apologize," she said.

Brieman plopped on the stool across from her. He eyed her. "You sounded stressed on the phone."

She slid the leather-bound book, no bigger than a postcard, toward him. "I think when you see this, you'll understand why," she said in a hushed voice.

He eyed the book still under her palm. "You mentioned a package in the mail. Is this it?" He grabbed the edge with his fingertips.

"It arrived this morning." A pause. "Mona overnighted it to me."

"Before she died, apparently."

Sabrina nodded. "My hunch is it must've been what the killer was looking for when he trashed her house."

"Why do you say that?" Brieman flipped through the pages. "Looks like a diary, or journal, of some sort."

Sabrina nodded. "Because it's related to the medical research Sanchez was working on at BioHumanity."

A server stepped over from a nearby table. "What would you like?"

Brieman pointed to Sabrina's glass. "I'll have the same."

"The pale ale?" the server asked.

"Perfect." Brieman smirked at Sabrina. "I like your choice." His eyes moved back to the small book. "What makes you think this is important enough to kill over?"

"I wish I knew. I mean it was obviously something she wanted me to have."

"No argument there," Brieman replied as the server arrived with his beer. He took a sip, read the first few pages, and then scanned the rest of it. "I don't get it. Seems like standard research notes on the trial he was working on."

She sighed. "Something's not clicking." Her attention was suddenly drawn to the front door. It was a man and a woman, both dressed in black. They were standing there, as if looking for someone.

Brieman leafed through the journal again. "This is interesting."

"What?"

"Take a look at the last entry. It's dated a few days before his death." Brieman spun the book around so she could see it. "He seems pissed about something at BioHumanity. He says: 'The test group of placentas contained the right number of stem cells as the embryo continued to double every few days. But I was unable to trick them into generating the heart muscle. This is consistent with the previous tests as well.' "

"And then he goes on to say: 'But they are pushing me beyond my ethical limits. I refuse to meet their demands and now they are blackmailing me. For the sake of humanity but at the risk of persecution, I have to go public with their intentions. I cannot, nor will I, accept and approve what they are willing to do.' " Brieman then flipped to the last page. "And then there's the last sentence in the journal: 'I will give them one chance to do the right thing. If they do not cease harvesting then I will go forward with my threat, regardless of how much it destroys me, BioHumanity, or the people that will benefit from our work.' "

"You're right. He seems on edge about something." She pointed to a set of initials and numbers underlined twice at the bottom of the page. "I wonder what this means."

Brieman eyed it. "You mean SI seven nine oh?"

A nod.

"I have no idea. Maybe it's the code for the project he's working on."

"Could be, but it was something he felt important enough to write in his journal."

Brieman shrugged his shoulders. "Maybe he was trying to remember it and just happened to jot it down on the page. Either way, we'll probably never know."

An uncomfortable pause settled between them. "Little did he know how far BioHumanity would take retribution," Sabrina finally said.

"If you believe BioHumanity's behind it, it must've been a helluva secret."

"No doubt. And how convenient he died a few days after the last entry," Sabrina said.

Brieman finished off his beer. He slammed the empty glass on the table. "What the hell is BioHumanity up to?"

"'If they do not cease harvesting …'," Sabrina said, repeating what Sanchez wrote in the journal. "What does that mean?"

"It could mean anything. In the medical field, harvesting is sometimes associated with organs ... but I'm not getting the connection with his work."

Sabrina looked back toward the entrance. The couple were gone.

"You okay?"

She focused on his eyes. They were as blue as a sparkling ocean. "I'm fine. I'm just a little jumpy, that's all."

"No argument here, especially since what's happened."

"It's just that I saw this couple near the door, dressed in black, and I thought they seemed out of place ... like they were coming for me."

He turned around. "I'm not seeing ..."

She shook her head. "They're gone now. It must've been nothing."

A smile. "I'm a little jumpy too." He gave her hand a nudge. "But you're with me," he said calmly.

She took a deep breath. "Thanks for being so comforting. Otherwise, I would've walked out of here by now."

He grinned. "Part of my job as a doctor."

She returned to the book. "What do you think of his comments about stem cells?"

"He seems to be talking about using stem cells in some sort of study, but that doesn't give us a lot to work with. I do know doctors and researchers are spending time and a lot of cash trying to understand the potential of stem cells."

"Potential to do what?"

"To solve a host of medical issues when your own cells die. Think diseases that affect organs such as the brain, lungs, liver, and heart ... and the spinal cord too. If you think about stem cells, they're usually associated with healing and repairing organs." He leaned back, folding his arms. "But there's a problem."

"Such as?"

"It usually requires a special kind of stem cell. I can't think of the name offhand but I want to say it starts with an M."

"Let's see what I can find." Sabrina pulled her cellphone from her bag and started tapping. After a moment, she replied, "Could it be mesenchymal?"

He snapped his fingers. "That's it. They're special because they seem to gravitate toward an organ's injured area."

"Any idea how you make them?"

"They come from bone marrow. But you would need a helluva lot of donors to do anything with it." He scratched his head. "I don't know. He mentions the placenta so maybe he's working on a new technique."

Sabrina pondered what he was telling her. "You said harvesting could be associated with organs. What does that mean?"

"I was just trying to connect the dots of what he might've meant. He could be talking about harvesting the family farm for all I know."

"C'mon! It has to be medically related."

"There's market demand for harvesting organs and selling them but I can't imagine that's what we're talking about here."

"That's sickening."

"When people are desperate, you'd be surprised what they'll buy and how much they'll pay for it."

Sabrina looked away.

"What are you thinking about?"

"I'm just trying to put this together. It's a lot to digest."

"Yeah, and there's still a lot of questions."

"The biggest one is what BioHumanity tried to push down his throat."

Brieman threw up a hand, trying to get the server's attention. "Maybe Sanchez didn't like how they planned on using his research."

Sabrina sighed. "But was it worth his and three other lives?"

Brieman eyed her. "As much as I want to make the connection to the other deaths too, we don't know that yet."

"No. You're right. But we need to." She ran a hand through her hair. "So how do we prove that?"

He leaned back for a few seconds and then snapped his fingers. He had a devious look in his eyes. "What about the coroner?"

Sabrina looked confused. "Coroner?"

"Yeah. To take a deeper look at the report."

"But they already ruled it an accident."

"What if there's more to it than what was released?"

"You don't think …" Her voice trailed off. She thought about it some more. She looked at him weirdly. "You're serious, aren't you? A corrupt coroner?"

"Wouldn't be the first time."

"What would we find?"

"Well, we know he was fishing the afternoon he died. What if somebody drugged or poisoned him and caused him to fall in the water?"

"Now you're jumping ahead."

"Touché."

She tapped the table. "Hmm. You do have a point." She always thought it wasn't an accident but she never thought about what might've caused him to die.

The server arrived with the check and Brieman threw twenty dollars on the table. "This one's on me."

"You don't have to do that."

"Happy to." When the server left, he asked, "So what do you think?"

She eyed him nervously. "I think it's worth a shot. But I really don't want to be another casualty."

"Hey." He reached over and felt her fingers. "I'll be with you the whole way. Nobody's going to be coming after you when I'm around."

"You promise?"

"Yeah, I do."

That comforted her. A lot. She moved from the stool. "Then let's see what we can find."

Chapter 40

"That wasn't the right time," Mannheim said to his passenger. They were in his black Jeep following a few car lengths behind the doctor's Porsche.

The woman, not about to agree, glared back. "How can you say that? We had them front and center in the bar."

"Did you not notice the twelve other people standing around? I don't know about you but I'm not interested in making a scene with that many witnesses."

"We could've done it discreetly. Besides, if someone realizes what's going on, you're very good at taking care of the situation. Remember how you handled the coroner?"

Mannheim laughed. She was irritatingly efficient as an assassin but had no concept of reality. "The coroner was a one-time deal. I seriously doubt I'd be able to bribe her again."

She shook her head. "I don't agree. She could've been paid off again. It was sick, it was so easy."

"I'm done arguing about this." He looked straight ahead at the doctor's taillights. "The decision's final," he stated. Out of the corner of his eye, he saw her turn toward the window. In the moment of silence, Mannheim focused on the car ahead, making sure to stay just out of view of their rearview mirror.

The Porsche suddenly braked hard and veered hard off Highway 101.

"Now what?" she asked.

"Continue following. That's what," he replied.

"And the journal?"

Mannheim stiffened. It was the one piece of unfinished business that was driving him nuts. "You sure it was there?"

"The reporter had it on the table," the woman replied. "I'm sure of it."

Mannheim pounded the steering wheel. "Damn woman. Now that makes two—"

The woman jabbed his shoulder. "Where are they going?"

Mannheim replied, "Don't know. But there's nobody out so now's the time."

A cruel smile washed over her face. "I'm thinking accident."

"Go on."

"What if she's killed, and we make it look like it was Brieman's fault."

"More collateral damage?" Mannheim replied. "I don't like it. We've had too many already. We'll be sunk if we have to pay off anyone else."

"But we'll take them both out with one shot," she pleaded. "It'll be the easiest way to clean this mess up."

He opened his mouth to retort, but changed his mind. Maybe she was right. "Did you bring the long-range rifle and scope?"

Her eyes lit with approval. She had won him over. "In the trunk."

Mannheim pushed hard on the brake. "Look!" He pointed ahead. The Porsche stopped in front of a gray building.

"Damn it," she yelled as she eyed the one story across the street. "They're going to the coroner's office."

"I know," Mannheim replied, his voice tense, "but that might be a blessing." The muscles in his body tightened. Adrenaline kicked in as if his mind and body were becoming aware of something that was about to happen.

"You need to relax," the woman noted. "The last time you acted like this, Mona was just pulling into the abandoned restaurant."

He ignored her. He was too focused.

"What are you thinking?"

"I'm thinking it's late," he stated. "That means there's going to be nobody around for blocks. It'll be just us and them in that office."

A smile started to draw on her face. "This is going to be easier than I thought."

Chapter 41

Brieman pulled off the main road—Rueppell Avenue—in downtown Pacific City and stomped on the brakes.

Two-story industrial buildings dotted the landscape indiscriminately along the street where they parked. It wasn't prime real estate, at least compared to what they had seen coming into town, but it suited an ordinary coroner just fine.

"What's the address?" Sabrina blurted.

"One two two one. It's the one over there." Brieman pointed to a pale brown building across the street.

She eyed the nondescript office as dimly lit streetlights cast a wide shadow on the tarnished brick. Everything looked chocolate brown, from the brickwork to the window frames to the door. "What a perfectly mundane building for a coroner."

"Government buildings," Brieman replied. "Always architecturally stunning."

Sabrina checked the car's clock. It was a half past midnight. The fear of someone coming after her was never far from her mind. She looked into his eyes. "I'm stressed," she blurted.

"I know," he replied. "But I told you I'm going to be here for you and I mean it."

She smiled gently. "That makes me feel a little better … but the Sanchezes and Mona probably thought they would be okay too. And that didn't work out so well." She paused. "I've been warned and I still haven't left. I don't know about you but it's obvious what they'll do next and yet …"

"You just can't seem to leave?'

A nod. "As much as I know it's the safest thing right now, I just feel like I need to figure this out, no matter what happens."

"Is that why you were helping Carla … you feel it's unfinished business?"

She looked away, pondering what Brieman had suggested. "You know, I hadn't really thought about why ... but maybe. Yeah, maybe."

He grabbed her hand. "Then we've got some work to do before you can truly go home."

She looked into his blue eyes and melted at the kind words sinking in. Why couldn't they have met earlier in her life? It would've made things so much easier.

Brieman zipped up his jacket. "You ready?"

Sabrina took a deep breath. "Yeah, I think so. But how are we going to get in?" For some reason, it was the thing she worried about the most—other than being attacked.

"Magic," he replied coyly. He pulled a plastic keycard from his shirt pocket. "Sometimes being a doctor has its privileges."

"Very nice. You had me worrying since we left the tavern ... you know that?"

"Sorry. Slipped my mind," he replied slyly.

"Probably because you weren't worried about it."

"Exactly."

"Men," she sarcastically replied. "Never do they tell you what they're thinking."

"Yes, but it keeps women on their toes." He flipped open the car door. "C'mon. I don't want to hang out here too long and ruin our welcome."

They hurried across the street to the front entrance. A single pale light sprayed on the door. Without it, they would've been grasping at the night air, trying to find the security scanner.

"How did you get the keycard anyway?"

"Sometimes I need to come down if a patient dies at the hospital. And people tend to pass at all hours of the day."

"Do you know the coroner?"

"Not well. Her name's Yori Wainer. She's standoffish at best and a bitch at worst."

"How does that compare to me?"

"No comment," he replied, smiling.

"Thanks."

Brieman chuckled lightly. "I hope you're used to my sarcasm by now."

"I hope you're used to mine."

He laughed as he slipped the card into the scanner. "Let's just hope I still have access. I haven't used this thing in a year."

"I suppose that's a good thing."

There was a click and then the red light casually went green. "See," Brieman said with a grin. "It's magic." He pulled open the brown-painted metal door. "After you."

She stepped inside a dimly lit waiting area. The only decor was a single window to their left with a hole cut out at bottom, like a teller's window. "Where to?"

"Down the hall." He pointed straight ahead. "Through the second metal door. Then take a left. They store their reports in the archive."

Sabrina led the way into a dimly lit room, the only light coming from a flickering, ornery florescent. She eyed the rows of black, metal cabinets against the back wall. "On paper? Who does that anymore?"

"They use both. They store the reports on paper so it can accompany the body when it's transferred."

"Seems like a lot of storage for such a small county."

"It is. But that's because it dates back to 1968. When you're the size of this district, you don't exactly have the resources of New York."

She scanned the alphanumerical digits pasted on the front of each file drawer. "Looks like it's sorted alphabetically."

He nodded. "It has to be. Chronological would make it a nightmare to find someone."

She ran her finger across the drawers until she came across S. She gave a tug on the handle. *Sage. Sahn. Sanchez.* "Here it is." She tugged on a reddish folder and flipped it open. "Let's see what we have."

Brieman leaned over her shoulder. "Case 92-18048," he muttered. "That's gotta be it."

"Yeah, that's the same report I pulled off Getty's desk."

"There's the cause." He pointed to the lower third of the report. "Death by asphyxia. It's right there."

Sabrina sighed. "That doesn't tell us anything we don't already know." She started flipping through the pages quickly. "Hopefully there's something I didn't see in the report."

Brieman stopped her. "What's that?" He pointed to a small yellow form paper-clipped to the end of the report.

"I don't know." She unclipped it from the back. "Looks like some sort of order form."

Brieman peered at it. "Looks like a toxicology report. It's usually required when the facts around the death are unknown."

Her eyebrows creased. "I don't understand something."

"What is it?"

"Look at this."

He looked where her finger was pointing. "Yeah, that's interesting. It looks like the pathologist found traces of Atropine in his blood."

"I'm confused. The coroner's report I read back at the office mentions none of this."

Brieman asked, "What's the date on the toxicology exam?"

"June 20."

"Isn't that two weeks after the coroner's report was released?" He turned and started pacing in the small room.

She eyed him. "Doesn't Atropine have something to do with the heart?"

"Yeah, it's a drug that can be used to stop it."

Sabrina gasped. "That could easily suggest he was murdered," she whispered. "So Carla's hunch was right."

"Yeah, and you were too."

"Do you know what this means? If a homicide occurred … maybe because of something he knew … that's probably why he wrote what he did in the journal." She pulled out her cellphone. "I've got to get a picture of this."

"If it's not a smoking gun then it's damn close," Brieman replied.

"There's one thing I'm not getting. If the toxicology report comes in after the report's been released, wouldn't the coroner rescind the report until it's right?"

"You mean the cause of death?"

"Right," Sabrina replied.

A quick nod. "It's just the right thing to do. That just means she buried it for some reason."

"Seriously," Sabrina said, "much to the chagrin of the family and their right to know."

"And the detective on the case."

"If the detective knew about this, I'm sure the case would still be open. There's just no other way," Sabrina said. "Maybe Mona and Carla would still be alive today."

A buzzing sound near the front entrance interrupted them.

Sabrina's covered her mouth. "What's that?"

"I don't know," Brieman replied before a door clicked open. "Shit," he said. "Somebody's here."

"This late at night?" she whispered. "Could it be the coroner?"

"Doubtful. Get the report back in the cabinet!" He spun around, searching with his eyes. "There's nowhere to hide in this damn room."

"Then we've got to confront them," she replied after slamming the cabinet shut. "We don't have another choice."

Brieman moved closer to her, clearly intending to keep his promise to protect her. Nudging her shoulder, he whispered, "I'm not sure who the hell it is but we're going to have to talk our way out of this. Let's keep the conversation short. And when I see an opening, let's take it."

She swallowed hard. Could the end be near?

They waited, bracing for whoever was here.

They didn't have to wait long.

A woman burst into the room, stopping abruptly when she saw the two of them. "Excuse me!" she said. She met Sabrina's eyes for a moment then turned toward the door. "Mannheim? I think we have something here."

"Who's Mannheim?" Sabrina blurted.

The woman ignored her.

Idiot, Sabrina thought. Drawing attention was not the way to go. She eyed the woman. Where had she seen her? And then it hit her: The tavern.

Mannheim appeared in the doorway. He sized up both of them as he pulled black gloves tight over his wrists. He took a step forward, his frame towering over everybody in the room, his biceps bulging from the tight-fitting black T-shirt.

Sabrina shuddered. It was clear they were both professionals.

"We need to get to the point. Quickly," Mannheim stated.

"Excuse me," Brieman interjected. "You're not—"

"Shut up." Mannheim swung his hand hard across Brieman's face, sending him crashing into the cabinets. "You'll talk when asked."

Brieman stormed toward him, right into the eye of a revolver. Brieman froze, then threw his hands up. "Okay. I get the point."

The man swung the barrel toward Sabrina. "No more tricks," he growled. "From either of you."

"It's our understanding you have came across some property that isn't yours," the woman stated.

Sabrina reached out and grabbed Brieman. She had a sinking feeling about the next few minutes. "I don't know what you want but we really need to leave," she replied nervously.

The man looked irritated. "Cut the bullshit. The black book. Where is it?"

"I don't—"

Mannheim cut her off. "The damn journal. Mona Frederick gave it to you."

"Look, the woman said she needs to go. What don't you get?" Brieman's stubborn tone suggested he was ready for a fight.

Mannheim's face lit with anger and he walloped Brieman's stomach hard with the butt of his gun.

"Ough!" Brieman gasped, stumbling backward. But it was the chance he wanted. As Mannheim retracted his arm, Brieman lunged forward, sending Mannheim tumbling onto the concrete floor. Sabrina, not missing a step, jump kicked the woman in the stomach, sending her crashing into the room's window blinds.

"Let's go!" Brieman yelled as he grabbed her hand. They flew through the door, down the hall, and into the night air. They ran across the vacant street and vaulted into the Porsche. Brieman kicked the engine into gear and sped through downtown Pacific City, back toward Highway 101.

Brieman glanced at the rearview mirror. "I hope we lost them. I'm not seeing anybody."

Sabrina turned around. "Yet," she whispered.

He swung a hard right onto Brooten Road. "Why do I get the feeling those two are tied to the Sanchez deaths?"

"No doubt. And probably Mona too." Sabrina paused. "And I don't think they like what Eric Sanchez wrote in his journal."

"Can we assume they're hired hands of BioHumanity?"

"You don't need to convince me."

Brieman shook his head. "I just don't get it. Who in BioHumanity is behind this? You just can't go around knocking people off."

"Unless BioHumanity has a huge bug up their ass."

Even though their situation was serious, Brieman couldn't help a chuckle. "That's the New Yorker I know."

She peered at the boyish face, his hair flowing freely in the night air. He had protected her, just like he said he would. "Thanks."

He glanced at her, smiling a second time. "It wasn't all me. Somebody in this car knows how to kick box."

"I learned in New York. Had to." After her sister's murder, learning kickboxing meant she could protect herself next time.

"How come?"

She wasn't about to recall that night anytime soon. "I don't want to talk about it."

An awkward pause followed. Then Brieman said, "You know, that's the second time you've said that when I've asked about your past."

Sabrina shook her head. She was mad at herself. "You're right." Maybe she should trust him, and open up. "I should tell you—"

Suddenly, a car roared onto the road, just behind them. Sabrina spun around as Brieman grabbed the rearview mirror. It was a black Jeep and couldn't have been more than fifty feet behind them.

"Is it them?" Sabrina asked.

"I don't know. I can't tell."

"It's gotta be."

"I'd prefer not to find out." Brieman popped the clutch into a higher gear. He then jerked the wheel, launching them onto the 101.

She looked behind them. Nothing there. "Did we lose them?"

"Doubtful!" he yelled over the noise of the engine. He glanced at the odometer. "We're at a hundred. I don't know how far I can take it before we hit somebody!" He swerved left and then right, barely avoiding a blue Ford.

Sabrina grabbed his arm. "Scott! The truck!"

He pulled the wheel right, just missing the tail of the semi.

"Where you going?

"Back to Neskowin, but you've got to get on the phone to Urbina and tell him what's going on."

"No! We're almost there with this, and I can't risk anybody messing it up."

He glanced at her strangely. "Even if it kills you?"

"Look, we're really close to solving this thing. I can feel it."

"But you could be a victim, just like them."

"Then that's the risk I've got to take."

He shook his head. "Something's got you going, that's for sure."

"How much longer?" Sabrina asked, pulling her seatbelt tight.

"A few miles." The road cleared so he kicked the speedometer past 110. He glanced in the mirror. "Shit! They're on our tail."

Sabrina whipped her head around. "How did they catch up?" Suddenly, a faint pop-pop-pop echoed behind them. "What was that?"

And then it became obvious. A back tire exploded. The steering wheel began shaking terribly. He grabbed the wheel as tight as he could but the car lurched left then right before fishtailing. "Hold on!" He slammed hard on the brakes as he tried to corral the wild machine.

And then he lost it.

The Porsche spun out of control, hit the guardrail on the opposite side of the road, and then whipped back across the highway, smashing into a sand barrier near a bridge.

The airbags popped, sending their bodies slamming into the inflating nylon.   Debris exploded everywhere.   An eerie silence followed.

Minutes passed.

And then Sabrina heard footsteps.   A voice shouted, "We're going to need an ambulance!"

Chapter 42

Mannheim adjusted the high-powered binoculars as he leaned on the hood of the Jeep. They were perched on a hilltop, just up the road from the accident.

"Is the assignment complete?" the woman asked.

"I don't know. I'm not seeing any movement ... at least not yet," he replied bluntly.

"Does it matter at this point?"

He peered at her. "If you mean the journal, yeah, that was easy. Once they hit the bridge, it wasn't hard to reach in the car and grab it."

"Where was it?"

"In the glove box, just where I saw her put it when they left the bar."

The woman shook her head. "All Mona had to do was tell us."

Mannheim spun around and glared at her. "Don't go soft on me. We agreed it didn't matter what she said. She needed to be disposed of because of her relationship with Sanchez. Anything tied to him is toxic. You know that." A pause. "And that's where ... we draw the line."

She refused to back away. "Maybe so, but I'm noticing hesitation in your voice."

"The problem is the reporter. She knows too much."

"You mean if she's still alive?"

"Right ... there's a lot she could say, especially if she figured out how Sanchez really died."

"But who's she going to tell? We've got them all locked up ... they're on our side."

"Urbina. She seems to have developed a relationship with him."

Sirens wailed below them. They peered at the developing scene and the collection of emergency vehicles.

"I'm seeing movement in the car," the woman said. "Do you?"

"You're right." Mannheim grabbed the binoculars. "I think it's the woman but they're blocking my view."

"So she's alive?"

"I don't know. Wait. Yes. She's sitting up," he replied irritably.

"What about the doctor?"

"Don't know yet … they've got him on a stretcher."

"Are they rushing him into the ambulance?"

Mannheim labored to get a better look. "Hard to say. If one of the paramedics moved, that would make it a lot—"

"What is it?"

"They're talking to him." He slammed the binoculars onto the ground. "Fuck."

"Oh for two today." She ticked them off on her fingers. "The bar. The accident—"

"Shut up!" His eyes flared with rage.

She held her ground. "If that bitch starts talking to the right people, the whole thing is going to be over."

"Nobody's going to believe her … at least initially. It'll buy us some time," Mannheim replied calmly.

"But you just told me you're worried—"

"I've thought more about it."

"Really."

"Trust me, nobody's going to believe her. It's too crazy of a story."

"And the doctor?"

"He doesn't have a single thread of evidence—he only has what the reporter's told him. She's the only living link to exposing everything."

"So what's your plan?"

"We have the journal. All we need to do is find the right time and the right place to finish her off. Once she's gone, that will eliminate any corroborating evidence to support whatever story the doctor tells."

"How do you propose to do that?"

"A single bullet to the head should take care of things."

"Beautiful."

Mannheim smiled. "Precisely."

And he wasn't just talking about the reporter.

Chapter 43

The bandaged area over Sabrina's left eye was tender to the touch and throbbed with pain, but she couldn't care less. She took a deep breath and looked around the small hospital waiting room, half wondering if the other visitors were as worried about their loved ones as she was about Brieman.

He's just got to be okay.

She had to believe he would be, otherwise she was never going to make it through the day. It was a terrible feeling watching him being rushed into the emergency room—with colleagues he probably knew better than his own family.

Now he was the patient.

Sabrina buried her head in her lap, making sure to keep her stitched face from rubbing against her thigh.

She started crying—at first discreetly but then uncontrollably.

Why was she doing this to herself? She should just go back to New York and save herself from getting killed. But then she thought about Sanchez and Mona. They had helped her in her quest to find the truth. How could she just let their lives go to waste? And Brieman. She felt so much guilt about asking him to come with her. The truth was, it was her fault he was badly injured.

He had to make it. It would eat her alive if he didn't.

A tap on the shoulder interrupted her thoughts. "Ms. Katz? Are you okay?"

She instantly recognized the gruff voice. "Detective Urbina. I'm glad you were able to come down," she replied, wiping away the tears.

"I had to … especially when there's attempted murder involved."

"You mean the gunshots?"

"Wasn't hard to figure out," he replied. "When I find five bullet holes, that's where I start."

"Five?" The sudden thought she was lucky to be alive made her queasy.

A nod. "It appears the one that hit your left tire caused the blowout. That's why Dr. Brieman lost control of the car."

She shook her head. "It all happened so fast."

"Do you know why they might've been coming after you and Brieman?"

"Yes—" she started. She was unsure how much she should tell but Detective Urbina seemed to be the only person she could trust right now.

He eyed her peculiarly. "You said 'yes'. What do you mean?"

"We were coming from the coroner's office," she blurted. "That's where they found us."

"They? How many were there?"

"A man and a woman."

"And what were you doing at the coroner's office after hours?"

"Checking out a hunch."

"About?"

"Eric Sanchez's death."

"Because you don't believe his death was an accident?"

"That's right. I didn't then and I still don't now. But now I can prove it."

"What are you suggesting?" the detective asked.

"We found something. Apparently, Eric Sanchez had Atropine in his blood."

Urbina looked away. "Causes heart attacks," he muttered.

"Exactly."

He turned back. "Are you sure? Because if it's true, it's a damn big thing to leave out of a coroner's report."

"I know … it was in the toxicology report but for some reason the coroner didn't include it in the final."

"The male and female that shot at you and Dr. Brieman … you think they were the ones that confronted you at the coroner's office?"

A nod. "My hunch is they knew we'd find something."

Urbina made a note in a small book he was holding. "Anything else?"

"Yes. It's about Gina."

He raised an eyebrow. "Go on."

"Sanchez gave her a journal—almost like a diary. She mailed it to me before she was killed."

"Now that's interesting. Can I see it?"

"I don't have it. It was in the glove compartment in the car. I think those two took it."

"I see. Did you find anything interesting in it?"

"A lot. For starters, Sanchez felt his employer, BioHumanity, was blackmailing him." She thought back to Brieman. "I just wish I could find that man and woman. I'd kick them both so hard …" Her voice trailed off.

A small smile. "I remember that attitude from the first day we met."

"Hopefully you remember more than just my attitude."

They were distracted by the neurologist trudging toward them, his navy blue scrubs soiled from surgery. Sabrina's eyes gravitated toward him. "How is he?" she asked hesitantly.

The doctor tried to smile briefly. "First, I want you to know he's stable. But on the way to the hospital, he started having seizures … so we got him a CAT scan and—"

Sabrina jumped to her feet. "What did you find?"

He paused, as if unsure how to say what was on his mind. "That's when we realized the swelling near the temporal lobes."

"Swelling? But how?" Sabrina replied. "He seemed fine … he was talking all the way to the hospital."

"That's where these things get tricky. When his head hit the dashboard it caused the brain cavity to shift toward the interior part of his skull. That caused swelling and a small brain contusion, which can be difficult to detect … that's because there's a delayed reaction after the initial trauma."

Her stomach tightened as she slid back into the chair. She looked away. "Is he going to be all right?" she whispered, afraid of the answer.

An awkward pause. "Like I said, he's stable. That's the good news. But we had to put him in a medically induced coma to reduce the swelling. Our hope is that with the temporary coma, the metabolic brain rate will decrease ... which will reduce the cerebral blood flow. That should reduce the pressure on his brain."

She started shaking. "And if it doesn't?"

"Then we're going to have to open the skull to allow his brain some more room. But we'll know that in the next twelve to thirty-six hours. We're going to do everything we can to save the healthy brain tissue."

"Oh God," she gasped.

The neurologist knelt down and put a hand on hers. "I know you're concerned. But I can tell you, once we make it to the other side of thirty-six hours, I know we'll be okay. It's just touch and go until then. The key is protecting his brain and that's what we're trying to do here."

"How long will you keep him in the coma?"

"I'd like to start getting him off the barbiturates within the next seven days. Once he's out of the coma, we'll do extensive neurological testing to see where we're at."

"So you don't know if he's had any brain damage?"

He looked into her eyes. "I'm an eternal optimist. And I believe in Scotty. He's a strong man, and if anybody can get through this, he certainly can."

She put her hand on his, resolved to the fact she couldn't do anything except wait. "Thank you, doctor. I know you're doing your best."

"This is family we're talking about. I'm very confident in the team and I know God will do the rest." He looked down at his phone. "Look, I need to get back."

Urbina placed a hand on her shoulder. "C'mon, let me take you home. You need to get some rest."

"No," she protested. "I can't. Scott needs me."

"You're not going to do yourself any favors staying in the waiting room. You're going to fall asleep anyway. Trust me."

The more she thought about it, he was right. A nod. "I am exhausted. It's been a long day."

He helped her up and led her to his unmarked police car, parked just outside the hospital's main entrance. As he drove her down Hill Road, Urbina asked, "What's next for you?"

Sabrina had nodded off but the question got her attention. She looked at him through the rearview mirror. "I don't know. I don't have a job anymore, a really good friend is life or death, and clearly someone's trying to get me killed."

"You should go home to New York."

"You remember where I'm from," she replied, ignoring the suggestion.

"You're a difficult one to forget."

"Thanks. I'll take that as a compliment."

He pulled up in front of her house and then turned toward her. "It's late. I've got a lot of work to do to find these guys ... but I want to make sure you're safe. ... So if it's all right with you, I'm going to put a forty-eight hour detail on your house."

"Thank you. It would mean a lot to me."

"It isn't a long time, and it's all I can afford," Urbina said apologetically. "But that should give you enough time to decide what you want to do. Once you do, let me know, and I'll make sure you get to where you're headed safely. And then let's spend some time talking about the journal."

She gathered her bag and stepped out of the car. "I'll do that. Promise."

"Sabrina ... there's one more thing," Urbina called out through the passenger window.

She turned.

"I'm going to give you a piece of advice but I'm only going to tell you once. After all, you're a big girl and can make your own decisions."

"What's that?" she replied wearily.

"First and foremost, you need to take care of yourself. Neskowin is always going to be here and Dr. Brieman's in great hands. There's nothing you can do help him get better. So I'd suggest getting as far away as hell from this town."

Sabrina nodded but unsure how to respond. He was more than right. But how could she just pick up and leave when people were dying? Someone had to be punished ... she couldn't just let the deaths of Eric, Carla, and Mona go unnoticed.

"Good," Urbina said. "I'll look for your call when you decide what to do. ... Just don't be alarmed by the squad car parked outside your house."

"I won't. Having them here will be the most comfort I've felt all day."

As Urbina drove off, she turned and walked toward the front door, her legs wobbly from fatigue. A car chase, the coroner's office, and the hospital had sucked the life out of her. She fumbled in her bag for the key and then entered her dark, quiet but comforting home. She dropped her bag on the floor, flipped on the nearest light, and collapsed onto the couch sighing. Without her body warning her, tears started flowing again. She didn't expect it but she also knew her body needed to release the intense stress and emotions consuming her ... ever since arriving in the Pacific Northwest.

"What am I still doing here?" she yelled at the wall. It was in that moment that she realized why Blogg had fired her. He was protecting her. He didn't want to see her get injured more than she already had. And sure enough, she hadn't listened to a word he said. "Why be so stubborn?" she again directed at the wall.

And then she suddenly understood what drove her to stay: Closure.

There were people, like herself, searching for something ... anything ... that would guide them past the agonizing pain they felt. Every day it steered their lives. But they just couldn't figure out what they were searching for: They didn't know how to deal with what life had thrown at them just as Sabrina didn't know how to make meaning of her own excruciating pain. But through her own actions since discovering Sanchez's body, it was clear helping others gain closure helped her own soul move on.

And in the process ... heal.

But she also knew she couldn't heal unless she protected herself. There was no sense in dying fighting what life had thrown at her. She touched her bandaged face. She was walking a precarious tightrope between danger and closure that was hurting herself and everybody around her.

She sat in silence, staring out the front window. *Enough is enough,* she thought. She would heed the detective's advice. Go home. Stay out of sight until she completed her journey safely.

A tapping sound near the rear of the house got her attention. She creased an eyebrow, wondering if it was the police officer.

Tap-tap-tap. Now it was a little louder.

She peered through the blinds in the front of the house. The squad car was there, the officer dozing inside.

Tap-tap-tap-tap.

Fear and anxiety vied for her attention. Should she alert the officer? But what if it's nothing?

Deciding she'd wait before alerting anyone, she turned on all the lights and walked toward the sound.

TAP-TAP.

She froze. Someone was knocking on her back door. She turned, half-expecting the officer to be behind her, helping her out.

BAM-BAM. Now it was a fist.

"What do you want?" she screamed. But there was no answer, just silence. She waited, hoping maybe her voice scared whomever it was off.

BOOM. The whole house rattled as the intruder slammed his body into the door.

She eyed the lock. It was holding but one more hit like that and he'd be in. She backed away—her only hope was the cop sitting outside. She just needed to reach him, and wake him, in time.

BOOM. The door slammed open into the kitchen, carrying the intruder right with it.

Sabrina trembled with fear. She was so spent, she couldn't even scream.

This is it. I'm doomed.

Chapter 44

"Ms. Katz?"

There was something in his voice that made her pause. She stopped trembling and turned toward him. He was on the tall side, maybe just over six feet, and looked to be in his early thirties. But everything about him was disheveled: His clothes were stained and seemed like he hadn't shaven in days, maybe longer. "You need to leave," Sabrina finally said.

"No … I mean … please Ms. Katz … I need to talk to you," the intruder pleaded.

"There are police sitting outside my house," she hissed. Her confidence was returning.

He took a step back, as if unsure how to handle her. "Trust me, I know. That's why I'm using the back door."

Sabrina crossed her arms, refusing to budge. "You owe me a new one."

"Yes, of course."

There was something in his voice that suggested a cry for help. Should she believe her instinct? "What do you want?"

"My sis … she's dying and I need your help," he replied, voice quivering.

Sabrina eyed him peculiarly. "From what?"

"Congenital heart disease."

Now she wasn't sure what to believe. "How do I know you're not here to rob me, or worse—" She stopped, refusing to let herself go there.

"Look at me. Do I look like someone who's going to rob or even kill you? I'm a mess."

Sabrina pulled back her hair with a hand and stared at him. He was right. He was a mess. Maybe she should be more trusting. But it was just so damn hard. "I'm sorry for you and your sister. But I don't know how I can help."

He stayed where he was. "Would you let me sit down and explain?"

She looked into eyes. Maybe he's telling the truth. Sighing, she relented. Pointing to a kitchen chair, she said, "I'll give you ten minutes. But I warn you … I'm trained in martial arts and won't hesitate to use it if I feel threatened."

He put his hands on the table, palms up. "Don't worry. I'm not going to do anything to you."

"And you're going to have to pay for a new door."

"Yes, of course. I already said I would."

Sabrina smelled something. Alcohol maybe? "Do you drink?"

He looked at her sheepishly. "No. Not anymore. I gave it up." And then he added, "But it's really hard when I'm this stressed. And that's been a lot lately."

She put out a hand. "Apparently you know my name. What's yours?"

"Excuse my rudeness." He shook her hand. "Gregory Archer."

"We're well past that. With that entrance, you've already proven you're rude." She thought about what he had said about his sister. "Your sister … I'll be honest, I'm not sure how I can help, but tell me about her."

His head dropped as he struggled to find the right thing to say. After a minute, he looked at her, tears welling in his eyes. "Blair was diagnosed about six months ago but it was only in the last two months that things turned for the worse."

"How so?"

"When we found out she had cardiomyopathy, the doctors told her, with the right treatment, she could very much live a normal life. But then things just got bad in a hurry. She started feeling extremely fatigued and then she fainted … twice in fact. When we rushed her to the hospital after the first time, that's when the doctor told us the bad news—her heart was failing more quickly than they originally thought. They said she wouldn't have much time to live … unless she received a heart transplant."

"How long did the doctors give her?"

"Two months, maybe three. But the bigger problem is she's way down on the U.S. organ transplant list."

Sabrina put a hand to her mouth. "I'm so sorry."

He wiped a tear away. "Thank you. It's been a rough few months."

"I can imagine." Sabrina walked past him, refusing to sit just in case he wasn't who he said he was. At the same time, her gut told her he was telling the truth. "But I'm still not sure how I can help."

"The gist of it is I need money to pay for the heart transplant and I thought you could help me get it."

"If you think I have money—"

He put a hand up. "No. No. It's not that at all. What I was hoping you could do is get the word out. Look, I saw your article in the Beacon on the *Little Johnny* statue and then I saw the editor's note that you were the new human interest reporter, so I thought you'd be the perfect person to help me put together a fundraiser."

"But I—"

"No!" Gregory said angrily, interrupting her.

"Excuse me?"

Realizing what he had done, he replied more tenderly, "Before you say no, let me explain. All I'm asking is for you to write an article that gives a little background on Blair's condition and mention that people can send donations or attend the fundraiser I'm going to hold for her. I'll take of the rest."

"I don't think you understand—"

"Please!" He lurched from the chair.

Sabrina backed away. She didn't like the turn this was taking. She stole a peek out the front window and wondered if there was a way she could alert the officer.

He threw up his hands. "Please ... don't say no. You're my only hope of getting the money I need; otherwise, she's going to die."

Sabrina briefly closed her eyes. Her confidence needed to show through, to get the tiger in the room to back off. "Mr. Archer! Will you please have a seat?" she demanded.

Gregory seemed surprised at her aggressive tone. He slowly nodded and then sat back down.

"You assumed I was going to say no, but what I was trying to say before you kept interrupting me is that I don't work at the Beacon anymore. They fired me ... almost a month ago."

"Really? I had no idea." His shoulders slumped. "I guess I didn't think your first article would be your last."

"Neither did I."

He again stood. "I'm sorry to have bothered you then. I guess there's nothing more for me here."

"Wait a minute." She reached out and grabbed his arm. "How much do you need?"

He looked at her outstretched hand. "The operation costs a hundred thirty thousand."

Sabrina gasped in surprise. "That's a lot of money. No insurance?"

He shook his head. "It's not an FDA-approved procedure. Truthfully, it's not being done here in the States at all."

"What? Then where is it being done?"

"Acapulco."

"Seriously?"

A nod. "That's where Blair is now, at the Acapulco Heart Center, waiting for me to give the doctor the balance due. I've already given him a down payment but it's not nearly enough."

Sabrina peered at him. "Are you sure this is legit?"

"I believe in it. It's a revolutionary way of doing heart transplants to save a patient when there's no donor available."

"Really. And how do they do that?"

"They've figured out a way to use stem cells to literally grow a heart that will be a perfect genetic match for my sister."

Sabrina looked at him oddly. Something he said intrigued her. "Stem cells?"

"Yeah." He peered at her. "Why are you looking at me like that?"

"I don't know. It's something somebody said." She took a deep breath and slumped into a nearby chair, suddenly feeling exhausted. "Do you know how they do it?"

"Yes. Dr. Vua—the Center's director—gave me a tour. It was incredible what they've done. They use stem cells from a woman's placenta and they modify them to create what they need—in this case a heart that matches the patient's cell type—and then they incubate it."

"Seriously?"

A nod. "I saw it with my own eyes. They have these rooms filled with incubators for the hearts to grow. Once the heart is ready, they transplant it into the patient."

Sabrina straightened. "No way."

"It's insane, I know."

"It's definitely that." She thought about what he said. Something didn't make sense. "Where do they get the placentas from?"

Gregory shook his head slowly. "That's where it gets a bit quirky. They pay women to have an abortion at the Center and use the cells from the placenta ... all right there. It's quite a process they've developed."

Her eyes bulged. "They pay women to have an abortion?"

"Yeah."

"Wow. No wonder it's not approved here in the States. Who runs the Center? They must have a lot of money, or investors willing to put their ethics on the line."

"A multibillion dollar company called BioHumanity invested in it." Sabrina's jaw dropped. BioHumanity?

Gregory continued, "And what's even weirder is my ex is supposedly down there right now."

"Getting an abortion?"

"I think so. Here name's Gina. I think she felt the placenta would be a match for Blair. And she could very well be right because I got a call from Dr. Vua not long after Gina told Blair."

"Why would she tell your sister?"

"They were like sisters while we dated.

"You are a soap opera."

"No shit."

"Do you know why she did it?"

Gregory replied, "I have a hunch. She probably planned to have an abortion anyway ... but once she realized Blair was doing this procedure in Acapulco, she decided to donate to the cause ... especially given the potential of the genetic match."

"You mean the placenta?"

A nod.

"How do you feel about it?"

Gregory thought for a moment. "You know, I was a complete prick to her so I deserve everything I have coming to me. And this just shows you what an angel she is. She did this to help my best friend." His voice wavered.

"Your sister."

"Yeah, my sister."

Her thoughts moved to his mention of BioHumanity. Something was bothering her about the connection. She reflected on what she read in Sanchez's journal. *Stem cells. Study. Mesenchymal stem cells.* And then to what Scott had said when they were talking about it: *You need a lot to do anything with it.* "Any idea what kind of stem cells this Dr. Vua is using to grow the heart?"

He shook his head. "Don't have a clue. He didn't say."

"Do mesenchymal cells ring a bell?"

Again, he shook his head. "It doesn't."

The journal's words continued to rush from her memory: *Organs … stem cells to repair organs … organs … blackmail … must go public … BioHumanity.*

And then it hit her like a wall of water. Her stomach tensed. She was sure she turned stone white. "Oh God."

Gregory moved toward her. "Are you okay?"

"There's something I haven't told you."

"What's that?"

"I've been investigating a murder … no three murders … since I wrote the Little Johnny article."

"What are you talking about?"

"A body washed ashore the morning of my first day at work. The police declared it an accident but something inside me told me it wasn't. And when I pressed them to investigate further, they refused—so I took it upon myself to find out what happened. But since then, it's gotten me into a lot of trouble," she said without taking a breath. She pointed to her head and then out the front window.

He walked over and pulled back the curtain. "That's why they're there."

A nod. "They're protecting me."

"From whom?"

"The killer. He ... or they ... don't want me around. So for my own protection, the police are on watch until the morning. That's when I'm leaving."

He eyed her, his mind obviously trying to process what she was telling him. "Are you saying there's a killer on the loose?"

"No doubt. There may be two. And it's not just because of the body I found. Two more were killed."

"What were their names?"

Sabrina started ticking them off with her fingers. "Eric Sanchez ... Carla Sanchez—Eric's wife ... Mona Frederick—she worked for Eric. And he almost killed a doctor who's a friend of mine ... not to mention me."

Gregory's eyes bulged. "And the police did nothing about it?"

"They were being treated as separate cases. I was the only one tying them all together ... until now that is."

"What a crappy job they did."

"More laissez-faire than anything." Sabrina regained her composure, almost excited to tell someone what she'd learned over the past month. "But there's more."

"Go on."

"Mona had a journal she had gotten from Eric Sanchez, that she tried to give me before she died. I think that's why they killed her. But she managed to mail it to me before they got to her."

"What did it say?"

"It turns out Eric was a top researcher at a pharmaceutical company and involved in stem cell research."

"So what's the connection with my sister? There's probably hundreds of studies going on with stem cells ... in this country alone."

"It's not just stem cells. It also involved organs. He was studying the use of stem cells, mesenchymal cells to be exact, to repair organs."

"Okay. Getting closer. But still not seeing a strong connection."

"The journal mentions how frustrated he was ... that he was being blackmailed because he refused to continue the study."

"Did he say why?"

She shook her head. "No, only that he was disturbed by what they were doing."

He seemed to be thinking it through. "That could mean anything. Who did he work for?"

"BioHumanity." Sabrina watched the reaction on his face as he connected the dots the same way she had five minutes earlier.

Gregory reached out and braced himself. "BioHumanity?"

"Yes, the same company that's supposedly helping your sister."

"Holy shit," he replied. He took a moment, his eyes darting back and forth as he tried to make sense of what Sabrina was telling him. "And so you think BioHumanity is behind his death?"

"I haven't been able to confirm that. I just think it's way too much of a coincidence that Sanchez was concerned about BioHumanity's research ethics ... and your sister is getting a one-of-a-kind heart transplant, run by BioHumanity."

"That didn't get approval in the States."

"Exactly."

"If that's the case, how are we going to prove a connection ... or that they're behind the deaths?"

Sabrina thought about how to answer him. She knew what the answer should be but it also meant not going home and risking her life further ... or worse, not being in contact with Brieman. Could she really do this? As she pondered what to do, the neurologist's words swirled in her memory: "Once we make it to the other side of thirty-six hours, I know we'll be okay."

The same question kept nagging her: How could she heal unless she gained closure for Eric? It was then she decided what to do. "We've got to go to the Acapulco Heart Center and find the smoking gun," she stated.

His eyes widened. "Are you serious? I wouldn't even know how we get in."

"Your sister." Sabrina replied abruptly. "We'll use your sister to get behind security."

He thought about it. "But her operation ... we don't have much time."

"That's why we've got to leave immediately ... like tomorrow."

"What are you expecting to find?"

Sabrina folded her arms. "BioHumanity's doing something they shouldn't be—something Eric Sanchez thought was unethical, if not criminal. Since they invested in a heart transplant procedure Eric probably worked on, somehow, somewhere, they've crossed the line, and we have to find out what that line is."

"Something worse than using aborted placentas?"

"Maybe. It's my goal to find out what that is … otherwise more people are going to die."

"Meaning you?"

"Meaning me, Scott, and now you."

"Me?"

A nod. "If somebody knows you're with me, then that's all the reason they need. Trust me."

Gregory swallowed hard. "But aren't you leaving for New York?"

She smiled. "I was but that was before you broke down my door. So … are you in?"

He shook his head. "You're one helluva strong-willed woman, I'll tell you that. You don't even know me yet and you'll travel four hours to Acapulco to investigate something that's nothing more than a hunch."

"I could tell you'd do the right thing just by the way you talk about your sister. You admire her. That means a lot to me."

"I do admire her."

"And because of that, I think you'd do anything if you thought your sister was in trouble. So?"

Gregory massaged his chin. "Okay, okay. You got me. Of course, I'm in. But you have to promise me one thing."

"What's that?"

"That we'll look for Gina."

"You think she's still down there?"

"I'm not sure. I looked into it when I was there with Blair. But they don't seem to have any record of her. What I do know is she's not at her house."

It didn't take more than a second for Sabrina to agree. "You have my word."

"Good." Gregory opened what was left of the back door and walked into the cool summer night with Sabrina close behind. He eased the door shut and looked at her. "It's urgent we get there before something bad happens to my sister … or Gina."

Sabrina was game for where he was heading with this. "I know. We should leave on the first flight out in the morning."

He whipped a credit card out of his wallet. "I'll take care of the airline tickets."

She put a hand up. "Absolutely not. You said yourself you're out of money."

A small smile. "But the credit is still good. Besides, I can't think of anything more worthwhile."

"Okay. Fine."

He eyed his watch. "It's after midnight. No doubt the first flight's around six in the morning."

"Doesn't leave much time for sleep."

"No, it doesn't … but we better get some while we can. I'll go home, pack, and book the tickets."

"I'll meet you at the airport later this morning."

"Of course." He stepped off the porch but then turned around. "Sabrina?"

"Yes?"

"I can't thank you enough for doing this."

She smiled and then responded, "I should be thanking you."

Chapter 45

Across the alley, the black Jeep sat barely out of sight.

Mannheim leaned over the hood and gazed upon the man and woman standing on the porch. He put down the sandwich he was nibbling on and picked up the high-powered binoculars resting next to him. He adjusted the focus and zoomed in on Sabrina's mouth. Back in the military, he had learned to read lips from a distance. And now was the time to use that expertise for his own benefit.

He slammed the binoculars down, perplexed at what he learned. *This cat has nine lives,* he thought. There was no reason for her to be here, pondering her next move. Any sensible woman would've cut her losses, packed up, and headed home. Apparently, she was none of that.

What a damn, stubborn bitch.

He slipped into the driver's seat and pulled out a metal case resting on the floor beneath his feet. As much as he wanted to take care of her now, he had something else on his mind. He flipped open the latches and pulled out the small revolver nestled inside.

"What are you doing?" his partner asked

"We've got the journal. We don't need her anymore. If I get a clear shot, I'm going to take it." But he was lying.

She grabbed his arm. "Are you nuts? Patience, Mannheim. Patience. Do you know where she's headed?"

"Acapulco. I could read it on her lips."

"You don't say," she replied. "And the man?"

"She doesn't know him, or maybe not well. He was trying to get her attention in the house before smashing the door in."

"And she didn't run out the other side toward the cop?"

"No. I lost them after they went inside, but seemed friendly with one another when they came out ... friendly enough to pull out his credit card and say he'd pay for airfare."

The woman smiled coyly. "I think we've got them right where we want them."

"How's that?"

"We'll take care of them in Mexico. They're going to play right into our hands."

A smile spread across his face. "I like your thinking. Nobody's going to connect the dots if we execute them there."

"Right."

"And you know what else? I think I'd make a damn good taxi driver."

She looked at him and frowned. "Where am I in all this?"

"Nowhere," he replied flatly.

"What's that supposed to mean?"

"I mean you're a drag on my style." He then turned the gun toward her and, without hesitation, pulled the trigger. The silencer whistled as the bullet hit its target. Her head jerked back and then she slouched over, against the window.

She didn't stand a chance.

Mannheim removed his sunglasses and studied the small bullet hole oozing with blood. Right between the eyes, maybe a quarter inch off.

But good enough.

Good enough to be worth her bonus when he finished the job —a bonus worth five hundred thousand dollars.

Chapter 46

The Boeing 737 touched down in Acapulco as gently as a swan landing on water.

Sabrina smashed a sweaty palm against the plane's window in seat 19A and looked out onto the tarmac and then off into the distance. She eyed the workers going about their daily life and wondered if any of them had a deep worry on their minds. A single bead of sweat rolled down her back as her heart—thumping faster and faster—tried to keep up with the extreme apprehension she felt having to make the awful decision to leave Scott's bedside while he was still in a coma.

"You okay, Señora?" The thick Mexican accent made it hard to understand him.

She grabbed the armrests and sighed. A frown settled on her face as she replayed his question in her head. She didn't know much Spanish but did know that Señora meant her neighbor in 19B thought she was married. She turned toward him. "Yes," she replied, not bothering to correct him. He was older, maybe in his mid-fifties, and his dark complexion suggested he was native to the region. "Just wanted to get an early view of Acapulco."

"Ah. I thought maybe you were feeling a bit of ill." A small smile formed on his lips. He patted her forearm. She looked down but didn't make any effort to move his hand. A sense of security brushed through her—a feeling she hadn't felt in a long time. "Are you visiting for family or pleasure?" His compassionate eyes suggested he sensed her anxiety.

"A little of both." It was all she could think of as an answer. And it was such a simple question too. She made a mental note to think of a better response the next time she was asked—just in case suspicion arose. The plane jerked to a halt. The fasten seat belt sign pinged off. After ten minutes of watching the other passengers shuffle obediently off the plane, she grabbed her only bag, a black backpack, from the overhead bin and headed into the terminal.

A few minutes later, Gregory appeared in the jetway with the last group of passengers. He had graciously taken the middle seat in the last row so she could sit up front.

Sabrina waved him over. "C'mon, we need to get through customs."

"Right."

They pushed their way through a wave of tourists—mostly older Americans without a sense of urgency—until they reached border control. The customs agent barely gave them a glance, stamped their passports, and waved them through.

"Follow me," Gregory said as he powered his way toward the exit. When he found the doors, he burst into the warm, Gulf of Mexico air. Everywhere, drivers were yelling, trying to get the attention of the arriving passengers. "Taxis?" Gregory asked no one in particular.

"Over there," Sabrina pointed to a sign, her backpack dangling over a shoulder. "We're in luck," Sabrina said. "Nobody's waiting."

A taxi pulled up within seconds and they collapsed into the backseat. "We're on our way," Gregory suggested as he wiped a bead of sweat from his forehead.

Sabrina nudged herself upright. "I didn't realize the Acapulco airport was so close to everything."

"Yeah," Gregory responded. "Second time down here and still amazed at how easy it is to get through."

"Adónde vas?" the cabbie asked behind dark glasses.

"Sí, sí." Gregory said as he fumbled for the address in his pocket. "Tres … Nuevo … Ocho … Hernán Cortes, er, the Bay."

The cabbie nodded. "Sí. En viente y dos minutos."

Sabrina eyed Gregory peculiarly. She wasn't quite sure what he had said, but then the two years of high school Spanish jogged her memory. "Twenty-two minutes?"

"Ah. Si, Señorita," the cabbie responded.

Sabrina nodded triumphantly. She touched Gregory's knee. "Thanks for booking this. I promise to pay you back."

He looked at her. "Absolutely not. I should be paying you. You're the one helping me save my sister, and maybe it'll even lead to getting my girlfriend back."

"I'm no matchmaker, if that's what you're asking."

"Only hoping. ... One thing I can tell you is we're in this together. There's no way you could do this on your own."

"And neither could you," Sabrina replied. No way she was going to let him talk down to her.

A smirk. "I get your point." He reached into his bag and withdrew a small brown flask. He opened the top and thrust it at her. "Want a little?"

She sniffed the bottle. "Whiskey?"

"I need something to take the edge off." He took a small swig.

Her face turned beet red, the anger suddenly swelling inside of her. "I will take a sip after all."

He handed the flask to her and she immediately threw it out the open window.

Gregory's eyes fumed with anger. "What the hell was that?"

"I thought you were done drinking. There's no room in this cab, or this trip, for that behavior."

"Whoa, lady." He put up a hand. "You don't tell me what I can and can't do."

"I just did so you better get used to it. The only way we're going to make sure your sister is okay is if we're both alert and smart about this, and the only way we're going to do that is if we're both sober."

When Sabrina mentioned his sister, his face lightened. He shook his head. "Sabrina ... you're one of a kind."

"I certainly hope so." For a few minutes, nobody said a thing. Sabrina didn't have to look at him to know he was flustered. She wondered if it made him less so when he drank.

The cabbie looked into his rearview mirror. "Hernán Cortes on Acapulco Bay, eh?" They both nodded.

"Do you think we're doing the right thing here?" Gregory asked. "We're walking on their home turf without a solid game plan. And without the cops involved."

Sabrina eyed him. "I just want to find that one piece of evidence that ties everything together. That's it. Once we have that, the FBI or whomever, can come in and handle it. Otherwise, I don't think much is going to happen." She sighed. "Besides, what I have so far is still circumstantial. If BioHumanity really becomes aware the police are investigating them hard, they'll crawl into a hole."

He turned toward her. "How do you know that?"

She really didn't want to argue but this needed to be decided. "I don't. But anybody in his or her right mind would do the same thing. These guys know what they're doing. I wouldn't be surprised if they've already paid off the law."

"Probably," he conceded. "But we're only two people trying to take on a powerful corporation. They've got a lot of money and resources … they could squish us like a bug."

"I know——"

The cabbie briefly caught Sabrina's attention as the mobile phone rattled next to him. He answered it in Spanish as he weaved in and out of traffic.

"If we find anything, who should we tell?"

"Detective Urbina, from Lincoln City," she replied confidently. "He's the only one I trust right now, especially after being there for me at the hospital."

The cabbie took off his shades. Those eyes! Suddenly, a sense of fear interrupted inside of her, as if she had seen them before. But where?

She jerked her head toward Gregory but he was lost in thought. She looked past him toward a gritty Acapulco street on display out the window. They were nowhere near the tidy roads she had expected the cabbie to take. She discretely nudged Gregory's arm, but hard. "Something's wrong," she whispered in his ear and then pointed out the window. For a moment, she didn't think what she said registered. She was going to nudge him again but then he jerked his head forward. "Cabbie, where are we?" he asked suspiciously.

Instead of answering, the cabbie yanked the steering wheel right—toward the curb—and slammed on the brakes.

"What are you doing?" Gregory asked angrily.

The cabbie powered down the window next to Gregory. Sabrina eyed a car slowly moving by in the opposite direction.

Suddenly, two gunshots fired from the car—blistering her ears. She shot a glance out the back window, trying to catch the identity of the driver, but all she saw were taillights as it sped away. She looked over at Gregory who had slumped over and gone deftly silent. Blood was dripping down his cheek and onto his shirt. She grabbed his face and turned it toward her. His eyes were still wide open, his thoughts frozen in time from just a minute ago. That's when she noticed the small hole over his right ear.

Sabrina screamed like never before—even as a little girl—as the shock of the moment blew through her. "Oh God! No!" She grabbed Gregory's wrist and checked for life. Nothing. She turned toward the cabbie who seemed to remain strangely calm. "Who just shot at us?" she asked frantically.

The cabbie spun toward her. "Associates of mine. I have many in Mexico." His English was perfect now, the Mexican accent gone.

"What ... are you talking about?" Her heart beat rapidly, not sure what he was telling her.

"Let's just say I call on them when the time is right." He gazed at her triumphantly. "You are a very lucky woman, you know that?"

"How so?" She would've said more but she was busy processing his voice. She had heard it before. And then it hit her—the coroner's office.

"Your friend just took a bullet meant for you."

"You!" she said hysterically. "You tried to kill me on the highway, back in Oregon. That was you!" She couldn't stop thinking about Gregory. He needed a hospital. Now.

"You seem to be filling in all the blanks," he replied flatly.

"Why are you killing everybody I know? What do you want?"

"I want your life," he replied coldly. Suddenly, the window next to Gregory closed.

She focused on the bullet hole nestled in the passenger door just to the right of her. He was right—she had been lucky. She eyed the door. It was locked.

"I wouldn't try that if I were you."

Was she out of options? She just couldn't die now—not with this madman, in this taxi, in Mexico. She just couldn't. Not after how close she was to figuring this all out. "I don't get it. You have the journal. Isn't that what you wanted? Why do you keep coming after me?"

"Because you won't quit. As much as I wanted to kill you earlier, I couldn't until I had control of the journal. Now that I do, you're disposable."

"Really? Was that stupid black book really worth killing Eric Sanchez over?" She was scared to death but for some reason her mouth was working overtime.

"Yes," he stated matter-of-factly, "when what's written in there can bring down everything my client is working for."

"You mean BioHumanity?"

He looked agitated. "I don't mean anything. Nor is it your business."

"But they have to be—" And then she understood. He was deflecting her away, refusing to talk about it. She wondered why. "You killed Mona, didn't you?"

"That was more messy than I would've liked," he admitted. "But when they pay you a bonus, you do what you have to do."

It made her sick just thinking about it. "Is this how you make your living?"

A nod.

The thought she was up against a professional killer suddenly petrified her more than she already was, if that was possible.

"Killing has no effect on you, does it?" she asked, her voice shaking with every word.

"Okay. We're done with the little chitchat." Mannheim pulled a revolver from an aluminum case sitting on the passenger seat. Sabrina swallowed hard. She was sitting in death's doorway and there was no way out.

Or was there?

"We need to finish some business," Mannheim said as he screwed a silencer in place.

She put her hand on the front seat, trying to judge how much room she had. *There might be just enough*, she thought. She took a deep breath.

It would have to be now.

She pointed out her window. "The police!" He followed her glance. She snapped her right leg in an arc, a move any kick-boxer would know, toward the killer's head. Realizing she had tricked him, he turned back as her foot slammed into his cheek, sending him crashing into the door, the revolver bouncing off the dashboard and onto the seat. As if she had practiced the move a hundred times, she swooped over the seat and grabbed the gun.

His eyes shot open. He had been outsmarted.

"Now it's your turn," she said coldly. She hesitated only briefly and then shot him—not once, but three times—her hand jerking back with each pull of the trigger.

She had killed him.

Chapter 47

Blood was spattered everywhere—on Sabrina, both bodies, the seat, and the windshield.

Her ears still ringing, she stared at the limp body slumped between the window and the dashboard. Her hand was shaking uncontrollably, refusing to let go of the gun or even point it away from the assassin.

Common sense crept back to Sabrina. Was he really dead? She had to be sure. She dropped the gun and reached over the seat —his wrist would give her a sign.

No pulse.

The warm Mexican sun made her nauseous. The dark vinyl seats were warm to the touch, and the bodies—a pool of blood forming beside them—were producing a sickening odor she had only smelled once before. But here it was, sending her into a dark anxiety she never wanted to experience again. She reached over the driver and popped the locks on the door. She needed fresh air. Now.

Her mind was spinning. Could she really stand outside a car with two dead bodies in it? She peered out the window. It was a sparsely populated street but that wouldn't last long, especially if the locals knew what had transpired. She closed her eyes. *Stay strong*, she thought. But how could she, or anyone for that matter, after all that happened? She was sitting in a car with two dead men—one she had killed and the other she had gotten killed. The guilt was unbearable. She had pushed herself to get involved, and then Carla and Gina, then Brieman, and now Gregory. She was in over her head and three of those four had paid the ultimate price for her stubbornness. She should've told Urbina everything she knew on that ride back from the hospital. *Why be so feeble?* A single tear raced down her cheek. Not bothering to wipe it away, it dripped onto her shirt. The sense of normalcy she had hoped for after moving from New York was as far away as ever.

The sound of sirens shook her back to reality. She looked out the blood-spattered window. The reflection of the flashing lights could be seen in the distance, maybe two blocks ahead. Were they coming for her? For this?

There was no way she could wait for that answer. Not in this country. She could be held for days, maybe weeks, while they figured things out—while her own investigation grew stale. She had to move on, if not for her livelihood, then for the memory of Eric, Mona, Carla, Gregory, and who knows how many others they disposed of.

She flung open the door and slid from the back seat, the humid air engulfing her like a blanket. Wait. She needed protection. Reaching in, she grabbed the gun she had dropped only minutes earlier, wiped the spattered blood off the barrel, and put it in her backpack. Shielding her eyes, she looked up and down both ends of the street. She needed to get away. Now. She spotted a small alley a hundred yards back of the car.

She ran—like she had never run before.

Panting heavily, Sabrina slowed to a walk, guiding her tired legs toward the harbor. Sweat was pouring from her face but she didn't care. For the moment she was alive, yet she felt only one step ahead of death.

Shielding her eyes from the blazing Acapulco sun, she turned every which way, looking up and down the unfamiliar city blocks. Less than twelve hours ago, she had vaguely researched where the Heart Center was and, for some reason, this felt right. By her count, she must've run at least a mile from the gritty neighborhood and the taxi she left behind, for this section of the city was vastly different. Gone were the piles of trash, the homeless, and the run-down storefronts. The city was now a sea of modern capitalism set along a glistening blue harbor—brick, glass, and stainless-steel buildings dotted the streets as if shiny new toys for wealthy corporations. Carefully designed street lamps and sandy-white brick ways completed the vibe. Just across the street, the water in the Acapulco Bay glittered under the cloudless sky. On any other day, she would have been happy to stand and stare for hours at the whitecap waves, but today was not that day.

Her anxiety intensified. There was nowhere to turn, nobody to help her unload the incredible burden she felt. And maybe worst of all: She still needed to find the smoking gun or every nightmare she had survived would be for naught.

Was it possible her intuition was wrong?

She eyed a pier entrance just on the other side of the road. Painted grayish blue, it extended for hundreds of feet into the Gulf. For whatever reason, a sense of tranquility seemed to float over the pier. Maybe it was the seagulls zigzagging back and forth, maybe it was the couple romantically enjoying the view. Whatever it was, it seemed to beckon her. Skipping down a set of cobblestone steps, she hiked across the wooden boardwalk. When she hit the end of the pier, she placed her hand over a metal railing and took in the view for a few seconds.

Something suddenly seemed to make sense to her: She should end it all right here.

She leaned over the railing, pushing her torso as far as she could toward the water. She hung there, watching the waves crash back and forth. It was so tempting to just slip into the sea and let the weight of her burdens drift away from her soul.

Why not? she thought. Four lives were gone because of her.

The temptation grew stronger, her arms shaking from holding her body in such an awkward position. She eyed the water, concentrating on a point of impact.

A thought occurred to her, making her laugh, almost uncontrollably. She hadn't been there for her sister and now—maybe—this was the price she had to pay. If she hadn't been so busy with her own life that morning, she could've walked down to the lobby with her—just like she did every day.

If she had, her sister Tonya would still be alive today.

She was sure of it.

Chapter 48

Three months earlier, the April morning started just like any other weekday. Sabrina was dabbling in the kitchen of her Manhattan apartment, adding her own twist to a soup du jour recipe she had fallen for years ago—just as she did every morning before heading into the culinary institute to teach.

"Hey Sabrina!" Tonya shouted over her sister's food processor. "Are you ready?"

"Not yet, sis. I'll see you down in ten." They were headed to Central Park for a short morning jog. "I got a bit of inspiration I want to see through."

"Okay. I'll warm up a bit and see you in the lobby."

"Right."

Ten minutes later, Sabrina gave the soup a once over with her spoon and then tasted it: *Hmmm,* she thought. *What a rich, savory taste.*

She looked at the clock above the oven. *Shit.* Her sister was going to kill her. She grabbed a pencil and jotted down the recipe of her new concoction, and then rushed out the door. As she hurried down six flights, she wondered what a squirt of citrus juice would do to the soup, and for a second, considered going back and adding it. *Not now,* she decided. Her body was screaming for exercise—especially after how late she had worked the night before at the institute. Running with her sister was the only way to burn off calories and the stress of a long day, especially since she was long retired from college gymnastics.

Sabrina rounded the fourth floor. Noises briefly distracted her but she thought nothing of it. Any number of sounds came from the rickety old building that had just been renovated into condos.

She heard the noises again.

It made her more alert as she hit the third floor landing. Were her steps causing the muffled taps? She softened her steps. *Maybe that would make a difference*, she thought.

It didn't. The taps turned into soft chatter and then she heard rhythmic scraping. Sabrina rolled her eyes. The familiar sounds of adolescent love. She returned to her normal trot. As she landed on the second floor, she wondered how kids picked places to explore their sexual desires. She just hoped they were somewhat dressed, saving the embarrassment they would all share.

Ironically, a bit of sadness passed through her. Because of her ambitions, it had been two years since she felt the intimate bond of a man wrapped around her.

She shuffled her shoes against the stair landing, hoping that might give them enough warning. Problem was, she was wearing her cushy running shoes. She grabbed the banister and swung herself around to within sight of the ground floor. As morning rays bounced casually off the glazed black and white floor, she surveyed the lobby. It was deserted—the sensuous sounds of just a few minutes ago gone.

She became cautious once more.

She tiptoed down the last few steps, moving her eyes from side to side, weary of what she might find. Something stirred to her left. She turned, just in time, to catch the blow of a hard object behind her ear. It spun her into a dizzy and she tumbled hard onto the tile. Blackness crept in from all sides, confusing her to what was real or illusion. Were there footsteps? The door seemed to open. Did it shut? She slid into unconsciousness.

The sun warmed her irises, prodding her to open her eyes. She mentally checked her body. Everything appeared to be okay, save for the throbbing pain behind her ear. A scraping sound caught her good ear. She propped herself up on her knees and turned toward the sound—the back of the staircase near the basement door. She looked around for something to fight off whomever it was. The best she could find was a discarded hanger. It didn't seem all that menacing, but maybe she could poke the intruder's eyes out.

As if stalking the intruder, she made her way toward the basement stairs. A shoe worked its way from behind the wooden risers and then another one. She bent over and grabbed one. It was a white and blue running shoe—a woman's—and it seemed oddly familiar. Sabrina dropped the hangar and fumbled her way into the dark corner. To her left was a discarded pullover. Slowly, Sabrina's eyes focused on a stiff female body. Silver tape was wrapped around her mouth. Her underwear was down around her knees. Her sports bra was still on but had been pushed up on the left side, exposing a breast. The shock of realizing who it was sent her crashing into a state of hysteria.

Tonya.

The familiar eyes of Sabrina's younger, twenty-seven year-old sister stared back. The most horrifying five minutes of Tonya's entire life were written on her face, and those minutes spilled onto Sabrina like hot ash.

It was a look Sabrina would never forget.

She had never been a mother but the urge to comfort her sister overtook her. She lifted the limp body off the cracked marble, nestled her into her lap, and started rocking her as if cradling a baby. A throbbing pain intensified near her ear but she ignored it —her battered, and motionless sister, was her only concern.

"It's going to be okay," Sabrina whispered to her.

There was no answer.

She caressed her sister's hair and just sat there—silently— hoping her sister would eventually come out of the brutal shock she was in.

Chapter 49

The stranger grunted as he pulled Sabrina back over the railing. As a small crowd formed, she embarrassingly murmured, "Nothing going on here." She stumbled forward as the blood drained from her head. "A bit dizzy," she whispered. He reached out and held her steady. She looked at him. He was a big, dark-skinned man dressed in black from his fedora down to his leather shoes. It was a warm day and yet there wasn't a spot of perspiration anywhere on his face. Not at all what she expected.

"Are you feeling any better?" he asked as he settled his bulky, muscular arms on the railing.

She wiped her face. "Yeah," she replied feebly.

He gazed toward the horizon. "I saw you as I was walking to pier's end and wondered what you were up to." His voice was warm and smooth, with a hint of American hospitality. "But then you jumped on the railing and I thought, *She's really gonna do it*. So I sprinted down and caught you just as you swung yourself over."

"It isn't what you think," was all she could muster.

"Are you sure you're okay?"

Watching the crowd disperse, she sighed. "I'm fine."

He looked at her as if she was lying.

"Really," she said quickly, hoping he wouldn't ask any more questions. "I'm just having a really bad day. And my emotions got the best of me. I'll be okay."

The man flashed a smile. "We all have those." Tipping his hat, he added, "I need to get going."

She reached out and touched him. "Thank you."

He turned and nodded, then drifted away, off the pier.

Sabrina eyed a nearby bench and collapsed onto the weathered wood. A sigh pushed out of her body, like a balloon letting out air. What now?

She had come to Neskowin to escape the nightmare of her sister's death. But—somehow—she ended up with more memories just as disturbing. *The story of my life,* she thought.

She thought about Brieman. She liked him. A lot. But now he was fighting for his life and it was all because of her stubbornness for trying to find the truth. Had she just gone to the police when her suspicions started checking out—or at the very least, persuaded Blogg to take up the story, things could've turned out differently ... for everybody. She sunk her head into her hands, and started sobbing, quietly at first and then uncontrollably. The self-pity soaked into her like a sponge, and she let it.

Finally the tears dried. She was mentally exhausted. With a swipe of a hand, she wiped the last few drops away and opened her eyes, half-expecting to be embarrassed by another crowd surrounding her. But there was nobody. The pier was quiet, the nearest couple more than a hundred feet away.

Maybe Brieman was right. Maybe her sister was the reason she kept putting her life in danger. After all, her sister's killer has never been found. But if she could somehow figure this out, at least others would have closure. Maybe that's just what she needed.

It can't end this way. She's a fighter. She's always been a fighter. It's the reason she took up kickboxing after her sister's death. And it had saved her life. She would find the reason behind these killings. It would be her mission.

She stood and peered toward the water. She ran through what still needed to be accomplished: She needed to talk to Blair—find out what she knew about Gregory's ex-girlfriend. Then she needed to find Gina. Once she knew the connection between Blair, Gina, and Sanchez's journal, she would have the smoking gun. She was sure of it.

But BioHumanity would be a problem. They were obviously fixated on making sure nobody knew their secrets and wouldn't hesitate to kill her if they knew she was still alive, especially in Acapulco. She needed a plan to derail them. Running through five in her head, she settled on one that made the most sense: She would walk through the front door of the Heart Center as if she was visiting a patient. From there, she would melt into the background—become an insider. And that would lead her to the truth.

She needed to freshen up—look like a visitor—otherwise she'd never be believable. She found a restroom at the front of the pier. Locking the door behind her, she rubbed the dirt and tears from her face, then pushed her growing hair into a wave. She placed her hands on the sink and viewed the face staring back at her—the lines beneath the eyes, the wooden look. The innocent girl from childhood was nowhere to be found—replaced by an untrusting adult who refused to give into the evil of life.

The next few hours will define the rest of my life, she thought.

Chapter 50

As the high Acapulco sun beat on Sabrina's strained face, she left the pier and crossed Avenida Costera Miguel Alemán 123. To her right a polished mahogany sign read in both Spanish and English: *You are entering the campus of the Acapulco Heart Center.* Looking up and down the street, she was amazed by the vibe of the complex: Stone, glass, and stainless-steel towered above her like contemporary palaces. Complementing the buildings were the same cobblestone walks she had seen earlier—lined with rows of violets, roses, and zinnias. About the only thing missing were crowds to enjoy it.

Straight ahead was the tallest of the buildings. Large letters above the entrance, in raised stainless steel, read *Acapulco Heart Center.* She looked around to see if anybody was watching her. Deciding she was relatively anonymous, she walked up the path toward the main lobby, her heart thumping from the plan she was about to execute. She pushed through the revolving door into a tall, airy atrium—not dissimilar to BioHumanity's own headquarters. "Can I help you?" a girl, barely in her twenties, asked in accent-drenched English.

"Yes," Sabrina replied confidently. "Who am I speaking with?"

"Salena Torres," she responded politely, pointing to a small placard just to her left.

"A beautiful name."

The woman flashed a quick smile. "American, I take it?"

"Yes, I'm visiting from Oregon."

The smile stayed. "Well, you're not alone. If we didn't have the Americans coming, we wouldn't be in business."

"It seems you're offering a wonderful service for those that have the resources."

"It's an exciting gift we're able to give here," the girl responded, falling into standard jargon she surely had been taught.

"Without a doubt."

"Who are you visiting?"

"Blair Archer."

The girl tapped and swiped a tablet sitting in front of her. "Oh," she finally said.

"Oh?" Sabrina repeated.

"Are you family?" Salena asked, her smile giving way to concern.

"Yes," Sabrina lied. She knew this questioning was a possibility when she walked in but she already had a story planned. "I'm her half-sister. We share mothers." A pause. "Why do you ask?"

"Because she's quite sick and we want to make sure she's resting as comfortably as she can, without any distractions."

A nod. "I know. The Heart Center is our last hope."

"And who shall I note is here to see her?"

"Katrina Meyer." She wasn't about to use her real name just in case they ran a check.

"Thank you." The girl tapped her name into the tablet and then gestured toward the elevators on the far side of the atrium. "She's on the sixth floor—in the intensive care unit … in room 608. Visitor hours are until seven tonight."

Sabrina slipped a look at her watch. It was just before two. "Thank you." She started toward the elevator, then paused. She needed to confirm one thing Gregory had mentioned. "Ms. Torres?"

"Sí?"

"Can you tell me if another patient is here?"

"Of course."

"Except she's not really a patient. She's a donor. Her name's Gina Hyde."

Again, Salena tapped on her tablet. "I'm sorry. I'm not finding anyone by that name."

"Are you sure?"

"Sí."

"Hmm. Okay," Sabrina replied, frowning. She needed to link Gina to the journal but obviously it wasn't going to be as easy as having a quick conversation with her. Then again, maybe Blair could help.

When the elevator pinged the sixth floor, she followed the signs to Blair's room. A dark-stained maple door, inset with smoked glass for privacy, marked room 608. Sabrina paused in front of the closed door and wondered whether she should walk right in.

"Can I help you?" a woman asked from behind, her accent lighter than the others.

Sabrina froze. Keeping the same story, she replied, "I'm looking for Blair Archer's room ... I'm her half-sister, Katrina." She turned to face a petite nurse dressed in maroon-colored scrubs.

"Oh. Yes, of course. The receptionist let us know. She's right behind you, in 608. Are you new to the Center? I don't remember seeing you here before."

"First time. But I know her brother, Gregory, has been here for her."

"Yes ... Gregory. I've gotten to know him well. ... Cares dearly about his sister."

"He does," she replied, voice quivering. Talking about Gregory, and knowing his death would probably devastate Blair, didn't sit well.

"Well, it's a good thing you're here now. Without the operation she doesn't have much time left."

A nod. "Gregory said as much. That's why I rushed down here." Sabrina pointed to the door. "Do you mind if I go in?"

"Of course. But she may be sleeping. We've got her on a potent beta blocker to keep her heart rate down."

Sabrina gently pushed open the door and walked into the darkened room. The shades were drawn but sunlight still seemed to slip through. Blair's eyes were closed but her hands were moving, almost restlessly. *Must be awake,* Sabrina thought.

"Blair?" Sabrina said softly.

For a moment Blair didn't respond but then her body stirred and her eyes opened. She eyed Sabrina strangely, and then asked, almost in a whisper, "Do I know you?"

"I'm a friend of Gina ... and your brother."

"Oh? What's your name?"

"Sabrina."

She shook her head slowly. "I don't remember them mentioning you before."

Deciding she needed to change the subject, she put a hand on Blair's forearm. "Don't worry about it. I'll explain later."

Blair looked at her and then turned away. "Yes, of course. I'm just not sure I'm going to have that much time."

"You have to stay positive."

"Have you talked to my brother then? I left a message earlier today but he didn't call me back."

"He's fine," Sabrina lied, her voice wavering a bit. "I just talked to him a few hours ago, before I flew down here."

"Everything's okay, right?" Blair asked, a bit of concern showing in her voice.

"Absolutely," Sabrina replied more confidently.

"That makes me happy," Blair whispered in response. "I don't know what I'd do without him. So how can I help you?"

Sabrina's heart melted as Blair's words sank in. *Stay strong*, she thought. "It's about Gina. Gregory mentioned she visited you back home."

"That's right. That's when I told her I wanted to have the operation here."

Sabrina took a breath and jumped into her made up story. "That's when I learned she wanted to come too. I tried reaching her for days but she never got back to me. I mean ... she didn't tell me she was coming ... not that she has to but I thought she would've at least left a note."

Blair seemed surprised. "And you flew all the way down here? You must be really close."

"Childhood friends ... but now we only get to talk every few months. Do you have any sense why she came?"

Blair stared at her for a few seconds, as if trying to figure out how much to share. She sighed. "It's a long story. And I'm not sure I have the energy for it."

"I understand." But Sabrina needed to push forward. "Do you know what she was thinking?"

"She was pregnant and wanted to donate her unborn for the benefit of others."

"Why here?"

"Because of me."

Sabrina's brow creased. "How could she help you?"

"Because the heart—the heart they're going to give me—is made up of incubated cells from the placenta. And the only way they can get the number they need is by using a lot of them. Abortions are the quickest way to do it."

This seemed to confirm what Gregory had told her. "So the stems cells are from the placenta ... and since they do the abortion here they own the production of the cells."

A slight nod.

But then where's the record of Gina? "Are you sure she came?"

"She told me so ... in a note." Blair paused, as if trying to get the energy to speak. "And not only that, she was going to be rooming with a friend."

"Really? Who's that?"

"Helen Mesona. She's someone Gina met at the clinic near her house. That's how she found out the Donor Center could help me."

"The Donor Center?"

"That's where all the volunteers go when they arrive. I hear they take care good of them over there."

"It's in a different building?"

She nodded briefly. "The sister building. You take the skyway."

Behind them, a nurse walked into the room. "It's nap time."

Sabrina leaned over Blair. "Thank you," she whispered. "I know you'll get better."

"I hope you're right," Blair whispered back.

The nurse looked at Sabrina. "You'll need to let her rest for a few hours."

"Yes. Of course." Sabrina waited until the nurse turned her attention to Blair. "But I need a little bit of help." She reached inside her bag and grabbed hold of the revolver.

The nurse turned. "How can I help you?"

Sabrina slid the gun out and pointed it at her. "I need your lab coat and ID."

"Are you kidding me?"

"No. I'm not," Sabrina replied coolly.

The nurse eyed the room's intercom.

"Don't get any ideas. I'm serious. Sabrina pointed the gun at her head. The odd thing was there was no way Sabrina could have done something like this yesterday. But today was different. She just didn't give a shit anymore.

The nurse swallowed hard and then slipped off her coat, the security badges dangling from the pocket, and handed it to Sabrina.

"Good. You made the right decision."

"You're never going to get out of here. You'll be arrested," the nurse hissed at her.

"We'll see about that." Sabrina nodded toward the bathroom. "You need to go in there."

The woman eyed the barrel of the gun. Deciding it was her only option, she walked into the bathroom. Sabrina pulled the door shut and then lodged the room's only chair underneath the handle. Tapping on the door with the butt of the gun, Sabrina said, "I wouldn't bother yelling. I'm going to wait ten minutes. If you start screaming, I'm going to open the door and put a bullet in you. Understand?"

"Yes," the nurse replied flatly.

"Good."

But Sabrina had no intention of waiting around. After double-checking the door was locked, she peered at Blair to make sure she hadn't witnessed any of this. She slipped the gun and lab coat into her bag and then cautiously peered into the hall. The nurse she had met ten minutes earlier was sitting at the station, buried in paperwork. Sabrina closed the door behind her and quietly headed toward the elevator. When the doors opened, she stepped inside, thankful she was alone. She tapped the skyway button. As the car glided upward she pulled the lab coat from her bag and slipped it on.

From now on, she would be on her own—guided only by her instinct.

Chapter 51

The skyway was aptly named: The walls and ceilings were made of large—maybe six feet across—V-shaped glass panels, causing natural light to flood the walkway from every direction. The black marble floor—polished to a high gloss—added the perfect complement to the bright ambience.

For some reason the moment struck Sabrina as humorous. She was standing in a glitzy Acapulco building—alone. Everywhere she turned, she was in danger. Yet she was as calm as her days as a culinary instructor. Maybe it was because she was so focused on finding the connection between BioHumanity and the murders that she had completely blocked out the danger she was in.

Or maybe she just didn't give a damn what happened to her.

Sabrina pulled the security card from her coat and waved it near a set of glass doors that blocked entrance to the Donor Center. After a second, a small LED light flashed green. She was in. Trying not to look like a clumsy visitor, she quickly took in the Center's seventh floor. To her left and right, sets of doors blocked access to the rest of the floor while an elevator stood straight ahead, much like the one in the Heart Center.

Now what?

According to Blair, a woman named Helen Mesona had befriended Gina. If anybody knew where Gina was, Helen would be a good place to start. She took the elevator down one floor, hoping to fine someone to ask which room she was in. When the doors opened, she eyed a small placard that read *Donor EV*. Ahead, a few nurses were gathered around a station.

Just what she was looking for. *Keep it simple*, she thought. *Act like an employee.*

Sabrina walked up to a dark curly haired woman parked behind the high counter. "Hola," Sabrina said with a fake accent. "I'm looking for Helen Mesona's room." She gritted her teeth, realizing it would be easy to notice her badge picture didn't match the face.

The nurse, dressed in navy-colored scrubs, scanned her for a moment then replied, "You must be new. You here for patient vitals?"

Sabrina paused, wondering if this would lead her down a path she didn't want to go. Folding her arms, she nodded. "I've got a list of donors I'm just trying to orient myself to."

After another once-over, the woman smiled and said, "Welcome to the Center. I'm glad you joined us." She placed a tablet on the counter. "Let's see what we have here." She tapped the screen a few times and then flicked through a set of pages. "Ah, there she is. She's in wing SV, on floor five."

"S … V?" Sabrina responded, as if confused. She wondered what the letters meant.

"Yes," the nurse replied. She tapped the tablet a few more times and spun it around so Sabrina could see. "See, we're in EV, which stands for East View. She's in SV, or South View."

"So four wings to each floor?"

"Actually, eight." She pointed to the tablet. "I'm showing you only half the floor—the side that faces the water—which is why it's called *V* for View." She moved her finger. "See this … this is the *I* side, which stands for Inland."

Sabrina nodded. She was getting it. "So there's an east, west, south, north wing on each side."

The woman nodded. "Since you're on the *V* side, all you need to do is take the elevator down one floor to five and head over to the south wing. She's in room SV-565."

Sabrina smiled. "Thank you so much."

"Of course. That's what we do here: Help the new staff so they can do the same for others."

Sabrina retraced her steps back to the elevator. As she opened the glass door, the nurse called out, "I look forward to seeing you around!" Sabrina waved a thank you. When she was out of sight, she took a deep breath and let it out slowly. If only the woman knew how much she had truly helped her.

When the elevator opened on the fifth floor, she pushed through a set of glass doors and veered right. Her mom had always complained she was directionally challenged. But today she needed to be right. Walking through the wing, she met another set of doors. She was right—a small placard announced she was entering South View. Now she needed to find room 565.

Staying close to the outside wall, she found the room near the back of the wing. The door was closed, as they all were in this part of the Center. She straightened her lab coat and put on as pure a smile as she could muster. Taking a deep breath, she thought about what she would say. And then knocked twice.

A woman—maybe in her mid-thirties with wavy, brownish hair held back by a headband—answered the door. She was dressed in trendy athletic wear—a plum tank matched with black bottoms. "Yes?" she asked simply.

"Hi," Sabrina began. "I'm from the Heart Center." She pointed behind her, as if that mattered. "I was hoping I could come in and let you know how much your generosity is helping the patients extend their life."

Helen's smile quickly faded. "Um ... not sure this is a good time."

"Oh? I'm sorry ... I didn't introduce myself." She stuck her hand out. "Theresa Carlos."

She eyed Sabrina carefully then replied, "Ms. Carlos ... thanks for coming but I'm leaving this afternoon and I'd really like to finish packing." She edged the door shut, as if confirming her words.

"I do understand. But look ... I think it's really important you take some time for this," Sabrina replied. "I really do."

Helen sighed, as if she didn't have the strength to argue. "Okay, but just for a few minutes." She pulled open the door.

Sabrina's eyes bulged at the room's decor. This was definitely not a hospital room; rather a lavishly decorated condo on the Mexican shoreline. The room basked in shades of brown and tan, accented by blues. "How beautiful."

"Yes, it's going to be hard to leave. You should see the bedroom."

"Do you mind?"

"Not at all."

Two beds shared the room—one with the sheets tucked nicely in place, the other cluttered with clothes and a suitcase. Banks of windows covered two of the walls, streaming sunlight into the room. "Great view," Sabrina said as she stepped up to a window. She looked at the glistening bay and the pier she had been on only an hour before.

Helen laughed a bit. "You must be new … or don't get out very much."

"A little of both," Sabrina replied, realizing she should act a little less naïve. She turned and pointed to the made bed. "Where's your roommate?"

"Really?" Helen shot back, her voice clearly agitated. "You should know."

Sabrina looked surprised. "I'm sorry. I'm new," she confessed.

"The Center … you guys … took her."

"Why would we—"

"Don't give me that. I was here."

"Where would we have taken her?"

"You really have no idea, Ms Carlos?" She stepped forward and eyed her badge.

Sabrina pulled away.

Helen pulled her eyes up to Sabrina's face. "That's not you, is it?"

"You don't understand." Sabrina replied, stepping back further.

"Now I get it." Helen's eyes were wide but there wasn't a hint of terror showing. "That's why you don't know a thing about this place."

Take control, she thought. *Be strong. Be forceful—just like I did with the nurse.* She took a deep breath. The anxiety went away, replaced by confidence she knew was always there. Whipping out the gun, she replied, "You're right." She aimed it at Helen's chest. "I don't."

Helen threw her hands up. Fear washed across her face. "Look … I'm sorry." She eyed the barrel of the gun. "Then who are you?"

Sabrina moved toward her until she could feel Helen's breathing. "I'm here investigating the murders of four people, one of them being Gina's ex-boyfriend Gregory. And the only way to find the truth is to impersonate a nurse's aide."

"What does that have to do with the Center?" Helen asked as her eyes moved between the gun and Sabrina's face.

"Maybe everything, it turns out."

Helen looked confused.

"BioHumanity is behind these murders, and I'm trying to find out why, and how."

"No way," Helen replied as if not believing.

"When I find out what they're up to, this whole place is going to go down, along with everybody behind it." She lowered the gun, hoping that might reduce the tension. "But I need your help."

Helen seemed to ponder what she was telling her. "Why should I help? I mean ... who do you work for? The FBI? The CIA?"

Sabrina grinned. "No ... nothing like that. I'm just a rookie reporter who happened to stumble into something I never should've. And the least I can do is make them regret killing all those innocent people."

Helen frowned. "Are you kidding me? A reporter? I'm sorry, but—"

Sabrina didn't have time for this nonsense. Jamming the gun into her chest, she said, "It's pretty simple. You help me find out why BioHumanity is killing people and the murders will stop. That alone is a reason to help. Look what they've already done to your roommate. I mean, who knows where she is. She could be dead, for all we know. But I'm running out of time. And I need you to help me."

"But I don't know how to help," Helen pleaded.

"Help me find Gina."

"But how's that going to—"

Sabrina interrupted her. "Because she knows something. I'm sure of it."

Helen shoulders slumped and gave a resigned sigh. "After seeing what they did to Gina, I've been waiting to spill what I know —someone I could trust." She pointed at the gun. "But you need to put that thing away and tell me your real name."

"Okay." She slipped it back into her backpack. "Now we're getting somewhere. It's Sabrina. And I won't hurt you, I promise."

The smile returned. "Then let's sit and talk."

Sabrina sat on the only clean area of her bed and started digging for answers. "What did they say when Gina disappeared?"

Helen shrugged. "Just that she had an emergency medical situation and they needed to take her to the hospital."

"But you don't believe them?"

"No. They didn't see me witness what happened. I mean … one of the staff came in, said a few words, and then the next thing I knew, they were taking her unconscious from our room."

"And no word since?"

She shook her head. "They say they don't have any updated information. It just doesn't make sense. She never mentioned anything to me about being ill." Helen looked toward the ocean. "We were outside sitting on the deck. She just went in to get a pair of sunglasses … and now it's like she's gone."

"How long does a donor normally stay here?"

"A week … sometimes two."

"That must've been weeks ago. Why are you still around?"

"Because I've been a basket case over the whole thing. And they've been very nice to me … told me I could take as much time as I needed."

Of course they did, Sabrina thought. "So you finally decided to go home?"

A nod. "It's time. But I still don't know where she is. I haven't heard a peep. I'm just hoping she's okay and back home."

"Can you think of anything that might lead to her?"

Helen shook her head. "Nothing."

Sabrina picked her words carefully. "I can tell you she's not home."

Helen's eyes widened. "How do you know that?"

"Because her ex, Gregory, went there. Nobody's there."

A sigh. "I didn't need to hear that."

Sabrina put a hand on her. "I didn't mean to make you more anxious."

"What about you? Is there anything you've learned that could help?"

Sabrina pondered what she asked. All she had were the interviews and what she remembered from the journal. A thought struck her: *What about the notes?* She grabbed the notebook from her bag—thankfully she had copied parts of Sanchez's journal while she still had it.

"What's that?" Helen asked, sitting beside her.

"Notes I took from a journal ... a journal from a man who knew BioHumanity very well."

"Who?"

"Eric Sanchez. He was a research scientist with them. He became so disturbed by what he saw going on at the company, he created a daily journal."

"Anything worthwhile?"

"I'd say plenty. I just haven't figured it all out. But I can tell you one thing: BioHumanity desperately wanted the journal back."

"Oh? Where is it now?"

"If my assumptions are right, I'd say they do. A hit man they sent recovered it."

"From you?" Helen guessed.

Sabrina sighed. She didn't want to relive that right now. It was still too traumatic. "Yes," she simply replied.

"How did you end up with it?"

"While I was investigating Sanchez's company, I met his assistant Mona. She gave it to me but then they killed her ... probably over the journal."

Helen covered her mouth. "Oh my God."

Sabrina looked at her hard. "They must've known she gave it to me because they've been trying to kill me since."

"How?"

"Car accident." And then she added, "The second one I've been in the last month."

"What do you think it all means?"

"What do I think it all means?" Sabrina repeated. She paused, thinking about an answer. "It means they're hiding something sensitive—so sensitive they're willing to do whatever it takes to keep it that way."

"Like what?"

"I know it starts with stem cells and ends with organ harvesting. I just haven't been able to make the connection."

"Where did you come up with organ harvesting?"

"Sanchez talks about it in his journal." Sabrina eyed her notes. "He says BioHumanity needs to cease harvesting. That's why finding Gina is so critical. If she mysteriously disappeared off the face of the earth as everybody seems to think, then there may be a reason. She may know something ... assuming she isn't dead ... that ties everything together."

Helen sighed. "I wish I could help you. I really do."

Sabrina flipped though her notes. What was the connection? Her eyes were drawn to the last page where she had underlined three numbers and two letters.

SI-790.

It was the last thing Eric had written in his journal.

Something occurred to her. "Helen, is the skyway the top floor?"

A nod.

"Is there a wing called South Inland?"

"Yes, you'll run into it ... once you walk through the elevator lobby that splits the two wings."

"Really."

"Yes, absolutely."

"Makes me wonder," Sabrina said as she circled the number. Could it be a room number here at the Center that was important to Eric Sanchez, important enough to write in his journal?

"Wonder what?"

Sabrina put away her notes. "I don't know. Just a hunch. I doubt it's anything." She couldn't risk Helen knowing where she was going with this, no matter how much she trusted her.

"What now?"

Sabrina stood. "I don't want to waste any more of your time. You've been a huge help." She gave Helen a quick hug.

"But I didn't tell you anything."

"You've helped me more than you can imagine."

"Where you off to?"

"To find Gina."

Sabrina walked out of the bedroom and then paused. "Congratulations on leaving today. I hope we'll get a chance to meet again on better terms."

"With Gina," Helen replied.

"Yes, with Gina," Sabrina repeated.

Chapter 52

The cellphone buzzed. Vua turned away from his seventh floor penthouse window and glared at the phone, squinting at the number blinking through. "What the …" he mouthed. He snatched the phone. "Yes?"

"It's Rico. We've got an intruder in the donor building."

"I see. Who is it?"

Silence and then, "It's unbelievable to say this, sir, but we believe it's the reporter … Sabrina Katz."

Vua's heart jumped. If it were true, then something went wrong with Mannheim … something devastatingly wrong. "Are you sure it's that damn bitch?" he replied, trying to contain himself. "She should be hours dead by now."

"I understand that but it appears to be true. I triple-checked the security feed coming in … from multiple cameras … it's definitely her. I'm a hundred percent sure of it."

"Then how'd she get in?"

"I … don't know. I'm backtracking the feed now to see when she walked in. I can tell you she picked up security clearance by stealing a nurse's lab coat and badge."

"From whom?"

"Theresa Carlos. We found her locked in the bathroom of one of our patients."

"So she was in the Heart Center too?"

"Yes."

He tapped his desk. "Which patient?"

"Blair Archer."

"Blair Archer?" *That bitch.* After hearing about Sabrina's friendship with Gregory Archer, he wasn't surprised. He made a mental note to pay Blair a special visit once the Center was secure.

"That's right. I'm going to cut off her clearance so she doesn't burrow in any further."

"No!" Vua barked.

"But—"

"I want the exact opposite. I don't want her knowing we're tracking her. Find out where she's going. When she gets there, distract her with Gina—and then… I'll join you."

A pause. "Sir … are you sure Gina's ready?"

"She's more than ready," Vua stated.

"And what are you going to do with her?"

A small smile worked its way from Vua's mouth. "Let's just say she won't be around for long."

Rico sighed. "BioHumanity can't authorize that. You know it's against our bylaws as an international corporation. It's why …" His voice trailed off.

"Just say it," Vua boomed into the phone.

"Sir, it's why we have contractors."

"I don't give a shit," Vua hissed. "I need this taken care of immediately. And I'm going to personally see it through."

"Then consider it done," Rico replied softly.

Vua flipped the phone onto his desk. *The bitch was poison.* But now he would witness her permanent demise.

He thought for a second and then pulled a second phone from the desk. He dialed Mannheim's emergency number—something he only used when it was urgent. It rang to voicemail. What was disconcerting was Mannheim never failed to answer knowing who was calling. Vua threw the phone back in the drawer and slammed it closed.

What happened in that taxi?

He eyed Sanchez's journal still half-open on his desk. He had the evidence. But now the reporter was in the building. The simple fact was he didn't need Mannheim anymore.

Ironically, the bitch had just saved him a million dollar payout.

Chapter 53

Trying to hide the rush she was in, Sabrina strolled briskly past the nurses' station outside Helen's room and headed toward the South Inland—or SI—wing. When the doors opened on the seventh floor she stepped out and froze. Was it the right floor? The wing looked nothing like the rest of the building. Sterile, pure white walls greeted her everywhere she turned. There was only one door: A simple stainless-steel one with no windows that seemed to emphasize the minimalist décor. To Sabrina, it looked like some kind of research wing; but whatever it was, the floor definitely was not meant for donors.

She turned toward the door and read the placard next to it. "S ... I," she whispered. She gave the door a tug, but it refused to budge. She eyed the security reader blinking red. Would her card possibly work up here? She swiped the reader and held her breath. After a second, the door clicked open. *I do have an angel,* she thought.

She cautiously peered inside. Stark white walls covered the hallway, with stainless-steel doors scattered along one of the walls the only thing breaking the monotony. She stepped through and closed the door gently behind her. Numbers were printed in a simple black font on the doors, starting with 770. Her target was close. She moved down the hall and turned the corner. "790," she whispered at the last door on the left.

Located next to the door was another security reader but this one seemed different. Wondering again if her card would work, she waved it in front of the reader but nothing seemed to happen. *C'mon,* she thought. She tried again. Silence.

Okay, now what? She peered closer and realized it was a thumbprint reader. For a moment, she pondered the switch in security. Obviously whatever was behind these doors needed to be more secure than anywhere else in the Donor Center. That was telling and meant she may be on the right path. But she also knew she didn't have much time. It wouldn't be long before they found the real Theresa Carlos.

She reached into her backpack and grabbed the pistol. She eyed the silencer fitted on the end, hoping it would be quiet enough for what she was about to do. Lowering the gun, she pointed at the reader and fired a shot from a foot away. The reader exploded, scattering pieces like a firework. But the main guts stayed attached, bouncing up and down like a yo-yo from the exposed wiring.

She crouched near the smoldering mess and counted the wires in the wall. She was no electronics whiz but she knew from her days as a culinary student that kitchen cookware and appliances went out all the time. And since she didn't have the money to replace them, she worked with a friend to fix whatever she could—and learned a few things along the way. She knew outlets had a hot wire—a white one that went straight to the source—while the neutral, usually red or black, went to the switch, or reader in this case. But this one was a bit different: It had red, black, yellow, and blue wires. When she traced the yellow and blue back into the wall, their route took them away from the door, meaning they weren't being used to open the door. So that only left the red and black. She traced the black one: It went up toward the ceiling. *Must be the power source*, she thought.

She grabbed the reader and pulled hard on the black wire until it snapped away from the reader. She did the same with the red wire. Biting her lower lip, praying this was right, she pressed the two wires together. The door buzzed and clicked open. Smiling at her success, she dropped the wires and pushed open the door. She stopped. *Not yet*, she thought. She swept the reader's guts into the room and then jammed what was left of the switch back into the wall.

At first she couldn't see much. Glass windows encircled the room, but they were tinted gray, giving the room a somber mood, even with a navy blue-tiled floor that seemed to run the length of the room. Sabrina took a few steps forward, knowing she needed to keep moving—it wouldn't take long for someone to realize her intrusion.

When her eyes adjusted, the room morphed into something she hadn't expected: A science lab. But it wasn't any lab she had seen before—either in college or on the Internet. Along the windows, lab computers and other machines blinked red, yellow, and green. Below a row of gray cabinets, vials of liquid capped red, blue, and black filled the counter.

Her eyes settled on something more fascinating: Aluminum rods—maybe fifty of them—hung from the ceiling across the room. Suspended from the rods were heavily tinted black capsules, the size of a small bassinet. She walked toward one and touched it with a hand. It was smooth, like a bowling ball. She bent over and cupped her hands against the capsule to take a look, but it was too dark to see anything.

She went to another one—still nothing to see. That's when she noticed a small touchpad next to each capsule. She touched the screen and it sprang to life, highlighting buttons like a mobile app. One of the buttons was marked *Incubator Light* so she touched it. A subtle reddish-orange LED light began to glow inside the capsule. As the lights took hold, she gasped.

A web of wires spun throughout its interior. But it was the middle of the capsule that caught her attention: Something small —maybe two inches in diameter—was suspended from the wires. At first it looked like raw chicken meat. But the more she peered at it, the more she realized it was something more—something much more. As she stared, she realized it was expanding and contracting —like a heart—but its beats were easily two or three times faster than a human one. *That can't possibly be a heart.* She walked around to the other side, placing her hand delicately on top of the capsule as she continued staring at it.

"Oh my God," she whispered. *They had done it. They had created a human heart.*

She turned toward another capsule and tapped its touchpad, bringing the incubator light to life. Another suspended heart, this time maybe half the size. She ran to a third capsule and flipped its light on. This heart was the biggest so far, the size of a baseball.

There was a sudden thud behind her. She froze. Did she hear something or imagine it?

"What do you think?" a voice said from the doorway.

Chapter 54

Sabrina whipped her head toward the woman's voice. "I don't know what to say. I mean … it's a miracle."

The woman came closer, but Sabrina could still barely make out her features, except she was tall, maybe five-eleven. She pointed to a capsule. "That incubator's for Marjorie. She's in NV-399, just days away from her life-changing event."

Sabrina felt for the pistol as she stepped toward the woman. She needed to regain her composure—quickly. "This is the most amazing place I've ever seen."

"Without a doubt," confirmed the woman. She moved near one of the incubators Sabrina had turned on, the dim light drawing out her features. She was dressed in a white lab coat over dark purple scrubs that were matched with gray Crocs. Her smile was welcoming, like she wanted to be friends. Dark, flowing hair stopped at the shoulders, making her look younger than she probably really was. Her eyebrows arched high, but her jaw was long, casting an oval shadow on her face. Overall, she was strikingly beautiful.

Sabrina stepped closer. "You must be a doctor. Are you responsible for the lab?"

The woman laughed. "Me? No … just a tech for the S-I wing."

Sabrina eyed her coat but didn't see the familiar security badge.

"I'm Gina Hyde … if you're wondering."

Sabrina's face flushed red, she was sure of it. "I'm sorry … did you say Gina?"

"Yes." A pause. "And you are?"

Suddenly, she forgot the name she had assumed. And then it came back. "Theresa Carlos, Bio Technician." She reached out her hand.

Gina didn't take it. "No, it's not."

"Excuse me?"

"For one, you did a number on the security scanner outside. That tells me you didn't have clearance for the room—"

"Me?" Sabrina replied defensively, interrupting her. "It was like that already."

Gina's smiled sweetened. "Sure it was."

"Whatever."

"And two … we just recovered Theresa from a patient's bathroom."

"No," Sabrina replied. "You must have—"

"Let's get real, Sabrina." Her voice turned sour. "We know your real name. And we know why you're here."

Sabrina was taken aback by Gina's sudden prickly personality. Maybe she was the one that caused Gregory to drink. "And why is that?"

"To ruin every patient in this heart center who's getting a second chance at life."

"No … that's not true!"

Gina ignored her. "Take the heart in the far corner. That one belongs to Kara Fischer, a dietician who ate all the right things in life. Her only fault? Genetics."

"And then there's Percy Strueger—a world-class executive at the top of his game. His only problem? High blood pressure."

"And then there's Blair Archer, a dear friend of mine." She paused. "She's here because of a chronic heart condition known as cardiomyopathy." Gina took a few steps to her left, tapping an incubator. "This is the heart she's getting … one that started in me."

Sabrina nodded. It was starting to make sense: It was Gina. "Why did you do it?"

"Because Blair needed the help or she was going to die. And they needed a transplant that her body wouldn't reject."

"And how do they make sure of that?"

"Through the stem cells they use—family is as sure a thing as you can get."

"But you're not related," Sabrina interjected.

"No, but my fetus is."

"What do you mean?" And then it hit her. "You're not saying …"

Gina nodded emphatically. "Her brother Gregory and I had a long relationship … and I'll confess it was filled with a lot of drama. Then I hit a wall … I just couldn't take it anymore so I decided to end it. But that's when I found out I was pregnant with his baby."

"Seriously?"

"Yes, but it's a secret. I only told one person—the person that matters the most."

Sabrina bit her lip. "Are you talking about Blair?"

"Yes."

She didn't have the heart to tell Gina Blair hadn't kept the secret. "Why didn't you tell Gregory? I'm sure he would've wanted to know."

Gina shook her head. "And then I would've been chained to him forever. I just couldn't let myself do that. Besides, I'm doing this for Blair. Gregory may not like the choice but he's going to like the outcome."

Sabrina's mind was racing. "So you had the abortion and BioHumanity used the stem cells to grow the heart," she replied, relating a conversation with Brieman to the one she was having now.

"Yes, it's the most satisfying thing I've ever done in my life."

"Then tell me something."

"What's that?"

"Why aren't you in the database?"

Gina seemed confused. "How do you mean?"

"The donors … like you … are supposed to be registered. I checked with the receptionist and you're not in the system."

"Really?"

"Yes, really. Any idea why?"

She thought about an answer. "Yes … it's because I'm part of the BioHumanity family now. It's a special honor … and so they give you special treatment."

"Why would you want to do that? I mean… I just met your roommate Helen and she's going home."

Gina's face brightened—the mention of her friend seemed to raise her spirits. "Helen … she's the second best thing that's happened to me." Then she added, "I want to stay because this is the only life I want—being here, helping these people."

"Hmm." Sabrina wasn't following her logic. "But Helen tells a different story. She says you found something … or know something … and they took you away. Is that true?"

"I don't want to talk about that," she replied curtly.

"Why not?" Sabrina interjected. "What do you know?"

"Let me be clear: It's not important." Her response was terse.

"The hell it isn't," Sabrina replied angrily. Gina took an aggressive step forward but Sabrina would have none of it as she pulled the gun from her backpack.

Gina's face flashed surprise and then anger. "What is wrong with you?"

"What's wrong with me?" Sabrina repeated. "Four people died because of BioHumanity, and you're telling me it's not important."

"That's complete nonsense." Gina replied.

"I don't think so." Sabrina shook the gun at her. "You are going to tell me exactly what you know."

Gina looked into her eyes, as if trying to understand how serious Sabrina was.

"Now!" Sabrina screamed.

Gina's frame shook from Sabrina's outburst and then her shoulders slumped. She sighed. "It doesn't matter anymore anyway—there's no way you're going to make it out of here alive."

"We'll see about that."

"I found a flash drive in my jacket," Gina started. "The demonstrators must've given it to me when I walked in."

"What demonstrators?"

"You didn't see them? Outside the Center?"

Sabrina shook her head. "Nobody was out there … just pedestrians."

"Steven must've figured out a way to remove them … maybe the Mexican authorities stepped in."

"What were they demonstrating against?"

"It looked like an organization against abortion—definitely US-based … there must've been twenty or thirty women chanting,

245

holding signs with pictures of aborted fetuses. Honestly, it was sick. But the Center was definitely concerned. They had extra security helping us get through the crowd. After that, I didn't think much of it because I knew what I decided to do was the right thing."

"How did you end up with the flash drive?"

"All I can think of is I remember one of the women bumping into me and she must've slipped it into my pocket."

"Was there anything on it?"

A nod. "A video."

"Did you watch it?"

Gina nodded, but her face was wretched with disgust. "I was so sickened by it."

"Take your time." Sabrina moved forward, anxious yet fascinated by what Gina might say next.

"A woman and a man were in it but I couldn't make them out."

"What were they doing?"

"They were in some sort of operating room. The female doctor was performing an abortion on a woman—but let me tell you the fetus looked big, almost second trimester big."

"So the demonstrators gave you a video of a doctor giving an abortion?" Sabrina replied, disappointment clearly showing in her voice. "Isn't that what they do here?"

Gina shook her head. "No, it wasn't just that. After she did the abortion, she ..."

"Take it slow," Sabrina said calmly.

She put a hand on her chest, her emotions getting the best of her. "I don't know how to say it." Her voice was trembling.

"Just give me the truth."

"The man took the fetus, cut open the chest and harvested the heart ... and then put it in some sort of solution. It was sick."

Sabrina gasped. "Oh my God!"

"And then it ended."

"But why? Why harvest the heart?"

"Don't you get it?" Gina screamed. "Look around. The Center doesn't have the technology."

"To do what?"

"To—"

And then without warning, the room went pitch black.

Chapter 55

Sabrina hit the floor, still holding the gun. She was panting heavily, trembling—scared that she had taken her interest in BioHumanity too far and now she was going to pay the ultimate price.

Stay calm. Breathe easy. Make it out of here alive, she thought. She let her eyes adjust to the deep darkness in the hopes a sliver of light would lead her to safety. But it was fruitless—she could barely make out a hand in front of her.

Then an idea hit her: What if she crawled toward one of the walls? She could then follow it in the direction of the door. Deciding it was the only rational idea, she slid delicately across the floor, stopping every few feet to see if she could hear anybody else in the room. After crawling through what seemed like a warehouse of darkness, she finally touched a wall—a wall anchored with cabinets she recognized were close to the door. Making sure the wall stayed within reach, she veered right toward the only exit she knew.

As she made her way, she thought about what Gina had admitted. *BioHumanity was harvesting hearts, from fetuses.* But she was confused. Weren't they growing and incubating hearts from the placenta cells? Why would they need to harvest fetal hearts? She sighed silently. If they hadn't been interrupted, Gina would've told her.

Before she could think it through further, she heard movement. Was it coming from behind her? She wasn't sure. There it was again. Scraping sounds, as if someone was sliding plastic along the floor, or maybe the wall. Where was it coming from? It grew louder. A second sound joined the first—almost in rhythm. After a few seconds, it stopped. Everything grew quiet—eerily quiet.

Maybe ten steps ahead, Sabrina could make out the light underneath the door.

She was almost there.

Suddenly, an arm swung around her neck and whipped her backward, onto her feet. The gun flew out of her hand, skidding across the tile.

"Gotcha," a male breathed in her ear. And then he said to someone else, "Secured. She's not going anywhere."

"Excellent," another voice said. "Make sure you have her tight. She has a knack for escaping death."

"Jonas … get the lights," a third voice said.

"Of course."

Rows of ceiling lamps hummed to life but still seemed too dim to make a difference. The men switched on their flashlights, spraying the room with more light. Sabrina looked around her. Other than the man holding her, there was one patrolling the door. Both seemed unarmed but were wearing high-tech goggles. *Night vision,* she thought. On the other side of the room was Gina—she was going from incubator to incubator, ignoring the commotion around her.

There was nowhere to go, or run. She felt nauseous at the thought she was not long for this world.

A man of medium build stepped from behind her. He was smartly dressed head to toe in black, and seemed to be of mixed Asian heritage. The only thing that seemed a bit out of place was his hair. Jet black locks were pulled back, curling at the shoulders. It gave him a certain boyish look. "Allow me to introduce myself," he said in a slight American southwest twang. "I am Dr. Steven Vua, CEO of BioHumanity."

Sabrina looked him up and down, and then did something she had never done before in her life. She spat on squarely on his face. "Don't you dare take another step toward me," she threatened.

He wiped the saliva from his eyes and cheeks, eyed the spit on his palm, and then laughed. The others joined in before he cut them off, and then he slammed the same palm into the side of her face, spinning her around in her captor's arms. "Oh!" she muttered, taken by surprise. A burning sensation rushed across her face like somebody had pressed a lit match against it.

"Now … let's try this again," Vua hissed at her. He stuck his hand out but she refused to grab it. "Fine, bitch. We'll do this my way."

"By murdering innocent people?"

He stared at her, his face popping with anger. "They were the ones intruding on my plan. Just like you are now."

"Then why didn't you have your assassin take care of me when you had the chance … like back at the funeral?"

"You're right," he admitted. "I should have but I underestimated your burning desire."

"So you bumped me off the road, hoping that would do it?"

"Something like that," he said. "Only a stubborn bitch would've ignored that warning."

She ignored the last comment. "You murdered Eric Sanchez."

"You have it wrong."

"Correction … your assassin did," Sabrina continued. "He told me right before I took care of him."

"I've learned you are quite capable of taking care of yourself," Vua replied, not denying her accusation.

"I had to. I learned long ago nobody else would give a damn."

"I like your attitude. You would've made a fine associate, and made a lot of money I might add."

"Maybe. But I prefer to live my life on the side of good."

He gritted his teeth and stared at her. "Are you calling me evil?"

"I'd prefer to call you a savage, but I'm too polite."

"You know nothing of me," he replied coarsely.

"No? Then why did you bribe the coroner?"

"What are you talking about?"

"I found it ironic the coroner didn't include in her report that Sanchez had Atropine in his body."

"Ah." A small smile worked across his lips. "You have done your homework."

"He was just a researcher, helping you with … with this repulsive house of cards."

Vua shook his head. "He wasn't just any researcher. He was BioHumanity's Chief Researcher and had access to everything we were doing. And he just wasn't … shall we say … on the same page as us."

"So you had your so-called associate dispose of him." Sabrina said.

"We gave him plenty of warning but he ignored it."

"And his wife?"

"That was unfortunate, but necessary … consider it collateral damage. Her love for finding the truth ultimately killed her."

"By burning her house down while she's inside? That is barbaric."

Vua waved her off. "How my associates dispose of someone is their own business." He stepped within inches of her, close enough she could feel his breathing. "The ironic thing is he didn't love her as much as his mistress."

"His mistress?" She tried turning away but her captor held her head tight. "What are you talking about?"

Vua laughed. "Oh, there is something you don't know. But I bet you know who it is."

She was lost. "Who?"

"Mona Frederick."

"That's impossible. They were just friends … besides, I met Carla. They were deeply in love."

"Yes, well, maybe they were at one time. But the fact is, that's how Mona ended up with Sanchez's journal. And I needed it back."

"Why didn't you just steal it from his office?"

"Because it disappeared a week before he died. We confronted him but he refused to acknowledge its existence even though the security cameras were right there. But then we got lucky."

"How?"

"We monitored Mona's conversation with you in our atrium. At that moment I was ecstatic you didn't decide to leave town. After all, you were doing all the dirty laundry for us."

Now she understood. "I was your bait."

"Exactly." Vua took a leather glove from his pocket and slid it on his right hand. "We had to keep you alive until we knew what happened to the journal."

Sabrina gasped. "And you had Mona murdered because she probably refused to tell you where it was."

"A brave girl. She never told. But not a very smart one." He wrapped the black leather strap around his wrist and snapped it in place. "Which brings us to you, my brave New Yorker." He pointed a gloved finger at her. "Even through all that, I gave you one last warning to wash your hands of everything, and you still refused."

"How do you mean—"

"The pictures—the ones of your dead sister lying in your New York apartment."

"You bastard!" she screamed as she thrashed around, trying to escape the grip her captor had on her. "Don't dare bring my sister into this." Her captor tightened his hold, almost choking her.

"Testy. Testy," Vua replied softly. "But now it's your turn."

"What"—she struggled to get the words out—"what are you going to do to me?"

"Ah, always the inquisitive reporter," Vua replied calmly. "You'll just have to wait and see." He then smacked her hard across the cheek with the gloved hand.

She slumped in her captor's arms, tears flowing from her eyes it hurt so much.

"Have you given up already?" Vua asked without remorse.

Sabrina tried to reach the tears but she only found the drops on her cheek. She gritted her teeth. No matter what he did to her she needed to know the truth. "But once you had the journal, I was —"

"Disposable? Yes."

"Then why didn't you finish me off?"

"You should thank two dead men for that—even if they didn't plan on it."

"Two?"

"Gregory Archer … and Scott Brieman."

Her heart jumped. Did he know something she didn't? "You're wrong," she spat at him. "Scott's going to be fine." She glanced over at Gina, who seemed taken aback by the mention of her ex-boyfriend.

"Believe what you want."

"Is what you're doing worth killing innocent people?" She looked around the room. "For this?"

Vua turned toward Gina, who was near the back of the room, and gestured toward her. "She knows. It was the reason she felt … compelled to join."

"You mean the harvesting?"

Vua smirked. "Did you learn that from Gina?"

"She just helped me understand the connection. But I'm not there yet … we were, after all, rudely interrupted." *C'mon,* she thought, *answer the damn question.*

He put his hand on a nearby capsule. "These incubators are saving people's lives. The problem is … there are people who just don't seem to see it that way."

"Like how?"

"Regenerative transplants. That's how. They are giving terminally ill patients a second chance they never thought they had." He eyed her curiously. "Everybody deserves a second chance, don't you think?"

She thought back to her conversation with Gregory. "Maybe. But my intuition says you don't give a damn about the patients. You just want the money … and when people are desperate, they'll give you everything."

Vua laughed but she could tell she struck a chord. "Look around. Do you think this should be a handout?"

"So you decide who lives based on how much money they have? Who gave you that right?"

He shrugged. "It's not my problem if someone can't afford it. Like I said, this isn't a charity."

He wasn't giving her anything. "Why are you doing it here? Why not in the States?"

"Because the U.S. government refuses to acknowledge the value of a regenerated heart."

"Why? I would think they'd love the innovation—MSC's are the one of the richest forms of stems cells you can work with."

Vua clapped. "Bravo, Ms. Katz. You have done your homework. And I agree: MSCs are a critical part of our process, but we needed … a boost. That's why we had our best research scientist on it—we just couldn't get the stem cells to grow in a reasonable time. But when we injected the cells into a catalyst, everything came together—it was like growing a Chia Pet."

Sabrina pondered what he was telling her: *They needed a catalyst.*

Oh my God, she thought. He didn't give a damn about the donors or the patients. He just wanted the fetal hearts so he could feed his empire and make him filthy rich ... all by deceiving pregnant women into believing what they were doing was for the good of science. The gravity of it made her want to vomit. "How many people are in on this?"

"All across the U.S. I have a network of associates working in clinics ... paid excellent commissions by the way ... who are providing me the donor supply I need to grow my business."

She shook her head. "You're a savage excuse for a human being ... you son of a bitch."

Vua chuckled, as if her words didn't matter. "No, Ms. Katz. You have it all wrong. At the heart of it, I'm just an entrepreneur supplying a market demand."

"And not caring a damn how many lives you destroy along the way."

Vua shook his head. "I think if I had enough time, you'd understand. You see, you and I have something in common."

"I don't think that's possible," she snapped back.

"Oh, it is ... we've both experienced the unthinkable."

"Such as?"

"We both lost someone very dear to us: Siblings. It hurts, doesn't it?"

She was not going to let his stinging words get to her. "Did you murder your brother too?" she asked sadistically.

"No, you bitch," Vua replied rudely. "Genetics killed him. He had a heart condition—similar to Miss Archer—that required a heart transplant. Unfortunately, he just didn't get it in time. But unlike your sister, something good came of it."

"You bastard," Sabrina hissed.

"Sometimes, times of pain can bring out the best in someone. And it was in that moment"—he raised his hands and looked up —"I saw the future."

Sabrina opened her mouth, but then stopped. Something made her ponder what he said: *We both lost siblings and it hurts.*

He eyed her. "You seem perplexed, Ms. Katz."

Sabrina looked at him as the thought washed away. "Just thinking about the day you're arrested ... once they find me," she said.

He reached out with his right hand and the guard stepped forward, placing a short nylon rope in it. "Don't worry, Ms. Katz. I'll make sure you're dumped well beneath the bay. Nobody will find you there—other than the deep feeders, of course."

"You seem very good at getting rid of collateral damage," she blurted. Her sarcastic comments weren't helping but she just didn't give a damn.

He snapped the rope in front of her. "Goodbye, Ms. Katz."

Eyeing the rope and hearing the finality of his words stung her, melting the courage and confidence she accumulated the past twenty-four hours. "Don't do it," she whispered, looking him straight in the eye. She was barely holding her composure.

He focused on her but the gaze seemed to pass through her as he started the chore of wrapping the rope around her neck. Within a few seconds, it tightened hard, making it impossible to breathe. She felt her captor loosen his grip but the lack of oxygen zapped her strength. Darkness swirled around wherever she focused—like a deep morning fog it seemed. Off in the distance— a hazy gray distance—she could've sworn she heard someone yell, "No!" A gunshot followed. And maybe another. Or was she hallucinating?

But it didn't matter.

Not anymore.

Chapter 56

With her face planted against the cold floor, Sabrina opened her eyes and began following the speckled blue and black pattern in the tile. Realizing she was still in the lab, she put her palms on the floor and tried lifting her head. A hand grabbed her arm and helped her the rest of the way up. "C'mon!" a woman's voice said.

Sabrina coughed hard, gasping for air as her neck throbbed with pain. She was dazed, confused—but didn't care who was helping her. She glanced at the woman, surprised whom it was. "Gina," she muttered. "Where are you taking me?" Her voice was hoarse, barely recognizable, but Gina seemed to understand.

"We need to get you back to the States before you get killed." She pulled Sabrina toward the doorway. "This way."

As Sabrina stumbled after her she glanced back and saw Vua and a guard lying still in pools of blood. "Oh my God! Are they dead?"

Gina grabbed Sabrina's hand and led her down the hall. "I don't know. I haven't checked their pulse but Vua was shot right where he deserved it—in the heart—so I doubt it."

"And the third?"

"He escaped … probably to get help. That's why we've got to get out of here."

"How'd you do it?"

"Your gun. It slid by my feet when they grabbed you."

"But aren't you … one of them?"

"Not a chance. But that's what I wanted them … and you … to think. It had to be that way otherwise they wouldn't be comfortable around me."

"What do you mean 'think'?"

"Think like them. They want everybody here to believe in their program."

"And if you refuse?"

"For the ones they want, they apply something called coercive persuasion to make sure they get the right behavior out of those that resist."

Sabrina gasped. "Brainwashing."

"Yep. And for the ones they don't want … I think you know what happens to them."

They reached a solid gray door with a sign above it that read *Salida*. Gina pushed it open, causing an alarm to sound. "I was afraid of that," she said. They hurried down the midnight black steel stairs. "We've got at least a few minutes' advantage but it's going to take some time getting to the ground floor." They hit the sixth floor landing and turned to conquer another set of stairs. By now Sabrina was under her own power, but barely able to stay with Gina's urgent pace.

"How'd they brainwash you?" Sabrina asked.

"They had me in a room for weeks … nothing but white walls … trying to break me through sleep deprivation." A pause. "It was the worst thing I've ever experienced in my life." Sabrina detected dread in her voice. "But then I had an idea: Make them think you've joined them. Then turn on them when the time is right."

"Like now?"

"Couldn't think of a better time."

They rounded the third floor landing. Sabrina stopped, trying to catch a breath but Gina grabbed her. "C'mon, we're almost there."

When they hit the ground floor they could hear voices above. Gina pointed to her right. "There … that's the door to the outside." Sabrina pushed open the gray-painted exit and burst into the blinding sunlight.

"Now what?" Sabrina asked, covering her eyes.

"We need to disappear into a crowd." Gina looked around. "By the harbor."

"But if Vua's dead, does it matter?"

"He's the leader but BioHumanity is a living, breathing enterprise and they'll do anything to keep us quiet."

They rounded the corner of the building and sprinted across the lawn toward the harbor. Sabrina's heart jumped as her eyes locked on a familiar figure standing across the street. "Detective Urbina!"

Urbina flashed recognition but then stared past them. Sabrina peered over her shoulder at two men sporting small handguns. Urbina nodded toward a maroon car parked alongside him. "Behind the car ... now!" The two women rushed toward the car just as a burly Hispanic man, police badge dangling from his neck, burst out of the driver's door holding a large caliber rifle. Sabrina grabbed Gina's hand and slid across the hood of the car, falling on the concrete curb.

"Todos al suelo!" someone yelled.

The women crouched against the passenger door, invisible to the pursuers. The same man hollered a few more words Sabrina didn't understand and then two shots were fired, the sounds echoing throughout the bay.

And then an eery silence followed.

The agony of not knowing stretched on. Sabrina crouched low and peered under the car: Nothing but darkness. *What's going on?* she wondered. Swallowing hard, she crawled around Gina.

"What are you doing?" Gina whispered.

"Seeing if it's over," Sabrina replied. She slowly stuck her head in front of the car's bumper and surveyed the street. When she realized what happened, her face lit with a happiness she didn't know was possible. She turned back. "They got 'em."

Gina's face burst with emotion. "Are you sure?"

Sabrina nodded slowly and then stood. "Take a look for yourself," she said, grabbing Gina's hand.

"Don't think about moving," the burly officer yelled at the attackers. He and Urbina had them pinned to the concrete with their knees and were securing their hands with white plastic ties.

Urbina looked up at the women. "Steven Vua ... where is he?" he hollered.

"He's dead," they replied simultaneously.

Urbina at first seemed surprised but then nodded. "That makes it easy."

As Sabrina watched the two attackers, she did something she didn't care if she would later regret. She walked up to one of them, bent over and whispered in his ear, "I don't know how much Vua was paying you but it couldn't be worth this."

"Screw you, bitch!"

"That's enough!" Urbina barked at the attacker.

With their hands tied tightly behind them, Urbrina and the officer yanked the two to their feet and dragged them over to the unmarked car. The officer threw them in the back seat and slammed the door shut. He turned to the women. "I'm sorry for being so rude," he said in heavily accented English. "My name is Carlos. I am with the Mexican Federal Police." He slapped the top of the car. "These men will no longer trouble you."

"It's over," Urbina said.

Sabrina stared at him. She heard his words but it didn't seem to sink in. And then she nodded. It *was* over. She wrapped her arms around the two men. "We both owe you so much for helping us. I don't know how you made it here but you did."

Urbina hugged her back. He grabbed her shoulders and looked her in the eyes. "Do you know how foolish you were coming down here," he scolded her.

"Then how——"

"How did I find you?"

"Yes."

"When my patrol officer found out you had slipped out during his watch, we ran a computer scan on your name and found the flight you booked to Acapulco."

"But it's out of your jurisdiction. Why come?"

"Because I knew you were in trouble—big time trouble."

"So you figured it out?"

"It was our conversation at the hospital. You mentioned Sanchez died of Atropine—which as you know, wasn't in the final report. So I went to the coroner's home that night and rattled her door until she woke up. I wanted to find out exactly what she knew."

"What did she say?"

"Let's just say her body language said it all. She knew she was cooked and told me everything."

"Like?"

"Apparently she had been paid off to withhold information on the report. A man offered what he called an 'incentive' if she left certain details out of the report."

"Bribery."

"Yeah. She was desperate … behind in her bills.

"I wouldn't doubt the man she met was their hired killer."

"No doubt. She showed me the check. It was issued from a shell address here in Acapulco … which, by the way, exactly matched the address of one of BioHumanity's buildings."

"Hmm. How convenient," Sabrina said.

"So I booked her and then headed for the airport." Urbina pointed toward his friend. "That's when I called my buddy, Carlos. I needed someone with jurisdiction to arrest Vua. I was determined to bring the whole thing down and I wanted to start and end with him. Plus, I knew I could trust Carlos over the locals who I'm sure BioHumanity had under their control."

"I'm finding Vua had a lot of people under his control," Sabrina replied.

He shook his head. "I just wish … I hadn't been so bullheaded. It caused me to miss the connection between the murders." He paused. "And by the time I did, you were here." He turned toward Carlos. "This woman's determination is unbelievable. Three of my men couldn't have done what she figured out."

Sabrina blushed before putting an arm around Gina. "You need to hear this woman's story. She's the hero in my mind. She saved my life."

Urbina eyed Gina. "A compliment from Sabrina? It must really be true."

They all chuckled. Carlos opened the driver's door. "I need to take these men in."

"Just to make sure they don't get any ideas, I'll join you," Urbina replied.

When the men pulled away, Gina eyed Sabrina wearily.

"What's the matter?" Sabrina asked.

"I've been dying to ask you if what Vua said is true—"

Sabrina put an arm around Gina to comfort her. "I'm so sorry."

Chapter 57

Dressed in a white and red patterned top matched with black pants, Sabrina sipped on a cup of cappuccino and gazed at the warm faces surrounding her.

She was at the Neskowin coffeehouse just around the corner from the newspaper. Three of her closest friends, some newer than others, were gathered around a table enjoying the breezy July morning. Sabrina wished one more person could've been here to enjoy the moment, but Detective Urbina was off helping the FBI and would be traveling a few more weeks. Besides, there was no way she could get him to sit for five minutes, let alone an hour, and have a cup of coffee. That just wasn't his thing.

Across from her, Gina put down the morning newspaper she was reading. "This is an amazing piece of writing," she said.

Sabrina smiled. "After all that family went through, I just had to write something that really showed people what Eric Sanchez stood for. He paid the ultimate price for being the first to speak up and I want people to understand what a big loss he is."

"But he wasn't all good," Helen added. "He did have an affair." She was sitting to Gina's left, clearly happy to be reunited with her ex-roommate.

"I know!" Sabrina said. "It's still hard to believe. But after meeting Mona, I felt like she didn't know what to do … and I don't think she had any idea what she was getting into. I mean, I still feel sick to my stomach for what they did to her."

"Maybe she didn't know he was married?" Helen pondered.

"That's possible. But she was his admin—she must've taken a call or two from Carla at some point."

The man sitting next to Sabrina raised his mug. "Well, I want to give a toast—here's to Sabrina's perseverance," he said, a baseball cap drawn low over his eyes.

"Either that, or New York stubbornness and stupidity." Sabrina replied, laughing.

"So true!" the three chimed in.

"Hey," Sabrina replied, faking hurt.

"I'm just glad Blogg decided to pick up your freelance piece and print it. It was the right thing to do," the man said.

"I think he felt guilty because he never believed a know-it-all rookie reporter knew what she was talking about," Sabrina surmised.

"Or he felt guilty for firing you," the man suggested.

"He's the one that looks like an idiot," Helen added.

Sabrina took another sip and gazed out the window. It had been forty-eight hours since that horrifying day in Acapulco, a day that branded a memory she'll never forget. But today felt different. She felt at peace with herself, with her sister's death, almost as if she was finally healing. It was something she so desperately wanted since picking up her life and moving west. Sabrina turned to the two women across from her. "Thank you so much for coming up. It really means a lot to me."

"I wanted to do it," Gina replied, "to support you anyway I can." She then said, "Besides, I would've been at home anyway … nervous … waiting for the news."

"I think we all are," Sabrina said.

As if on cue, Gina's cellphone rattled on the table. She looked around at the others and then whispered, "It's the hospital."

"What are you waiting for?" Helen said, handing her the phone.

Gina pressed it to her ear. "Thank you so much!" Gina replied after a minute. "That's the best we can hope for. We'll just have to wait and see now." She put the phone down. The others crouched forward, eager to hear the news. "They just finished the operation. Everything looks good so far. Blair is in the ICU, heavily sedated, but the heart transplant seems to have taken. It's beating on its own!" she said excitedly.

"Oh, Gina," Sabrina said, "that's great news."

"And from what they can tell, her body doesn't seem to be rejecting it."

"That's definitely what we hope for when a donation comes from a sibling," the man said.

Sabrina nodded. "And thank God the emergency crew was trained in handling organ donations."

"Agreed," the man replied. "It made a huge difference when they attached Gregory to a medical ventilator to keep his heart going."

"I just wish it could've been different," Helen said. "I mean, it's not fair Blair had to lose her brother just to stay alive."

"He so loved his sister … would've done anything for her. That's the saddest part," Gina said.

Helen looked at Sabrina. "So what's next for you?"

"I think I might stay here."

Helen looked surprised. "Even after all you've been through? And still no job?"

A nod. "I'm serious. This town's been through a lot … we've been through a lot … and I can't just pick up and leave. Not now. Not when things are just starting to become normal again." She turned to the man next to her, the baseball cap hiding the shaved head and bandaged temples, and put her hand on his. "Besides, if I left, I would lose the man I've fallen for."

Brieman returned the favor, putting his hand on hers. He then said, "If she only knew she had me when I first laid eyes on her."

"Oh, I knew. I was just playing hard to get."

Brieman smiled. "Besides, we've proven we're a good team."

"No … a great team," Sabrina interjected.

"I'll drink to that," Brieman replied, taking a sip.

Suddenly, the coffeehouse door burst open and Blogg and Getty walked in. "Sabrina!" Blogg said, beaming with excitement. "I'm glad I finally found you."

Sabrina rolled her eyes when she saw them both. "Sure. Now you need me," she replied wryly.

"Have you heard the news?" Blogg asked.

"No, not this morning. I've been trying to take it easy the past few days." She paused then said, "I needed a little down time."

Blogg and Getty each pulled up a chair. A rare smile flashed quickly across Getty's face. "It seems our little hometown paper has been flying off the shelves since your article was printed," Blogg said.

"Yeah, well, just remember I did it for Eric, not you."

"Touché … touché. But it also seems we've gotten noticed by the networks. The big four called the office and want to do an interview with you."

"What?" Sabrina said, barely containing her excitement.

"No way," Gina added.

"Yeah, your story was definitely your coming out party. I put it on the wire last night. Headline News picked it up, mentioned it briefly, and now people are jamming their email and Twitter handle, clamoring for more details. The public is shocked an American company was somehow able to pull this off."

"Of course, when you bribe and murder people, that's bound to shut people up and keep things quiet," Sabrina said.

"BioHumanity is collapsing," Blogg declared.

"How so?" Brieman replied.

"We have reports this morning the Mexican government has completely shut down the Heart Center on pressure from the U.S."

Helen shook her head. "What about the people waiting for a transplant? They must be devastated. I mean … this was their last hope."

Sabrina nibbled on her lower lip. She had been thinking about that possibility the moment she left Acapulco. An idea, born yesterday while finishing her article, just might help them.

"There's more," Getty stated. "The FBI apparently got wind of their network and raided all the clinics they had records on. … It's gotten ugly for a lot of people."

Sabrina eyed Getty, sporting his usual checkered shirt and grizzly face, and shook her head. *He's such a lumberjack*, she thought. "So why are you here anyway? To sing my praises or throw me under a new bus?"

Getty looked her straight in the eye. "You know I'll always say what's top of mind."

"Certainly know that."

"When I screw up, I'll admit it. And I screwed up. It wasn't fair what I did to you. I just might've been a little territorial."

"You think?"

Getty let out a sheepish grin. "Deserved that." He held out a hand. "Maybe we can start over."

"So you're apologizing?"

"He's really not that bad of a guy once you get to know him—a helluva writer, but just a little rough around the edges," Blogg said.

Sabrina eyed Getty closely, then replied, "I'm not sure we'll ever share a drink over dinner but I've been taught to give people a second chance." She grabbed his hand and they shook.

Getty leaned back and studied her. "Can I ask you something?"

"That depends." She was half-serious.

"There's more to this, isn't there?"

Her demeanor became serious. "How do you mean?"

"The pictures—this was personal, wasn't it?"

Blogg jumped to his feet. "C'mon Getty. That's enough."

Sabrina grabbed Blogg's shirt and pulled him back down. "Jim, it's okay. It really is."

"Are you sure?"

Sabrina nodded. "Seriously. It is." She turned back to Getty. "You're right. It was personal. But I also realized why I was so determined to investigate Eric's killer—it was part of my own grieving. I just … needed to find some closure for my own sister's death."

"And now?" Getty asked.

Brieman put an arm around her. She thought for a moment and then a smile spread like sunshine on a warm day. "I'm in a good place. Yeah … a really good place."

About the Author

M.G. Scott, author of numerous short stories and long-form fiction, has earned accolades from a number of writers associations for his dialogue and creative storylines. As a veteran of technology companies from the Bay Area to Boston, M.G. uses this experience to form the backbone of his novels. M.G. lives in the Chicago area with his family and several pets, including a black Labrador and guinea pig.

Savage Heart is M.G.'s first thriller.

www.ingramcontent.com/pod-product-compliance
Lightning Source LLC
Chambersburg PA
CBHW071134170626
46809CB00002B/621